DEATH AND THE SECURITY GUARD

nick moore

cover art by sarah moore

for detective r. a.

and
for sarah

1

The Body

"Everything is the truth, or else it's hypnotism." Adam vaguely remembered being told that by someone once, but he couldn't remember who. And he wasn't remembering it at all, on this particular night, as he sat in the little metal guard shack, surrounded on all sides by windows and night. Beyond the windows, under the night, were the parking lots and driveways of the former shopping mall—now some kind of corporate headquarters for an internet company. Wearing the white shirt and black pants of a security-guard uniform, Adam was a solitary presence, a gate arm on either side of the guard house, and Adam keeping watch over the breach in the long black perimeter fence, that this entrance and exit represented.

At two other places along the perimeter fence, Adam knew, were two other guards, in two other guard houses, maintaining their noble vigils. And there was also the shift supervisor, who drove about the property, in an intrepid electric golf cart, looking for crime or graffiti, and shuttling between the stationary guards, providing them with coffee-and-bathroom breaks.

Before Adam, as he sat in his guard house, were two computer monitors each containing many live camera feeds, monitoring various locations around the outside and inside of the facility. Every few seconds his eyes would scan the few most important of the cameras, and then return to the magazine he'd propped up against one of the computer screens. The magazine's cover declared its title: *Detective Stories Magazine*. In this, the era of blogs, Adam found it comforting to receive this magazine in the mail every month. Since childhood, a detective story had stirred in him an excitement that nothing else did, and he allowed himself the fanciful idea that, as a security guard, he himself was participating in something akin to a detective's profession.

The most regularly featured reoccurring character in *Detective Stories Magazine* was a private investigator named Douglas Tent. Like Sherlock Holmes of old, Inspector Tent was a detective who advised the police, in their pursuit of the secrets of mysterious crime, and, like Sherlock Holmes, Tent's adventures were purported to be chronicled by a trusty sidekick —who, in the case of detective Tent, possessed the obnoxious nom de plume Lucy Truthteller. Also, like Sherlock Holmes, in his day, the adventures of Douglas Tent were widely believed to be based on a real detective, who, unlike Sherlock Holmes, was widely believed to be operating out of Texas—the very state of the union in which Adam found himself to be a citizen and a security guard, on this very night.

In the near distance, just beyond the access road to Interstate 35, Adam heard and saw a train cut through the outskirts of his field of responsibility. High light poles tinted the blackness milky purple as the train sped past the Olive Garden and the Applebee's located just outside the perimeter fence that enclosed Adam's jurisdiction. The horn of the train announced a forlorn moan, and time continued to pass, in the night, in San Antonio, Texas.

On one of the security camera feeds, Adam noticed the shift supervisor's electric cart, the orange light on its roof blinking as it went, glide swiftly and determinedly across the vastness of a nearby parking lot. It was headed his way. Usually, the shift supervisor was an affable overweight nerd in his 30s named Roland. Earlier tonight however, a different supervisor had appeared at the guardhouse. He was a small, thin man, Hispanic, in his 40s. He spoke with one raised eyebrow, as if slightly disapproving of any given state of affairs. Adam noticed that the uniform he'd been issued was obviously too big for him, but this wouldn't be the first time a new hire had trouble getting the right-sized uniform. When the new supervisor had introduced himself earlier that night, Adam had made a joke about the overnight guys never being told anything (because he hadn't heard that there was a new supervisor), and they shook hands. In the mental fog that sometimes resulted from Adam's nocturnality, he had neglected to remember what the new supervisor had said that his name was. Adam attempted to get the information from the fellow's ID card, but it happened to be turned the other way, as it hung from the lanyard around his neck. Now that the supervisor appeared to be about to visit Adam's guardhouse for a second time tonight, he would have to make a point of detecting and remembering the new guy's name.

The supervisor's red and white golf cart pulled alongside the guard house, stopping in the midst of the outgoing lane. As Adam exited the guard house, he realized that the ground was wet: a mist hung damply in the air. Light from light poles in the adjacent parking lot reflected whitely, here and there, on the cracks and texture of the blacktop.

"I have something urgent to report, Officer Hume," said the supervisor, as he joined Adam on the patch of pavement behind the guardhouse, between the incoming and outgoing traffic lanes.

"What's that, sir?"

"There's been a dangerous mental patient, who's escaped from the home for the criminally insane, a few miles away. The police are currently looking for him."

"Really?" Adam stared for a second, as if at something mesmerizing that was floating in front of his face. "Wow."

"Yes, so, you know, just be on the lookout for anything unusual. If you see anything unusual, call me on the radio, and I'll call the police, if warranted."

Adam touched the two-way radio clipped to his belt, to remind himself that it was there. Adam reflected that tonight had suddenly turned into one of those rare, proverbial nights, in a security guard's professional life: the kind of night in which something actually happens. Still, what were the odds that this escaped nutcase would wander into their industrial facility, from however many miles away? Adam reassured himself that tonight, in all likelihood, nothing would really, actually happen.

"So, don't call the police: call you, and you'll call the police."

"Yes," said the supervisor, his one perpetually raised eyebrow raised. Suddenly his body and face flinched slightly, and he immediately gave a brief cough, as if to mask the flinch. In the distance, the lights of a police car were visible, speeding down I-35. Adam wondered if the police car was related to the escaped criminal or not.

Just before the supervisor turned to leave, Adam glanced down his torso, to where he expected the supervisor's ID card to be hanging on its lanyard, in front of his white uniform shirt, only to discover that the card was tucked into the shirt, between buttons, completely obscuring it. So, Adam's social detective work was thwarted. The supervisor's golf cart drove away, into the shadowy distance and dark of night, across the parking lot, toward the structure of the former shopping mall, the cart's orange light blinking on its roof, as it receded swiftly and quietly away, and Adam felt alone.

He shuffled into the little guardhouse, pulling the door closed behind him. Suddenly, he was aware of the door, as an ally against danger. He considered whether or not he should lock it. He imagined it locked, and a scruffy, crazy-eyed lunatic outside scurrying and clamoring to get in. Could the lunatic smash the windows? What were these windows, anyway, plastic? Would the lunatic circle the guardhouse manically, waiting for Adam to exit, waiting for some way in? Adam felt that he was on display. It was a source of great strategic annoyance to Adam, that the protocols of his post required him to leave the lights inside the guardhouse on, despite the resultant glare causing the windows to be hard to see out of, into the night beyond, the night which contained all of the things he was supposed to be guarding. Now, stranded there, illuminated in his transparent container, in a vast expanse of darkness, he heard the heavy quiet of the lateness of the hour; and he heard distant industrial hums from the dormant business beyond the parking lot, and its attendant machines. And he felt like a blind goldfish in a bowl on a floor, in a room with a hungry cat.

Adam decided that he was freaking himself out, by remaining in the guardhouse, and imagining its potential to be attacked. He stepped out of the guardhouse door, onto the small, raised patch of pavement behind the guard shack, between the incoming and outgoing lanes, and he breathed in the night air. A breeze was blowing. He was more exposed, but less afraid. He looked at the incoming gate arm, and the outgoing gate arm (each located on their respective sides of the guardhouse), and he was comforted by their stalwart presence, each in its prohibitive downward position. He'd been told by someone or other that any car could easily drive through these gate arms virtually unimpeded: but, still: they symbolized something reassuring: an uncompromised perimeter.

Adam had barely had time to adjust to his new more preferable mix of fear and hope within him, when the radio on his belt crackled to life.

"Supervisor to Gate One. Come in, Gate One."

Adam unclipped the radio from his belt, and brought it to his mouth in one single-handed motion. "Go for Gate One," he said. Before the supervisor could answer, a sound broke through the quiet and hum of the lateness of the night: the crack of a gunshot. Adam had rarely heard gunshots in his life, but he was fairly certain that this had been one. He waited for his radio to say something. Nothing was said. A few long seconds passed. "Did you hear that, sir?" Another long second.

"That's a negative," the supervisor replied, through the static the radio added.

"It sounded like a gunshot," Adam said.

"Yes, you're right. The Active Shooter Computer has

registered a gunshot in mechanical room 3, first floor, next to the maintenance office. Do me a favor, go and check it out. I'll meet you there."

"Are you going to call the police, sir?"

"No, let's confirm what it is, first. It could be a false alarm. This is part of the fun of what we do, Officer Hume."

"Yes, sir, I'm on my way."

Adam returned the radio to his belt, and re-entered the guardhouse. He made an internal effort to remain focused and calm. He took a ring containing many keys, attached to a carabiner, and clipped it onto one of his belt loops. He checked that his miniature flashlight was in his left pants pocket next to his wallet. He checked that his pocket notebook and pen were in his right pants pocket, next to his housekeys. A flashlight, a notebook, a radio, and keys would be paltry protection against an escaped mental patient with a gun. But he had something more: he had the uniform he was wearing, and the sense of authority and responsibility that came with it. It was this sense that compelled him to exit the guardhouse, and begin the foreboding walk across the mostly dark and mostly empty parking lot (despite the occasional light post, and despite the occasional car) toward the windowless exterior doors of mechanical room number three.

As he walked across the parking lot, he attempted to maintain a respectable security-guard sort of posture, while his speed was modulated by a combination of wanting to get where he was going, and not wanting to get there. He was aware of his surroundings, and the soft, wet sound of his shoes against the blacktop.

As he walked, though it was a relatively short walk, he had time to reflect on the strangeness of the supervisor's instructions. Shouldn't Adam have stayed at his post, instead of leaving his opening in the perimeter vulnerable to any lunatic that might decide to stroll in? True, all the doors to get into any of the facility's buildings themselves required an access card be scanned at the card reader next to whatever door was being entered, in order to unlock said door, and generate a record of who was going where. But, still, it made Adam uncomfortable, to leave his position unguarded, and he was uncomfortable at the thought of some unauthorized person being able to enter past the perimeter fence.

Adam arrived at the heavy metal doors, on the outside of a near building, that represented his intended destination. He removed his miniature flashlight and clicked it on, while, with his other hand, he reached across to the badge reader next to the doors, to hold the ID on the lanyard around his neck in front of it. With a beep, and the flash of a green light, the doors were temporarily unlocked. Adam pulled one of the doors open, and, as the shadowy darkness beyond the door was revealed, Adam wondered what he would do, if he encountered a madman with a gun.

Stepping into the space, he began to wave the beam of his miniature flashlight around the inside of the mechanical room, among the pipes and wires and square metal-box machines that he didn't understand. From some distant corner, he barely perceived the sound of a single drop of water land on some hard surface, when the door fell shut behind him. He couldn't remember how one turned the lights on, in this room. Suddenly his flashlight's beam danced across something immediately surprising and wrong. It was human skin. A person lay on his side, in a relaxed fetal position—motionless, perhaps, Adam feared, lifeless. The person was male, naked, except for underwear, and lying near the room's far wall, his back to Adam. As he approached the body—for that's what it appeared to be: a body, not a person—Adam's flashlight cast a grotesque shadow against the wall, which grew in size as he approached. The fascinating yet sickening crime-scene photos that he'd seen in true-crime documentaries came to mind, and a hollowness nestled in his stomach.

The hollowness instantly deepened, when Adam achieved the proper angle on the body to see its face. It was Roland: the usual third shift supervisor. There was a rigidity and jaundiced color to the body, that told Adam that Roland was dead. He was also told by what looked like a bullet hole in the side of Roland's head, and a dark pool of blood which was visible between Roland's head and the floor. He considered jostling him, by poking his shoulder, to check for any unlikely life left in him, but then he decided against it. Moving the circle of light from his flashlight around, he found a gun—a revolver—on the floor near one of Roland's hands. He noticed the hand was entwined loosely around the wrist with rope, as if Roland had worked his way out of being tied up, before getting shot to death. Adam remembered something, and so moved his light to illuminate a metal cabinet that was against the wall nearby.

This was the cabinet where security kept their emergency guns. Security guards did not normally carry guns at this site, but there was a supply of them—and ammo—kept in this cabinet, in case of emergency. Only supervisors, and above, had the key. One of the doors of the cabinet was ajar, the keys still in the lock, and Adam could see that at least a shotgun was still inside. Shining his flashlight back down to Roland's body, he noticed a cell phone, and wallet, and car keys on the floor next to a nearby chair, which was against the wall. Adam reasoned that this was the contents of Roland's pockets, taken out and left, after his pants were stolen.

The beam of light shined on the frozen look of disgust and surprise spread across Roland's dead face. Adam remembered the only conversation he'd ever really had with Roland, on the topic of Roland's love of playing video games. Roland would never play another video game again. Adam felt sorry for him, and considered how he should report all this to the supervisor, on the radio. As Adam's hand reached back to unclip his radio, he was struck with a terrible epiphany. In his mind the nakedness of Roland combined with the bagginess of the new supervisor's uniform, and suddenly Adam realized that the new supervisor was not the new supervisor. The new supervisor was the madman who was on the loose. He had killed Roland and stolen his uniform. Adam had just enough time to begin to appreciate the gravity of his situation, when a wooden board, swung forcefully by someone hidden in the darkness at his periphery, connected with Adam's chin, and instantly he was unconscious.

2

The Detective

Adam became aware that he was in a hospital. His eyes opened, and became adjusted to the light, despite residual blur and dryness. His jaw was sore, but he felt no other pain. He was lying in a hospital bed, with an I.V. in his arm. He felt the familiar sensation of polyester against his skin, and looked down to see that he was still wearing his security-guard uniform. The bed he lay in was perpendicular to an off-white wall behind him. Projecting from the wall, on either side of him, a light-blue plastic curtain, hanging from a track in the ceiling, encircled an area immediately around him, creating a makeshift room.

"Oh, you're awake. That's good to see. I'll get the doctor," said a nurse standing to one side of him. She disappeared into the curtain. Adam dozed off again, for some unknown amount of time, and was awoken again by a man in a white coat entering through the curtain. He was young, and wore glasses of a small and fashionable type. He sat on a rolling stool next to Adam's bed.

"Well, how is our patient, tonight? You had a good wallop on the head there. Do you know who the president of the United States currently is?"

Adam thought for a second. Then he furrowed his brow in disbelief. "Is it Donald Trump?"

"Yes, I know. It's surprising," said the doctor. "Can you tell me, what your name is?"

"Adam Hume."

"Very good, Mr. Hume. Let me just bring you up here." He pressed a button on a controller connected to the bed, and

Adam was brought to a sitting position against the now upright upper half of the bed. The doctor took a metallic pen-shaped tool out of his pocket, and pointed it into Adam's eyes, a penhole of light shining out of the end of it.

"Follow the light with your eyes," said the doctor, as he brought the pen from side to side, in Adam's field of vision, a few inches from his face, and then up and down. Adam cooperated with the test.

"Do I have brain damage, doctor?" Adam asked.

"Well, technically, whenever someone loses consciousness from a blow to the head, the brain has been damaged. But there are no signs, on your scan, of any long-term effects. Is there someone who can take you home, after you leave the hospital, and wake you up once per hour, for the rest of the night?"

"No, I don't think so."

"You'll probably be okay." The doctor put the light pen back into his pocket and stood up. "You have visitors," he said, and exited through the light-blue curtain. Adam faintly heard the doctor say something outside, which was responded to by multiple other voices, speaking softly and mixing with the low din of hospital noises swirling outside the curtain.

Through the curtain now appeared a gruff but kind-seeming man, with balding red hair, and a bushy red mustache, in an expensive-seeming, loose-fitting suit and a tie. Adam's eye was drawn to the police badge on his belt, next to the handle of a gun, protruding from behind his suit jacket. Standing behind the first man was a taller, more gangly gentleman. He had piercing green eyes, and dark, slicked-back hair, with sharp facial features, and a Roman nose. He wore a more tightly tailored suit. In one hand he held a wool fedora.

"Mr. Hume," began the man with the gun and badge, "My name is detective Richard Bethany of the San Antonio police department. If you don't mind, I'd like to ask you a few questions."

Adam looked helplessly at the men, and ever so slightly nodded his head.

"The facts of this case pretty much speak for themselves:

an initial investigation has made it clear to me that the escaped lunatic—man by the name of Dio Macina—wandered onto the property you were guarding last night, came across the security guard named Roland Bellwether in the mechanical room, and under duress—provided through the use of a handgun—convinced Roland to let our suspect steal his clothing. (Our suspect—Mr. Macina's—clothing was found tossed aside, elsewhere in the mechanical room.) Mr. Macina, having successfully stolen the guard's uniform, and acting from a deranged and depraved mind, then convinced you and the other guards working that night that he was a new, supervising employee at the facility."

Adam's mind went back to the grim images he had encountered in the shadowy mechanical room, before he had lost consciousness. It felt like remembering a bad dream, and he struggled to accept that any of this was real.

"Roland is dead," said Adam, in a faraway tone.

"Yes." He paused. "We're sorry about the loss of your coworker: by all indications a competent security man," said the police detective, glancing back at the gentleman behind him, just so that he could look somewhere, as if to reset his mind before continuing with what he was determined to say. "The suspect, Mr. Macina," the police detective continued, "then returned to the mechanical room, shot Roland, and summoned you to him, via the radio. At which point he knocked you unconscious, with a board, ready at hand, lying around in the mechanical room. An open-and-shut case," said the police detective, glancing again behind himself, this time as if to express annoyance at the presence of the man there.

"The crazy man: is he still on the loose?"

"Well"—Detective Bethany's jaw tightened—"Yes. But we've got an all-points BOLO out on him, so it's only a matter of time."

"I see," said Adam. A moment passed, in which Adam wondered what would happen now. Then the taller, thinner man stepped forward.

"If I might be allowed to add a few observations—" the

man began, in an upper-class, English accent. Detective Bethany rolled his eyes, and stood aside, as if giving the stage, for which Adam was the sole audience member, over to the new man. "Detective Bethany's thoughts on the events of tonight are, as usual, admirable for their working-class charm, and correct in some of their details, but are also completely insufficient to lay hold on deep truth."

Inspector Bethany folded his arms, and deepened his glare at the new speaker.

"I have had the opportunity to inspect the crime scene. Several physical facts, when considered logically, contradict the theory that the madman killed your coworker." As the man spoke he paced from side to side, next to Adam's hospital bed. His bright green eyes pierced through atmosphere, as if cutting into the images he was conjuring before his eyes, dissecting them. He gestured with his arms, with reserved theatricality, occasionally touching the brim of the wool fedora he still held in one hand to his chin.

"There is the inconvenient matter of the gun," the Englishman continued, "a revolver. It was among the weapons that security kept in the firearms cabinet, in case of emergency. One of the other guards on duty was able to show me an inventory that identified that specific handgun by serial number."

"So, the madman got the gun out of the cabinet. Why is that hard to believe?" asked Detective Bethany.

"But think of what your own theory posits," replied the Englishman. "You deduce, rightfully, that the madman—Macina—must have had a gun, in order to rob Security Officer Roland of his clothing. But the keys to the cabinet were in Roland's possession to begin with." The Englishman turned to Adam. "Isn't that right?"

"Yes," said Adam, "Supervisors are the ones who have the keys to that."

"So, you see," continued the Englishman, his piercing eyes piercing all the more, "The madman must have brought a gun of his own. He will probably have it on him still, when he is found—if he is found. The madman used his own gun to undress Roland, and tie him up in the chair by the wall. He then left Roland there, tied up, with his possessions, including the keys to the cabinet, on the ground nearby."

"Why wouldn't Macina take the keys to the gun cabinet?" asked Bethany.

"Because, of course, he would have had no way of knowing that that's what they were. He had wandered into the facility, somehow, in the grip of lunatic caprice, and he stole Roland's clothing for the same reason. Once Roland was left alone, in his underwear, tied to the chair, he began to work to release his wrists from the rope that confined him."

"Okay, so he got out of the ropes..." said Bethany, softened by curiosity.

"Yes, he got out of the ropes, picked the keys up off of the ground where they lay, opened the cabinet, retrieved the revolver, loaded it, and shot himself to death."

"What! Why on earth would he do that?" Bethany demanded.

"That," said the Englishman, "is a mystery."

There was a long pregnant silence, wherein Bethany alternated between looking at the Englishman quizzically, and looking at the blue curtain contemplatively. Adam's general disbelief about his current circumstances only deepened now, as he sat vulnerable and amazed, in the upright hospital bed. Why would Roland kill himself? He had seemed a content, albeit awkward person. And why kill himself, directly after being stripped and bound by a lunatic? Adam eagerly awaited more information from the gangly, green-eyed Englishman.

"Well, why did he hit me in the face with the board?" Adam inquired.

"Simple," said the Englishman. "After dissembling himself to the guards on duty, Macina returned to the mechanical room, to check on his prisoner. Before arriving he heard the gunshot, and entered the room, to find Roland shot. In a panic, and fearing that you were onto him, he decided to knock you unconscious and run away past your now unguarded security checkpoint."

The others considered this, and the Englishman continued:

"Roland was a more profound individual than most people could realize. Detective Bethany, here, on the other hand, is a Presbyterian," the Englishman said to Adam. "Does that strike you as odd?"

Adam's eyes narrowed. "I'm sorry…what?"

"He's a Presbyterian, I say. And he is a police detective. This strikes me as very odd. The science of solving crimes is a kind of math, because everything is a kind of math, really. Everything, if we understood it, would be a kind of numerical machinery, humming away. And yet, here is a man, a police detective—Richard Bethany—who goes to a building once per week, called a church—"

"Sometimes twice per week, " inserted Bethany.

"—a building called a church, and begs and pleads with the unforgiving machinery of the universe to stop being logical —to stop being logical, so that he doesn't have to die—him, a man, whose job it is to understand logic, and to understand death."

"I think this witness has probably answered enough questions for now," said Bethany, causing Adam to reflect that he had been asked, and had answered, practically no questions.

A sudden melancholy seemed to drape across the Englishman's face, and a gathering of moisture in his eyes. "It's just that everything is so damned boring," he said. "That's the real hell of things."

He suddenly departed through the blue curtain. When he was on the other side, Detective Bethany and Adam heard the distinctive sound that is made, when a man quickly and forcefully snorts cocaine up his nose.

"Okay, where were we?" the Englishman asked, as he re-emerged into the space, briefly rubbing one of his nostrils.

"You were saying something incomprehensible about

my being a Presbyterian," said Detective Bethany.

"Can I ask another question?" said Adam. No one responded. "You said," he said to the Englishman, "That Roland was a more profound person than most people realized. Were you a friend of his?"

"I was a friend. And more than a friend. We were partners in the solving of crime. He was a security guard overnight, but during the day we worked together. Of course, most people would know Roland Bellwether better by his ridiculous pen name: Lucy Truthteller."

Adam's eyes widened. "Roland was Lucy Truthteller!"

"He was," said the Englishman.

"Then you must be—" Adam started to say.

"I am Douglas Tent," the Englishman said.

Adam's mind, which had, at about this point, started to become numb to surprise that night, now began to swim and explode with this seemingly imaginary and fantastical turn of events. A hero from—he had thought—fiction, had walked off the page, and stood now before his mildly brain-damaged consciousness.

"You needn't be bewildered, or star-struck," said Douglas Tent. "Besides some artistic exaggerations, the stories written by Roland about me—about us—and published in *Detective Stories Magazine* every month, have been the chronicle of true events. It is to my strategic benefit, that my professional anonymity is partially maintained, by the widespread belief that I am a fictional character. Since I work almost exclusively as a consultant for the police, most in the public have no occasion to discover that I am a real person."

"I can't believe it," said Adam affectionately.

"To be fair to the accuracy of Roland's memory, despite being of a generally superior intellect to Detective Bethany here, Roland did, like Detective Bethany, feel the absurd need to attend a church of his own. Last Baptist Church of San Antonio, I believe it was. On Backwoods Road."

"It's a big relief that you're on the case, Mr. Tent," said

Adam. "I think I've read all of Lucy Truthteller's stories about you. You inspire me to be a security guard. I'm sure you will get to the bottom of what Roland's murder really means."

"Nothing really means anything, not ultimately" said Douglas Tent. "If you want the cold, mechanical truth of things, that I will find for you. If you want to start assigning grand ideas about meaning to things, then go to church."

Douglas Tent placed his wool fedora on his head, and exited through the curtain.

3

The Pastor

As Adam made the drive to Last Baptist Church of San Antonio, his car's external temperature reading declared it to be a hundred degrees. It was one of those usual Texas days, wherein the heat is dry and hot against the skin, like the atmosphere inside an oven. Adam drove through the signs of civilization resplendent in the glare of the sun, among the occasional palm tree and cactus, and got onto the 1604 loop—the outer border of San Antonio proper—and headed south, toward Backwoods Road.

Adam had two reasons for wanting to interview the pastor of Last Baptist, whomever he was. He wanted to find answers about the murder of his coworker Roland Bellwether. But there was more to it than that. The police and Douglas Tent were on the case. And, true, Adam did harbor fantasies of being a detective, and a murder at his workplace was too tempting to pass up —as an opportunity to have something to investigate. But there was more to it than that. It had been three days since Adam had left the hospital—three days since he'd discovered Roland's body, and they'd been the worst three days of his life. A black ball of existential dread had appeared in Adam's soul, since that night, and he couldn't shake it. Its effects were torturously physiological. It felt like panic, sheer panic. He tried to go about his usual activities, in denial against the dread. But he was only barely making it. As he walked, as he worked, as he laid down to sleep, the dread was there. It was one long panic attack, for three days. He had gone to the movies alone, to try to distract himself, and the themes of the film—even though it was a comedy —minor themes related to death, reminded him, in the empty weekday theater, that the dread was still there.

Death was what his dread was focused on, he realized. The dread seemed to be expressing to him that he would die one day, inevitably as does everyone, but delivering the message in a more viscerally real way than he could have ever imagined. It was as if he were on death row, and he knew the escort was coming to take him to the electric chair in exactly two minutes. It was the feeling of the last two minutes of life. And he felt it all the time, that feeling of ultimate doom, with no possible escape. The image of Roland's dead body flashed before his mind's eye, with exhausting regularity. But he was not burdened with remorse for Roland, his friends, or his family. Adam's crisis was purely about his own mortality, and the seemingly cold machinery of the universe—the machinery Douglas Tent had spoken so blatantly about—which was grinding toward him, to crush him in only a matter of time. He wanted to solve Roland's murder. But he also wanted to solve his own.

As he continued to drive he was now in a rural area. On either side of him was yellow grass stretching out forever, and before him was the impossibly expansive Texas sky. Blueness full of grand white clouds. Sky like a painting of the sky. Adam suddenly remembered a memory, that was ten years old. Adam had been camping with his friends. It was a cold, breezy night, in December. There had been drinking of whiskey, with lime juice in it—a "snake bite" he seemed to remember the drink being called—and he remembered two tents erected, on different sides of the fire, in the small area among the trees that was their campsite. As the night wore on, a nagging sobriety had broken into Adam's consciousness, and at around that moment he had wandered into the woods, to relieve the pressure he felt in his bladder in private. But before he'd found an attractive tree to pee on, he realized that he'd taken too many turns, walked too far into the woods, and that he now didn't know where he was, and couldn't see or hear the campsite. He didn't have a cell phone. He didn't even have a watch.

As he had continued walking, aimlessly, with increasing

desperation, in unknown woods that night, ten years ago, his worry grew into serious concern. Around him were trees and underbrush, above him the night and stars. Everywhere was nature's quiet. Then, in the distance, the sonorous howl of some natural beast. The realization struck him, like cold water in his face—destroying whatever was left of alcohol's effects on him—he was lost. He stopped walking, because his walking might only be making his situation worse. He was at a spot, where, looking up, he had a picturesque view of the moon. All in an instant it happened, as he stared up at the moon, in that moment, showered by its light, in the woods, looking up, at the glow, the roundness, the realness of the craters in the regal floating thing. An infinite presence took hold of Adam. A feeling of total, overpowering love. It felt, for all the world, exactly like the presence of God, which was wordlessly communicating to Adam, in that moment, that he was loved, and that everything was going to be okay. He basked in that feeling, in the moonlight, staring upward, for an unknown amount of time. Then, when the time was right, Adam's consciousness came back down to earth, he began walking, took a certain number of turns, as if being guided, and suddenly he was back at the campsite. He heard the convivial voices, saw the light of the fire, just before he appeared back where he'd started. They hadn't even noticed he was gone. And he told no one about his spiritual adventure in the woods.

In the days, weeks, and years after that experience, Adam hadn't often remembered it. In its immediate aftermath, Adam had confidently dismissed it as proof of anything supernatural. A scientific explanation was ready at hand, in his mind: over the millions of years of evolution, that his ancestors had muddled through—he reasoned—there must have been some benefit to, every once in a while, a caveman being overcome by the feeling of the presence of God in the woods. As an explanation, it was vague and untestable, but relieved Adam of the burden of having to consider a spiritual world. And it wasn't until now, in the midst of his current panic attack, that Adam felt a willingness to consider again his holy encounter.

Adam found Last Baptist Church on Backwoods Road, near the spacious expanse of a cattle ranch. The church was across from a remote gas station, and set off from the road, by a driveway that opened into its front parking lot. As Adam drove down the driveway, he saw a barn next door to the church, on the other side of an electrified fence. Next to the barn were horses standing around, swinging their tails, not thinking about religion. The church building itself, rising proudly beyond the sizable parking lot, was a formidable complex, mostly red brick, with a white steeple surmounting the white shingled gable of the sanctuary, above the red brick of the lower gables and the portico of the main entryway.

Adam parked, and walked toward the church. It made him feel young again. His last memories of church were going there as a child, to a Presbyterian church as he recalled. He vaguely remembered a kindly older man in purple vestments, and a children's sermon, during which the kids in the audience would come down and listen to a short lesson on the carpet, while the pastor sat on the steps to the altar—before the children were dismissed to Sunday School. He vaguely remembered having the subjective feeling that the grownup portion of the service, before the children were released, took an interminable amount of time. And he remembered cookies being available after everything was finished. Probably his most palpable childhood memory of church was the cookies.

Walking under the entryway portico, to the four adjacent sets of glass double doors within, he found that the first door he tried was unlocked. Entering into the carpeted lobby, there seemed to be a lightness in the air—maybe it was spiritual. Around the lobby, on various tables, were pamphlets offering sundry types of life advice. On the far end of the lobby were three sets of wooden double doors, leading into the sanctuary—which were closed. On one side of the lobby was a door next to a window with its blinds closed, that seemed to offer the possibility of being an office area.

Adam looked at his watch. It was 2 pm on a Wednesday. Adam had visited the website for Last Baptist Church, which had informed him that service times were Sunday morning, Sunday evening, and Wednesday evening—the Wednesday evening service commencing at 7 pm. A portion of the website, entitled Meet Our Pastor, had introduced Adam to the pastor of Last Baptist Church, Pastor Moses Lacuna, who was a clean-shaven, white haired man in his 60s, with black thick-rimmed glasses, who was pictured smiling in a sea of children and grandchildren, next to his smiling wife.

At just that moment, Pastor Lacuna himself came walking alone toward Adam, down a hallway which led off from the lobby. He had the white hair and glasses from his picture, wore a dark suit jacket, white dress shirt, tan pants, and a necktie of many colors. Upon seeing Adam, he extended his arm for a handshake, and said, "Hello". "Hi," said Adam, taken a little off guard, and they shook hands. The Pastor's light-colored eyes gave a hospitable look, and he casually put his hands in his pockets.

"Hello, Pastor, my name is Adam Hume. I'm a security guard," Adam began, and then considered how to continue. "I don't know if you have a minute."

"I may have a few," said the pastor.

"The thing is, a coworker of mine was murdered, and he was a member here. I—" Adam was surprised by a sudden gathering of sadness within him, and his eyes filled with water. "I—" He tried not to give vent to the stress that wanted to express itself in tears.

"Here," said Pastor Lacuna, taking keys out of his pocket, "come into my office."

He unlocked the door off the lobby, and opened it to reveal a cramped, unoccupied receptionist's area, past which was a small office with its door open. The pastor flipped on the lights in the first area, then walked into his office, and lifted the blinds of his office window, which looked out onto the mostly empty parking lot.

"Come in," said pastor Lacuna, as he shuffled around various papers and books splayed messily upon his desk, before sitting down in his desk's chair, a bookshelf resplendent with theological erudition lining the wall behind him.

"Thank you," said Adam, sitting in a chair that was already positioned to face the pastor's chair. "I appreciate your talking to me. As I say, I'm a security guard, not a police officer. But, I always did want to be a police officer, or a police detective. Or a private detective."

"We're all on our own search for truth," said the pastor, leaning back in his chair, his interlaced fingers in his lap, his elbows on the armrests of his chair.

"Yes... And I—" Adam found that his earlier episode of emotion was subsiding, and he felt focused by the mission he was on. "I wanted to ask—was Roland, do you feel, was he suicidal?"

"No, absolutely not. And I can tell you, his family feels strongly as well that he was not. I should tell you, his funeral is this Saturday afternoon, if you were wanting to attend."

"Yes, I would," said Adam, knowing that he wouldn't. The dread would not allow it.

There was a pregnant pause, and then Adam said, "Pastor..."

"Yes?"

"Roland believed in God?"

"Yes."

"Why, I mean, why does a person believe in God?"

"Oh, well," said the pastor, sitting up in his chair. He looked at his watch, then looked down at his desk, and finally out the window, composing his thoughts. "That's a very good question."

Adam looked forward, relaxed and interested.

"If we're just speaking of generic belief in God, there have been, historically, arguments and evidence given, why God's existence makes more sense, philosophically, than his non-existence. Different people are convinced by different things. For me, I would say that the two things that cry out to be explained by reference to God are the existence of the world itself, and also the existence of human consciousness."

"Those things require reference to God, to be explained?"

"Yes, I would say so—to be explained as best as possible. From a Biblical perspective, if you look around the world that we find ourselves in, the splendor of nature, the beauty of things, even the possibility of evil. It's all intended to be an obvious miracle. The Bible says, 'The heavens declare the glory of God.' A person preoccupied about being inappropriately scientific will disbelieve in Christianity, because he thinks that miracles are impossible. But, from a Biblical point of view, miracles are obvious, because we're sitting in a miracle right now, which is creation. And where you have a miracle, you have God."

"But, what about scientific explanation: the theory of evolution?"

"The theory of evolution is only plausible to people, because they've already assumed that miracles are impossible. Once you assume that, then you're stuck with evolution, because it's the only non-miraculous explanation that anyone's come up with. But it's not even science, it's atheistic philosophy. There are not mathematical laws, that describe what evolution supposedly does, and if there were, an experiment to test them would take four billion years. How the world was created is a question for philosophy and religion.

"Any estimate I've ever seen of how likely a random mutation is to help an organism, coupled with an estimate of how many such mutations would be necessary to make anything useful happen, ends up proving that the universe would die and grow cold, before you'd get a single-celled bacteria. So, evolution is a great scientific theory, except that it isn't scientific, and it's mathematically impossible."

"What do evolutionists say about mathematical impossibility?"

"I've not heard them address it. Again, because they don't feel they need to. Based on their preconception against miracles, evolution just has to have happened. Therefore, there must be some way to make the math work, that we don't understand yet."

"So," asked Adam, "God exists, and the world is not cold machinery blindly turning?"

"Not even close. Do you believe in God?"

"Well," said Adam. "I did as a child. But as an adult I haven't. It occurred to me as a teenager that God might not exist. And so I didn't see any good reason to keep believing in him. You said also that the human mind proves that God exists?"

"Yes," said Pastor Lacuna, suddenly distracted. He took his phone out of his pants pocket, looked at its screen, and then returned it to his pocket. "I'm sorry, I'm needed elsewhere in the church. I hope we can continue this conversation soon," he said, standing up behind his desk.

Adam stood as well. "I suppose I failed to ask you very much about Roland. The reason I came was to investigate—to see if you had any idea what might have happened to him. Did he have any enemies that you know of?"

"To be honest, I didn't know Roland personally, very well. His family are members here. His attendance was infrequent. My specialty is the mysteries of the universe. I'm afraid I'm not much help in a murder investigation."

"I've met with a private investigator who's on the case. I supposed I should try to work with him."

"It was good talking to you, Adam." The pastor shook Adam's hand. The two men stepped out of the office area, and Pastor Lacuna locked the outer door. "I will pray for you to find the truth," the pastor said, then walked away, down the hallway through which he had arrived.

Adam turned to go, and suddenly became aware of the three pairs of wooden double doors leading into the sanctuary. Each one had a narrow, vertical window in it. Adam approached one, and looked through the glass. He saw the largeness of the space beyond, the rows of long cushioned pews, on top of flat green carpet, surrounding the raised wood-floored stage, at the center front of which stood a pulpit equipped with microphones.

Standing on the carpet, in front of the stage, were a group of people: men, women, and children, dressed in varying degrees of formality, that appeared to be practicing a song, led by a man in a suit jacket, who was facing them, and conducting with his hands. Adam stood for a moment and observed the wholesomeness of the event. He could faintly hear them singing.

4

On the Case?

Arriving at the office of Douglas Tent's one-man detective agency, Adam was filled with hope for his mental health. The dread was still there, in the background always. He sometimes found himself imagining that it had lessened in intensity, or frequency, only to realize that it had not. The shudder in his heart, the flashbacks to his encounter with death in the mechanical room: they could only be distracted from, for various amounts of time.

Adam had called the San Antonio police department, and spoken to Detective Bethany, in order to get the address of Douglas Tent's office, which was, it turned out, nowhere to be found on the internet—which mostly regarded him as a fictional person. Adam was happy to discover that the detective agency was only a few minutes' drive away from his apartment. To think that his own literary hero was not only real, but had been solving crime all of this time, mere blocks from his apartment, and working with Adam's own dorky coworker?

Adam didn't know if he believed anything the pastor had told him about evolution or not. But, for the first time since childhood, he was curious to learn more about the Christian point of view, to see what relief from his mental anguish it might promise. When Adam was a child, going to Presbyterian church, he had a definite belief in the existence of real good and real evil in the world. He remembered thinking, at that time, that, in such a world—one in which exists real good, and real evil—a man must endeavor to grow up to be one of the good guys. The most obvious way to accomplish this, it seemed to Adam as a church-going child, was to become either a preacher or a detective. Around ages ten to twelve, he had been an avid watcher of police shows on television and detective movies, a reader of detective-themed books for kids, and thought all the time about being a solver of mysterious crimes. But some combination of puberty, and his parent's divorce—and the subsequent ceasing of Adam being taken to church—had caused Adam to abandon his crime-fighting dream. All that remained of it today was his love of reading about Douglas Tent in *Detective Stories Magazine*, and the enjoyment he took in his profession of security guard, which he imagined put him vaguely—potentially—in the good-guy category.

But now Adam wanted, desperately wanted, for Douglas Tent to allow him to be his partner in solving the case of the murder of his coworker Roland Bellwether. Adam was uncertain what Christianity might do for him. If the universe was a cold, heartless machine, as Douglas Tent insisted, then the only meaning to be found in life would come from values in the human heart, put there accidentally by biology. Perhaps such is the case. But, then, what value is higher in the human heart than the conviction that a murderer must be brought to justice? And, then, who is nobler, whose existence is more meaningful, than a detective bravely on the hunt for a murder's solution? Yes, Adam would join Douglas Tent on his quest to solve this case. And then, maybe, hopefully, the light of truth would drive away the shadows of dread bristling in Adam's heart.

Adam arrived at the address the police had given him, to find that it was a small, two-story brown-brick office building, located solitarily on the corner of a block, across a side street from a gas station, and otherwise surrounded by the trees adorning that portion of Jones Maltsberger Road, in San Antonio. It was a clear, relatively cool morning. Pulling into the parking lot, Adam observed that the sign at the entrance of the lot only identified the building as being the location of a dentist's office. Adam parked and approached the building's front entrance, noticing that the first floor was surrounded by tall, tinted-black windows, stalwartly reflecting the day's traffic back to itself.

Entering the building, Adam found himself in a small entry way, with stone-look linoleum flooring, a small multi-tiered fountain to one side, and a small wrought-iron patio chair-and-table set to another. Daylight streamed dimly through the tinted windows. Down a hallway from the entry were other office spaces, that Adam assumed belonged to the dentist. Because, immediately in front of him, as he stood in the entryway, was a mahogany door, the top half of which contained a cloudy glass window on which was hand-painted in black lettering: Douglas Tent Investigations. As Adam summoned the courage to turn the door's knob, an older blond woman in scrubs, carrying a brown bag from a fast-food place, walked past him, and disappeared into the dentistry area beyond. Finally Adam mustered himself, checked in with his dread—still there—and walked into the detective agency.

As he entered an electronic chime sounded and Adam was immediately struck with the feeling that he may be intruding. Adam found himself in a room that presumably was once a lobby area. To Adam's left was a large wooden desk, that a receptionist might have once used, which was now crowded with papers, books, files, unlabeled pill bottles, and various sizes of brown chemical bottles with black plastic safety caps. On the right side of the room was a table, completely occupied by dozens of stacks of file folders, stamped "Confidential" in red ink. Some of the contents of which—various papers stapled together—lay sloppily atop the folders. A book shelf stood against a wall by the table, which housed thick softcover books with titles like, *The Science of Fingerprinting*, and *Surveillance Law in Texas*. In the back of the room, to Adam's left, was a door which stood open, beyond which appeared to be Douglas Tent's personal office. In the right back corner of the lobby, a hall led off to somewhere else. Against the backwall, facing Adam, was a wood sideboard, above which was hung framed newspapers, with headlines such as "Kidnappers Apprehended" and "Missing Jewels Found". At multiple locations, on the floor, were wastepaper baskets surrounded by wadded up balls of legal notebook paper. Also, on the floor were multiple ash trays filled with cigarette butts. A scent and visible smog of cigarette smoke hung in the air.

Suddenly Douglas Tent swept into the room, unshaven, and wearing a blue kimono-style bath robe. In his mouth was a lit cigarette. In one hand he held an antique saber in its scabbard. With his other hand he dramatically drew the flat sharp stainless-steal sword, tossing its sheath aside, and aiming its tapered point at his visitor. He slightly rotated his hand around the axis of his wrist, causing the ornate handle, handguard, and hilt of the weapon—as well as its end beyond—to describe a small circle upon Douglas's view of Adam.

"Who goes there?" demanded Douglas Tent triumphantly.

"Hello, Mr. Tent, Detective Tent," said Adam—not shaken by the display. "I'm sure you remember me—Adam Hume. I was the security guard whom you interviewed in the hospital… about the murder of Roland Bellwether."

"Yes, of course." He held the blade perpendicular to the floor and turned it from side to side. "A gift I received for solving a case. Nineteenth-century weapon. *The Case of the Chinese Russian.*" Douglas Tent placed the sword carelessly on top of the piles of file folders on the table, walked to the desk with the chemical bottles, and began considering them, as he took a puff on his cigarette.

"What brings me here today, sir, well… I know Roland was your friend and partner in crime fighting." Douglas Tent glanced at Adam, and then back to the chemical bottles. "His murder has affected me too," Adam continued. "And, sir, what makes me a good security guard is, I believe, well—it's always been my ambition to be a detective, to be a private investigator. And, as someone who happens to be close to this case—" Adam looked down at his feet, then back up to where Douglas Tent stood. "Well, I believe, sir, that I could be of help to you on this case. I don't expect you to pay me. But, I'd like to learn what you could teach me about being a detective. I feel—I feel that it's my calling in life."

There was a pregnant pause. "I'm working on a chemical experiment," said Douglas Tent. "I've created something—yet another something—that I believe could be useful in fighting crime." As he said, "chemical experiment", Douglas Tent held up a white ceramic mortar and pestle that had been hidden among the chemical bottles, then placed it back down again. "My system is quite compromised by other chemical experiments currently, therefore, I require an average test subject. Are you average, chemically, Adam Hume?"

"Umm.. yes, I think so."

"Very good." Douglas handed him a coffee mug from among the chemical bottles. "Drink this."

Adam held the mug, and looked down into it. The fluid in the bottom was too shallow, and too masked by shadow to admit any information about itself—color, texture, viscosity. In that moment, Adam's desperation, brought on by his troubled soul, combined with the hope in him, of being a detective one day, and throwing back his head and the coffee mug, he swallowed the mystery in the cup. It was tasteless, and therefore, all the more unnerving.

Suddenly, the muscles in Adam's legs tingled, and in the next instant, his legs had gone completely rubbery and numb, leaving Adam finally in a collapsed pile of himself on the floor.

"The purpose of the drug," said Douglas Tent, "is to cause temporary paralysis of the legs, in the subject. Which, as we can see, it has done. He pulled a pencil and pocket notebook out of a pocket in his bathrobe, and started jotting things down.

"Um.." said Adam, shakily, "How long does the paralysis last?"

"Eight hours, " said Douglas Tent. "But, of course, there is an antidote."

Douglas put the notebook and pencil back in his robe, and suddenly stared at the blank wall beyond the receptionist desk, taking a drag on his cigarette.

"Global warming is killing us all," Douglas Tent declared with resignation. "Do you realize that? Of course you do. I am currently writing a paper which explores a, hitherto, unstudied contributor to global warming."

Adam continued to lie on the floor, his legs still paralyzed, attempting to be patient and a good listener.

"Consider what happens when a criminal person—or a criminologist studying crime—cooks cocaine into crack, in order to smoke it. Cocaine powder is combined with water and baking soda, and then heated. The bicarbonate in the baking soda has an acid-base reaction with the hydrochloride in cocaine, forming crack and carbonic acid. Continued heating causes the carbonic acid to degrade into water and CO_2. You see? CO_2. And global warming is thereby accelerated."

Adam considered this. "Is very much CO_2 released in this fashion," he asked, still looking at the ceiling.

"So far, we don't know," said Douglas Tent—and as he did, he lifted a small skinny glass pipe from among the things on the desk, held the flame of a plastic lighter to its end, and inhaled smoke through the mouth piece.

Adam looked over to Douglas Tent, from where he lie on the floor. "Did you just smoke crack?"

"Yes, I did," said Douglas Tent. "For science." Adam considered this. Douglas returned the pipe to its former hiding place among the desk's clutter, retrieved his cigarette from the ashtray that had temporarily held it, and returned it to his mouth for a drag. He then found a second coffee mug among the chemical bottles, and handed it to Adam. "The antidote," he said.

Adam drank it. It had a strange, bitter taste, and Adam felt the feeling immediately returning in his lower extremities. He sat up, then stood up apprehensively.

"You see," said Tent, taking the coffee mug from Adam, and returning it to the mess on the desk. "The effects are completely reversible."

"Mr. Tent, about the case—" continued Adam, undeterred.

"To be a scientist is to face the cold truth of things," interrupted Douglas. As he spoke, he turned away from Adam, and looked at the framed newspapers hanging on the opposite wall. "Especially to be a student of crime. It is to look, unflinchingly, into the evil in men's hearts, and to accept it as meaningless ugliness, and biological malfunction. Tragedy is not redeemed in the end. It can only be documented, and understood as a natural phenomenon. Science is not always comforting, but it is the only path to truth we have. Are you willing to be a detective, a scientific student of crime?"

"Yes."

"Then take my advice, and don't work with a partner."

"But, Mr. Tent, you and Lucy—you and Roland—you were partners, sir. I've read all of your cases."

"Then you know that Roland and I were in constant danger. And you know that Roland is now dead. It was irresponsible of me to expose a second person to the rigors of my calling. A man of science, a detective, is doomed to a lonely existence."

"No," said Adam. "There have been great partnerships in science, and in crime-solving. Look at Watson and Crick or Batman and Robin."

Douglas turned to face Adam, a redness in his eyes. "Batman's exposure of Robin to that rogue's gallery of criminal maniacs is reckless and wrong," he said. "He is obviously, subconsciously, attempting to alleviate his own sense of helplessness, at watching his parents die as a child, by exposing another child—Robin—to such ridiculous crime-fighting risks. How many Robins have to die, before he realizes that?"

Adam took a moment to wonder whether or not Douglas Tent thought that Batman was a real guy.

"If you insist," said Douglas Tent, "then I will tell you some of what I, so far, suspect about the case of the murder of Roland Bellwether. When you have heard what I have to say, then, hopefully, you will understand why I must work this case alone. Step into my office."

As Adam sat in the chair facing Douglas Tent's desk, he looked around the small office. It was as cluttered as the lobby, a disarray of files, papers, and ashtrays everywhere—the smell of cigarette smoke lingering on everything. To Adam's left, the building's big tinted windows took up one wall, letting in their tepid light, and giving a covert view of the parking lot, and persons coming and going from their dentist appointments. To Adam's right was a table, framed by two floor lamps, beyond which was a bookshelf, with more volumes about criminology and forensics, all of which sat on the carpeted office floor. The L-shaped office desk took up much of the space. On it, among the files, papers, and books, Adam noticed a padlock, with lock-picking tools inserted into it. The lock was made out of clear plastic so that the metal tumblers within were visible, so that the lockpicker could practice tripping them, and thereby defeat the lock. On the walls were more framed newspaper articles, about solved cases, presumably ones that Douglas Tent had secretly helped the police to crack. Across from Adam, behind the desk, sat detective Douglas Tent.

Douglas put a fresh cigarette in his mouth and lit it, tossing the pack and the lighter into the melee upon the desk. His movements slowed, he looked carefully at Adam. Finally, he began, "Captain Ahab had the white whale. Sherlock Holmes had Professor Moriarty. I have Malcom Esperanza."

Adam's eyes widened, and his mouth fell open. "Holy shit! Is he real too?"

"Real, yes. And yet unreal somehow." Douglas stood up, still in his bathrobe, and turned to put a hand on the sideboard, that lined the wall behind his desk. On it was a silver tray, with glass tumblers and bottles of alcohol. His head pointed downward at a bare place on the cabinet top, as he examined the images he was constructing in the emptiness.

"Malcom Esperanza is an expert at bank robbing, at seduction, at art forgery. He is an ingenious pastry chef."

"*The Case of the Muffin of Death.*"

"Precisely." Douglas took a long drag on his cigarette, then returned to sit again in the chair behind his desk. His slicked back hair had become disturbed, and errant strands were hanging chaotically out of place. "No one knows what he looks like, who he really is. He is a master of disguise, whom I have met in various forms—without even realizing it until it was too late. Malcom Esperanza, naturally, is only one of many names. His true identity is a complete mystery. He could be someone I've unwittingly known for years."

"He could be a woman," offered Adam.

"Yes, I suppose he could." Douglas Tent retrieved the pocket notebook and pencil from his robe, and jotted something down on it, that appeared to be about the length of "He could be a woman." He then replaced the pencil and notebook, and went back to smoking his cigarette.

Adam's body felt frozen in his chair. "Do you think that Malcom Esperanza had something to do with the murder of Roland Bellwether?" he asked.

Douglas's eyes narrowed, as he stared at Adam across the desk. His mouth was tight, as he took another long drag on his cigarette. He flicked its long ash onto an a pile of paperwork, missing the ashtray three inches away.

"One thing that I have never revealed about Malcom Esperanza, one thing that is not in the stories—"

Adam sat slightly forward, unconsciously holding his breath.

"It has never been revealed that Malcom Esperanza is perhaps the greatest hypnotist on planet earth."

"Wow," said Adam Hume.

"Think of it: why would Roland, after freeing himself from the bondage of the madman Dio Macina, proceed to walk over to the firearms cabinet, unlock it with his key, sit back down in the nearby chair, and shoot himself in the head?"

"Why?"

"Because...he was under the influence of a powerful hypnotic suggestion."

"Wow," said Adam Hume. Douglas took another drag of his cigarette.

"Hypnosis," continued Douglas Tent, "can, in the wrong hands, be a powerful tool for crime. Physical force is a blunt instrument. A true criminal artist, such as Esperanza, relies on mental prowess, trickery, and misdirection. And the manipulation of the mind." He went to his book shelf and selected a volume that was out of place among the modern paperbacks. As Douglas removed it, Adam saw that it was old, and leather-bound. He sat back down behind his desk, and opened its yellowed pages.

"This book," said Douglas, "is an only known copy. It is a defense of atheism written in 1889, by a philosopher who has since been forgotten to history. As far as arguments for atheism go, it's nothing groundbreaking. But I have found that this book has an amazing, one might say, magical quality. But, of course, we know that magic is merely science poorly understood."

"Of course."

"There is a quality to the tone and rhythm, created when a person hears the words of this book read aloud, that cause the hearer to go into a hypnotic trance. It works with every part of the book that I have tested. It's quite remarkable. I've been using it to hypnotize myself."

Wrinkles appeared in the space between Adam's eyebrows. "Why would you want to hypnotize yourself?" he asked.

"To fight fire with fire, you see. I put myself into a hypnotic state, by reading myself a few sentences from this book. And then I implant suggestions into my own mind. I tell myself that I am comfortable and at ease with my place, in the godless universe in which we find ourselves. I tell myself that I will fearlessly pursue a search for truth, using science, and eschewing philosophy and religion. I use the enemy's weapon against him. It is a very new technique, begging to be analyzed and further understood."

"I see," said Adam.

"The amazing thing is, that the words of the book don't

appear to have any special qualities, when you hear them. For example," Douglas looked down at the time-worn pages and began to read, "'Atheism, its tenants, its insights, its moods and beliefs, have been extant since time out of mind, offering sobering divulgement into the *nuit blanche* of human life. There is an apocryphal reminiscence transmitted apropos of the Greek philosopher Democritus, whereby Democritus is said, on a peripatetic excursion, to have come upon a moribund olive tree—"

Adam suddenly opened his eyes, not realizing that they had been closed. He felt that he had nodded off for a fraction of a second. Douglas didn't seem to have noticed.

"Fear not," said Douglas Tent. "That's not enough of it to put you into a trance. As you can see, the writing is unremarkable. But it turns out to have an amazing effect on the human mind, for reasons that I cannot yet explain scientifically. I tell you these things to impress upon you that this case is too dangerous for me to, in good conscience, take you on as a partner. I must remain vigilant, through rigorous logical thinking, and through the mental buttressing provided by self-hypnosis. I hope I've been of some help, but now I must be alone."

Douglas Tent extinguished his cigarette by rubbing it into an ashtray, and stood up.

"But, detective Tent, you don't understand. I need this. I need to solve this case."

"As I say, being a detective is a lonely quest. The state of Texas requires that a person have a license to investigate cases for money. But nothing is stopping you from investigating this case for free, on your own. Being a student of crime is, in this way, like being a painter, or being a streaker. No one can make you a streaker. You are one as soon as you pull down your pants and start running. Please let me know if you find anything out."

"Thank you for your time," said Adam, and left the office of Douglas Tent.

5

A Theological Interlude

"If you're curious about what a Christian—and specifically a Baptist—believes, we'd love to have you attend a church service."

"I don't think that I'm ready for that," said Adam. He was back in the cramped office of Pastor Moses Lacuna, cloistered off of the small office area—an inner sanctum. He was again addressing him across the clutter on his desk. His desk's clutter, Adam noticed, felt more wholesome than the clutter he had seen on the desk of Douglas Tent. Both heavily featured papers and obscure books. But Douglas Tent had the occasional chemical and weapon, and peered into the dark side of things, with no hope of any final redemption. The desk of Douglas Tent was dedicated to understanding evil. Pastor Lacuna's desk was aimed at knowing the good.

"My problem," said Adam, "is that I realize now that I have to hunker down, and investigate this case on my own. The detective I mentioned, he doesn't want to work together with me on it. But, I think, if I can make some progress on my own, then he might be impressed enough to let me work with him."

"I see."

"But my mind's not right. I mean, based on what the detective told me, about what he believes is going on, with this case, a really evil guy is behind it. A criminal mastermind."

"Interesting." Pastor Lacuna took a piece of gum out of a pack on his desk and started chewing it, all the while, maintaining polite eye contact with Adam. He was a practiced listener.

"So, I figure, Pastor, that my mind has to be right, if I'm

going up against evil. But, it isn't. It hasn't been right since I saw Roland dead in that shadowy room. So, since then, well—I feel like you might be able to help me. To prepare me. I think I need to decide what I believe about God. What you were saying before…"

"Yes, where did we leave off?" Pastor Lacuna straightened himself, by scooting his butt to the back of his chair.

"You were going to tell me how it is that the human mind proves that God exists."

"Yes, oh, yes—that's right. Well, it's not a deductive proof. Like the thing of creation being a miracle, it's more a matter of brushing aside the misinformation that clouds the issue, so that you can see that, on a basic intuitive level, it just makes more philosophical sense to believe that the mind, like creation, is an obvious miracle. And where you have a miracle, there you have God."

"So, you're saying that, like the creation of the external world, the internal world—the mind—must have a supernatural cause?"

"Yes," said Moses Lacuna. "And like the world, it should be obvious, but we've become blind to it, through familiarity and alternative theories that don't really make sense.

"Consider what the mind is," he went on. "Consider what happens when you turn your mind's eye upon a memory, or an imaginary something. The word 'angel' conjures a specific mental picture. Many imagine a benevolent-seeming man with wings. A person can employ his imagination to examine this fictitious angel in his mind; he can see it in detail, how the angel is dressed, its face, its posture. But, where is that angel?"

"What do you mean?"

"I mean, where is it? There's nowhere in the world that it can be. You won't find it in the brain. In the brain there is just tissue and chemical reactions. True, there may be certain chemical reactions that my brain undergoes, specifically when I'm thinking about an angel. But that is not an angel. That's not what my inner eye is looking at."

"Okay, I think I see what you mean."

"That is why there is a difference between the brain and the mind. The brain is the lump of tissue in the world, that goes into various chemical, electrical states, depending on what's going on in my mind. But my mind is something separate. My mind is where the angel is."

"So, then, where is the mind?" asked Adam.

"Throughout the history of philosophy—until just recently—it's been understood that the mind must be its own substance, separate from physical matter and energy. Just as physical matter and energy have certain definitional properties, so, too, mind is a substance—albeit an immaterial, supernatural, if you will, substance—that has its own particular properties. Most importantly it has the property of containing thoughts, and imagined things, like angels."

"How do we know that the brain doesn't contain imagined angels?"

"Well," the Pastor answered, "because it just doesn't. We can see that the brain is a physical thing, and that there are no angels in it. No matter how complicated it is, it's still a physical thing. Whereas, we can introspect, and observe that the mind—and the imagined angel in it—is obviously a non-physical thing, with totally different properties than the brain. Therefore they are separate. They obviously have some causal connection between them. But they are distinct, and made of two different substances."

"I suppose that makes sense. It kind of makes me light-headed to think about it."

"One important attribute of the mind, that proves it to be non-physical—to be supernatural—is that it possesses free will."

"Okay." Adam considered this. "How do we know that we have free will?"

"Again. It's obvious. Can you imagine what it feels like to fall down stairs?"

"Yes," said Adam, "I can." He grinned. "In my mind."

"Well, that's what being under the control of the laws of physics feels like: it feels like being out of control. Whereas, a free action—" Pastor Lacuna picked up a yellow sharpened pencil from his desk, and held it level in front of him. "Picking up this pencil is a freely chosen act, using my free will. It doesn't feel like falling down stairs, because it wasn't determined by the laws of physics. It was determined by free will—it was caused by the supernatural substance that is my mind, feeding motion into the physical system of the world."

"So, then, every free-willed action breaks the laws of physics?"

"You could say that, yes. Or you could say that the action of an immaterial mind adds something into the otherwise-closed system of physical determinism. So what it adds isn't determined by the system. It's only determined by the mental state of the immaterial mind at the time it acts. That's free will. God's actions, likewise, are not determined by physical law. When he adds something in, it's called a miracle.

"So," Lacuna concluded, "it should be obvious—from noticing that the contents of our minds are not themselves physical, and from noticing that we have free will—that an immaterial mind—or soul, if you will—exists, separate from the body. In fact, if you think about it, we never actually experience the world directly. All we ever actually experience is the contents of our minds: thoughts, memories, perceptions. We only assume that they are caused by an external world—which is a logical conclusion. But, it would actually make more sense to accept mental substance, and be skeptical of physical substance —which, of course, is the opposite of what the atheist does."

"Fascinating." Adam rested his head on one hand, and looked out the window, thinking this over. On his face was the look of incredulity teetering on the brink of defeat. It lightly started to rain.

"I see what you're saying," said Adam, "about these arguments for God's existence being obvious. That the world exists, and the inner mind, and that these cry out for God as an explanation. And that the natural explanations aren't sufficient."

"By their very nature, they can't be."

"You make that case well. But, of course, you aren't just a theist. You don't just believe in God. You're a Baptist. You believe in the Bible, I assume. And something about Jesus."

"Yes," said Pastor Lacuna. He took another piece of gum out of the pack on his desk, put it in his mouth in addition to the one that was already there, leaned back in his chair, and began chewing it into the first.

"If God exists, then a natural question arises," said Pastor Lacuna, "Is he giving us the silent treatment, or are there things he wants us to know? Seems like there would be. We believe that God has communicated authoritatively to man, through prophets in the past, and that this revelation is collected, for us today, in the sixty-six books of the Christian Bible."

Moses Lacuna gave a friendly pat to a sizable book, with a soft imitation-leather cover on his desk, that bore—in gold lettering—the words "Holy Bible".

"But there are multiple conflicting scriptures from various world religions, and there are even multiple versions of the Christian Bible, are there not?"

"Yes," continued the pastor, "but for it to be true that God has communicated with man, there need only be one true book, that comes from God. The false ones, then, come from someone else."

"The devil?"

"Yes." The pastor continued. "We believe that the Christian Bible is the word of God, and that it has been preserved through the ages, with only inconsequential variations. In this Bible we are told that the central dilemma of the human condition is that God is infinite and perfectly holy, whereas we are finite and sinful. Therefore, God had to do something to save us from the alienation between us and him, because we cannot save ourselves."

"Okay."

"That is why there had to be the Incarnation. God's justice is perfect, therefore sins must be punished. But God's love is also perfect, therefore he pays the ultimate price to save us—he sends his Son to die for our sins on the cross, two-thousand years ago. Only God could save us, but only a man could die for the sins of man. Therefore, you have God, come to earth as the only sinless man: the man Christ Jesus."

"Okay, but which is it? Is he God, or is he the Son of God. I remember from when I used to go to church as a kid, that there is a Trinity. Why is that the case?"

Pastor Lacuna raised both eyebrows and looked into the middle distance, as he absent-mindedly put a third piece of gum into his mouth, and started chewing. The collected mass of the three pieces of gum proved overwhelming. He removed the wad of gum from his mouth, considered it for a second, and then disposed of it beneath his desk, presumably into a trash can.

"The Trinity is taught in the Bible," he said, "and various teachers have constructed different analogies to try to understand it. The traditional formulation is that God is one God, and three persons. But what does that mean? The way I think about it, there is one perfect, divine mind—one God—that is experienced by three separate consciousnesses—hence three persons."

"I see. But why is that necessary?"

"My own opinion is that it has to do with time and space. God the Father is the divine consciousness that dwells outside of space and time, whereas Jesus—being a man—experiences the divine mind bounded by space and time. God, being God, has the properties of omniscience, omnipotence, and omnipresence. The Father has these qualities outright. The Son, acting in space and time, is omniscient and omnipotent, but, as man, isn't omnipresent. That's why we have the Holy Ghost, in my opinion: he acts as the omnipresence of Christ, directing people to the Savior. And that's why there is a chain of command, from the Father, to the Son, to the Holy Ghost. I would say the Trinity is a consequence of a timeless God interacting with a timebound, space-bound world."

"Interesting. But, does that mean, that the Trinity began with the world?"

"No," said Pastor Lacuna, "Because the world is the expression of God's nature. He is by nature triune."

Adam sat and regarded Pastor Lacuna from across the desk. The patter of the rain outside had increased in volume. Soil drank plentifully from the sky, and the sun still shown from behind dark clouds.

"I have this distinct feeling, Pastor Lacuna," said Adam, "consciously or subconsciously, that if I can figure out what happened to Roland, that it'll bring peace to my mind. My mind has been so troubled, since I found him dead, there at work. And yet, what brings me here today, is that I'm afraid that I can't be effective as a detective, with such a troubled mind."

"The detective that you mentioned, whom you want to hire you, is his mind at peace?"

"No, it's not…not at all."

"I hope I've been of some help," said Pastor Lacuna. "The best advice I can give you is, 'The truth shall make you free.'"

6

On the Case!

Adam considered all of the philosophy that Pastor Lacuna had introduced into his mind, as he drove the red supervisor's security golf cart, through the refreshing breeze at work late Friday night. Since Roland's murder, there was a hole in the work schedule, that needed to be filled. Against his reluctance to do so, Adam was now promoted to weekend supervisor, on the overnight shift, to help cover the needed hours. Despite not wanting to do it initially, on this, his first shift as supervisor, Adam instantly enjoyed the freedom of his new position. Rather than being stuck in one of the guard houses along the fenced perimeter, Adam was now free to drive the electric security cart about the grounds, through the spacious outdoor parking lots of the converted shopping mall, keeping a trusty, solitary patrol against crime. Wind came through the half opened plastic windshield of the cart, splashing against Adam's face and the polyester of his uniform, the moon looking on in the adventurous promise of the weekend night, and Adam meditated on the first investigative step he would take, in the solving of the murder of Roland Bellwether, the dead man whose position he was now filling. He felt vulnerable, yet capable, as he remembered that Dio Macina was still out in the world somewhere, as was whoever had caused the death of his former coworker.

Adam pulled up to a remote corner inside the facility's tall, chain-link perimeter fence. He got out of his vehicle and took a few deep breaths. Beyond the fence were silhouetted trees, beyond which were the lawns of residential houses. Malcom Esperanza. Malcom Esperanza. What in the world would become of all of this? Was Adam going to get himself murdered by an evanescent criminal genius? And, equally of interest: what would happen to Adam's soul afterwards? The breeze was cool but humid. The night stood stalwart in its coy repose. What in the world was going to happen? Adam knew he would have to risk everything, if he was going to pretend that he was prepared to really investigate the murder of Roland Bellwether. But he was beginning to understand that it is the essence of the human condition that risking everything is unavoidable. We're all going to die someday. We've all got to decide which God to believe in, or whether to believe in any. There is no safe middle ground.

Adam looked up at the moon: bright and regal, floating and far: calling out to him. He remembered that night that he was lost in the woods, and suddenly the feeling of the presence of God was again in his heart, nagging and expansive. His soul was warmed and excited. The overall effect of the discussion with the pastor, Adam realized, had not been to convince him of any specific logical point, but rather—he now found himself realizing—it had left Adam with the conviction that God's existence is not impossible, or unreasonable. Whatever the merits of the individual arguments, Adam now understood that belief in God was a viable option. And, if so, then why shouldn't Adam decide that his feeling of the presence of God—the feeling he was now, again, feeling—why not decide that it is, in fact, what it seems to be? That it is a holy message from God declaring himself and his love? Adam, in that moment, realized that he trusted the feeling, and that he was now a believer in God. At the same moment he realized that the dread he'd been feeling all week—with its unbearable ideation of death—at once seemed to part like the Red Sea, seemed to clear away like fog, to be replaced by this inner witness from God that Adam was embracing. Tears welled up in Adam's eyes, and the inner pressure from his week of torment flowed out of him, as he wept alone, on the remote and empty pavement. Now he knew, he was ready for risk.

Adam walked toward the Security Operations Center, with a plan to trade deception for clues. The Security Operations Center (or SOC), was in a windowless room, in the heart of the internally sprawling internet company's complex, housed in the erstwhile shopping center. To get there he walked across the dull-colored carpet, past escalators dutifully rising and falling, among the multiple abandoned floors of cubicles and coffee stations, disappearing into every direction, all decorated by kitsch pop culture references—strewn about desks, and painted officially on some of the many garishly-colored walls.

Before entering, he crumpled up a grocery-store receipt, that he had happened to find in his pocket, and threw it into a small trashcan nearby. Then he scanned his ID badge, which—now that he was a shift supervisor, at least tonight—unlocked the heavy maple door, and he walked confidently into SOC. Adam had been curious about this room, ever since he had started guarding this site. It had an air of prestige and omnipotence about it, the way it was referred to. Whenever a guard, at one of the guard houses along the perimeter fence, had a question about procedure, or needed to clear a visitor for entrance, protocol required the guard to "radio SOC" for guidance. It appeared to be a special breed of guard, that was selected—brought up from the ranks—to slave mentally away in the Security Operations Center, answering—it was said—emails, and monitoring cameras—from not only this facility, but from the company's facilities in Mexico, London, China, and all around the world.

The visage of the inside of SOC, when Adam had first seen it earlier in the week, did not disappoint. The SOC guard sat facing a counter full of computers and monitors. Above the computer monitors were two large flat-screen television monitors on which were dozens of camera feeds, showing live footage from areas all over the labyrinthian facility. Above these, just below the ceiling, was a row of analog clocks, their arms aesthetically clashing, as each clock declared different times, and each subscribed by white letters on a black strip that indicated, "London", "Mexico City", "Amsterdam", "Singapore", and a few others. To the right of these monitors and clocks, the rest of the front wall was filled up with two more big-screen television monitors, each of which had a different digital map of the world displayed. One map seemed to be reporting, in real time, gun shootings in the east, and wild fires in the west, as they occurred with surprising regularity. The other monitor was tracking something else, which Adam couldn't make out. The rear wall, from waist-high and upwards, was covered, along the length of it, with a white board, on which various lists of words and numbers were written all along it, by a variety of colored markers, according to some system of organization that Adam had no idea about. Between these two walls—in the middle of the room—were four adjacent work stations, populated with the odd pieces of personal flare—like personal work areas are—owned by the company's higher level, internal security people, that would only be there during the day. At seemingly random locations around the room were fireproof containers, and security gadgets and equipment, that Adam was not authorized to understand.

  The only thing that spoiled the otherwise enjoyable experience of being inside this miniature fortress and shrine to the security profession was the identity of the security guard occupying the chair in SOC tonight. Jack Burnwood. Jack, when he had been a guard in the perimeter guard houses, had been the bane of everybody else's existence. He was not a smart man, but he was possessed of a singular obsession, which empowered him with a kind of genius when in pursuit of his calling. His calling was to get his coworkers fired. He was known to employ note-taking, surreptitious sound recording, and frantic calls to corporate hotlines to carry out his quest. Multiple site supervisors had fallen by his sword. Again, not a smart man, but he knew certain catch words, that would send his complaints up the chain of command: words like, "harassment", and "sleeping". Probably pushing 50, but with a youthful quality that oblivious stupidity sometimes brings, Jack was lanky, and over six-feet tall. His salt and pepper hair was always carefully combed back and styled into a pompadour, and, behind large thick glasses, his froglike eyes seemed to blink in an unconvincing show of innocence. Putting all of the pieces together, Jack Burnwood was a pure, old-fashioned dickhead.

"Hello," said Jack Burnwood, as Adam entered, not turning around or taking his gaze from the computer screen in front on him.

"Hello, Jack," said Adam. "Here is last shift's paperwork." Adam placed a small stack of papers he had been holding onto a table. "Do you need a break?"

"No, I'm good."

Adam grimaced, unseen by Jack. Him taking a break was crucial to Adam's plan for clue acquisition. "Are you sure, because I've got some extra door checks to do tonight. So, it might be a while before I can get back here again."

"No, I'm good." Then, after a few frustrating seconds, "Well, okay. I do actually need to do a number two." Jack turned his swiveling chair to the side, and then stood up. His show of pleasantness was present, and hollow as always. Adam noticed that Jack reminded him of the late actor and director Harold Ramis, when he was heavier, if he'd been lobotomized. Jack, in his clean and well-pressed security-guard uniform, sauntered out of SOC, and Adam waited for a few tense moments before sitting in his chair. The SOC chair, seat of all power. Behind him Jack had left, to one side of his computer screen, a tidy arrangement of metal lunch box, thermos, and a large, leather-bound Bible. What kind of Christian was Jack Burnwood? Adam glared at Jack's lunchbox briefly, and then remembered his mission.

Word had gone through the security-guard grapevine that week, that SOC officers had been combing through the dozens and dozens of camera feeds always filming throughout the plant, looking for relevant information about the death of Roland Bellwether. Some said that the police had already made a digital copy of all camera information for that night. Some said that the police were asking security to review the footage, and deliver anything suspicious that was found. Perhaps both. Then, just yesterday, a memo was printed out, displayed in all guardhouses, and personally mentioned to all guards, by each shift supervisor. The guards in the guardhouses had access to some camera feeds, though not as many as the guard in SOC. The memo said that accessing camera footage from last Sunday night—the night of Roland's death—was forbidden, unless specifically authorized to do so, and that doing so without authorization would result in disciplinary action "up to and including termination".

Accessing this footage was exactly what Adam intended to do tonight. Rather than accessing it from one of the guardhouses, which would require combing through various feeds, the navigation of which he was not fully familiar with, Adam reasoned that he would try to find out what footage SOC had syphoned out for reportage to the police—if in fact they had done so. It might be a long shot, but Adam would poke around a little, in SOC's computer, to see what he could find.

The idea of doing this while Jack was on a bathroom break sent a cold chill up Adam's spine. But, for all he knew, the clues that may be on the SOC computer may be given to the police and erased tomorrow. He had seen, on one of the many camera feeds, on one of the big-screen monitors, which bathroom Jack had gone into. Jack had said he would be doing a number two, which Adam desperately hoped was a lengthy procedure for Mr. Burnwood.

His first problem was that there were many different windows and programs open, in accord with the many digital things SOC officers were called upon to do during a shift, that other guards—including Adam—had only vaguely heard about. In order to leave no evidence of what he was doing, Adam found a way to minimize all windows at once, so he could view the desktop icons. He scanned the many files and desktop icons, which were a conceptual mess to him. A panicked voice in his head told him to put Jack's windows back up, and get out of his chair before it was too late. A slideshow of the decent smiling faces of the guards that had fallen at Jack's hand started playing in Adam's mind. He shook his head to focus. He glanced at the camera feed on one of the big flat-screen monitors above, showing the hallway outside of Jack's bathroom. No movement.

Adam's mouth felt dry, the surface of his skin was cooled by fear and the beginning of sweat. He decided to give up. But then, he saw it, a single yellow file folder among the mess of things, simply labeled "CONFIDENTIAL". He opened it, with a click of the mouse. There were only three files in the digital folder: a text document labeled "FOR POLICE ONLY", a digital picture, and a sound file. Adam clicked on the text file. It opened to reveal a report, written by security, for the police, about what they had found on the surveille cameras. Adam found himself rereading words, and restarting sentences, as his comprehension was impeded by nervousness. Pull yourself together, Adam, he told himself. He was finally able to skim the document sufficiently to realize what it was saying: all relevant footage had already been turned over to the police. However, some new things had been found. There had been no camera in the mechanical room, wherein Roland was shot. However, a nearby storage room did have a camera, which had been thought to be broken. However, as it turned out, the camera, while it didn't record video, due to some unknown malfunction, it did record sound for a few seconds every hour. A digital file would be provided to police, of a few seconds of audio that the camera had happened to record during Roland's death. Also, a car had been identified, apparently occupied, parked in a visitors' spot, outside the perimeter fence. A crimson Nissan Versa. No owner for the car could be located among company employees, and the car was there for much of the night, including the time period in which Roland would have died.

Adam was frozen by the revelation that a sound file existed, which perhaps had captured Roland's death. He felt a warm blush break out on his neck and checks. Sweat gathered at the hairline of his forehead. He closed the report, checked Jack's bathroom hallway camera for movement—nothing—then clicked the digital picture file. It was a still, taken from a camera feed, that pictured the crimson Nissan Versa in question, an undistinguishable figure perhaps occupying the driver's seat. Adam closed the picture file, and opened the audio file. He didn't want to hear it, but didn't have time to brace himself. The computer's media player window opened and the file played.

It displayed a totally black picture, provided by the blind camera. The effect was overwhelmingly eerie, as the black screen was suddenly accompanied by the muffled sound of the legs of a chair scraping chaotically on a cement floor. Then the faint, guttural sound of a man struggling, as if with constraints. It's Roland, Adam realized, a droplet of sweat falling to his eyebrow. Roland is freeing himself from his restraints, in the chair. In his mind, he could see, with unforgiving clarity, Roland in his underwear, tied to a chair in the stark mechanical room, a human being losing against fate. The struggling stopped, and a relieved sigh was heard. Roland was free. Then, inexplicably, the muffled sound of a cell phone ringing. Adam remembered that the mad man had left Roland's phone behind, when he had stolen his clothing. Then he heard Roland's voice—his dead co-worker's voice—immortalized on this piece of digital evidence. He merely said, hello, by way of answering his phone. There was a momentary pause, while Roland, presumably, was listening to the one who had called him. It seemed to last an eternity. Then, suddenly, horrifyingly, Roland started screaming. The scream cut through the muffle of the concealed, broken camera, it cut through the flaws in the digital file, it cut through time and space. The dead man was yelling one phrase over and over, shattering the serenity and safety of SOC. He was yelling, "I'm blind! I'm blind! I'm blind!" The yelling must have concealed the sound of the gun cabinet being opened. After the blood-curdling proclamation was made maybe two-dozen times, a gun shot rang out. There were a few seconds of utter silence, and the media file ended.

Adam only had a second to be stunned, before the realization came to him, that he hadn't been checking the camera covering Jack's bathroom! How long had it been? Adam looked imploringly at the camera feed of that hallway. No sign of Jack's ridiculous gait. He glanced at some other cameras, that looked at nearby places. With horror, Adam's eyes landed on a camera feed which was pointed at the door to SOC itself. Jack was extending his ID card to the sensor, to electronically unlock the door. There was no time to restore Jack's computer to its original condition, and to get out of his chair. Adam's security guard career—which he loved—flashed before his eyes, and he struggled, in his heart, to bid it goodbye.

Then, miraculously, on the camera, Adam saw Jack withdraw his ID card. Then he bent at the waist, the tall, uniformed thinness of him folding in half, so that he could put his face into the small nearby trashcan. He was meticulously examining something in it, with his eyes. Adam quickly closed the confidential digital folder, restored Jack's windows and programs, stood up, and positioned his chair as he remembered it being. He had just finished wiping the sweat from his brow with one sleeve, when Jack appeared in SOC.

"Hey, Jack," said Adam. "Was it a refreshing number two?"

"Oh, yeah," said Jack, who breezed past Adam without giving him much regard, and retook his place in his chair, his gaze once again locked onto the work he had to do.

Adam knew what had occurred. The receipt that he had crumpled up and tossed into the trash can. Jack could not resist inspecting it. Because, you see, it might have had information—anything—that Jack might have been able to use against someone—anyone. Jack was a kind of detective himself, always looking for information to be used for evil. In this case, Jack's curiosity had backfired, costing him a golden opportunity for causing misery.

As Adam left SOC—left Jack to rule over the powers of surveillance that the higher-ups had unwisely granted to him—Adam said a prayer of thanks, for the delivery from termination that God had provided him just then. He was delighted to have God to thank, and to believe in, at that moment. What a better world this was. If the only eye in the sky had turned out to be Jack Burnwood, then the world would certainly be doomed.

7

Surveillance

The next afternoon, after a few hours of day-sleeping, Adam found himself inside an ancient gold-colored station wagon on a stakeout with fabled private detective Douglas Tent. The car's windows were cracked, as the Texas heat radiated in. Because running one's vehicle's engine would defeat the stealthy purpose of the surveillance investigator, the car's motor—and hence its A/C—wasn't running. Instead, inspector Tent had placed a spare car battery in the back seat of the station wagon, attached to an AC-to-DC power invertor. This device consisted of a pair of metal clamps that affixed to the terminals of the car battery, and connected to a small metal box with two power outlets in it. Into one of these power outlets was plugged a small up-tilted oscillating desk fan, whose breeze blew sweetly across the back of the necks of the sunglasses-wearing crime-fighters seated in the front seat—Douglas Tent explaining some of the finer points of the art of surveillance to Adam, as they continued to watch their target location.

"Before I go out on a surveillance," Douglas Tent was saying, behind his cheap, aviator-style sunglasses, "I always print off pictures of a missing child, from the internet."

"Why do you do that?" Adam asked, from behind his cheap, movie-star-style sunglasses.

"Because," said Douglas Tent, "Someone asks you why you've been parked suspiciously for hours in their neighborhood, and you say that you're a private detective on a case, and you hand them one of the missing-child posters. After that, you'll usually have the neighbors bringing you food and drink, to assist your heroic efforts in defense of the missing child, including maybe even the douchebag whom you've actually been hired to take pictures of."

"Interesting," said Adam Hume.

The gold-colored station wagon, whose age was proven by its working cassette player, had limo-level tent on its side and back windows. This made its occupants nearly undetectable, as they sat, sweaty and detecting. The unassuming surveillance vehicle sat in the front parking spaces of a convenience store—the Buy-N-Leave Food Store—whose two gas pumps appeared to be perpetually out of order. The store shared its building and half of the building's façade with a barbershop for dogs called The Fluffy Bitch. As the detectives sat in the station wagon in the convenience store parking lot, meditating on the details of crime detection, various of their fellow citizens of San Antonio were coming and going behind them, dropping off their beloved dogs, and then picking them up again four hours later, their nails and fur having been shortened by cheerful women in flower-print scrubs.

The main mystery, however, on Adam's mind at that moment, had nothing to do with dogs, but rather concerned the question of why he and the world-famous private detective Douglas Tent were in that station wagon at all, and why they were surveilling the large reflective windows of Douglas Tent's own detective agency—in the building he shared with the dentist's office—from across the street.

"When doing surveillance in cold weather, to avoid one's windows fogging up, apply shaving cream to the glass, and then wipe it off," Douglas Tent advised. "This will cause fog not to gather." He looked wistfully into the middle distance for a moment, as if remembering the fogs of England. "I've considered what you said before," said Tent, "about Malcom Esperanza being a woman. It was an insight so obvious, that the powers of my genius had overlooked it. Often when Roland and I would discuss a case, his average powers of human reasoning would, through an accident of chance, stumble upon a missing piece that—while he was impotent to appreciate its significance—would turn out to be the secret ingredient the master chef of my intellect had been grasping for."

A memory of Roland flashed into Adam's mind. This time it wasn't the one that had plagued him in his former atheism —the image of Roland's rictus of death. Rather, he was now, for a second, transported to a visual image of Roland, during a normal uneventful night at the security-guard jobsite they had shared. When Roland was speaking of his love of video games, and giving no indication of his secret life as an investigator's assistant and biographer.

"Don't we know, old chum," Tent continued (Had Adam been promoted to the status of "Old chum" already, or had detective Tent been smoking crack again?) "Don't we know well, that it is part of the psyche of the human female, to bide her time, to have a superhuman patience, when waiting to serve the cold dish of revenge?" Adam began to wonder what storied catastrophes the annals of the universe must contain, filed under the rubric of "Douglas Tent and Women".

"A woman," Douglas Tent continued, "who is also a savant of law-breaking, a Picasso of banking fraud, the Georgia O'Keeffe of bodily dismemberment. Such a one would be insidious enough to worm into my very daily life without my detection of it. She would take the most innocuous of forms: just salient enough not to be thought to be hiding, but hidden enough to be overlooked: a character at once annoying and anodyne."

Adam had no idea what the detective was talking about, and again wondered how altered his state currently was. But, then, was this not the master of detection, that had solved all of the cases Adam had pored over with delight in *Detective Stories Magazine*? Adam had faith that Tent's substance abuse—which had, in fact, been at least hinted at in the stories—was an integral part of his unique and powerful mind. He was a kind of artist of thought. He knew what he was doing.

Adam suddenly became afraid that Malcom Esperanza —woman or not—was at that moment planning a devastating physical attack on Tent's office, and that that was the reason for their surveillance of it. He imagined an ear-shattering boom erupting from the tall reflective windows that encircled the first floor of the building. He imagined glass and fire ejaculated toward them—metal, brick, and shards of window landing all around them in a traumatizing cacophony. Adam adjusted his sunglasses pointlessly, and decided to slightly change the subject.

"As I said before," said Adam, "I found some clues, at work, in the case—"

"As I said before," said Tent, "We are not working together on that case. It's too dangerous. I can't stop you from investigating it on your own. But we can't be partners. I've agreed to give you this brief tutelage in stationary and mobile surveillance. That is all."

"I understand. I don't hold you responsible for whatever happens. But couldn't you give me some feedback? Not as a partner, just as advice. As a teacher? Let's say it's hypothetical. Let's say, suppose, in a case like Roland's murder, a certain clue was found."

"What clue would that be, then, hypothetically?"

"Let's say it was an audio recording—no video—capturing the fatal shot sustained by Roland. But here's the strangeness of it—"

"Good clues are always strange," said Douglas Tent.

"Roland's voice is on the audio. Right before he shoots himself—if that's in fact what happened—he is heard screaming, over and over again, 'I'm blind! I'm blind! I'm blind!'"

Adam looked at the detective, ready to gauge his reaction, ready to absorb his guidance. Detective Tent was still for a moment. Then he slowly removed his aviator sunglasses with one hand, and, with the other, ran fingers and thumb soothingly along his eyebrows, with his eyes closed. Then he opened his eyes, and lifted his head.

"I told you, remember, that Roland was under the influence of a hypnotic suggestion—that is why he shot himself.

Malcom Esperanza found a way to induce a trance-like state in Roland, without him realizing it, after which he implanted the instructions to commit suicide, once the trigger words were received."

"Oh," inserted Adam, suddenly realizing he'd left something out. "Right before Roland starts screaming—before he shot himself—his telephone rings. He answers it; he's listening for a few seconds; and then he starts screaming, and then the gun shot, and silence."

Tent's sunglasses-less eyes gave Adam a look of annoyed amazement.

"Well, of course! That clinches it. The trigger words were given over the telephone. Esperanza, or one of his associates, had Roland's number and called it. They knew enough to know that he had access to guns at work, and implanted him with the suggestion to use them on himself, when prompted." His eyes were stern with terrible realization.

"And the attack from the madman Dio Macina was just a coincidence?"

"I believe so, yes," said Tent. "Ironically, if Macina had tied him up better, it would have saved his life. He would have been unable to answer the phone when it rang. The fact that he was in such close proximity to the guns, when he received the call, is also unfortunate."

"Yeah." Adam considered this morbid and fantastical idea. "But, I've heard it said, detective Tent, that a man cannot be hypnotized to do something against his will?"

"Ah, yes." Tent replaced his aviator sunglasses. Their twin surfaces gave a steely reflection, like the windows of the dentist's office and detective agency they were presently surveilling. "That is where the apparent blindness comes in. Think about it. Roland was the teller of the tales that we lived together. He was the eyes of our audience, watching along as we quested against evil, looking for truth. It pained the black heart of Malcom Esperanza, to see glory given to the good guys, through the undefeatable medium of the written word. He had to silence Roland. He—or she—had to put out his eyes.

"Roland wouldn't have killed himself, simply because the suggestion was implanted in him to do so. His very soul would have balked at that. But, Roland was a writer. His identity depended on the light of his eyes, on being able to turn them bravely upon life's rich pageant—upon crime, and evil, and truth, and friendship." Adam saw Tent's Adam's Apple tremble, and he wondered if, behind his sunglasses, he was crying.

"You see? You see the deep evil of it all?" Tent asked. "Esperanza knew that it was not in Roland's nature to kill himself, unless he thought that he was permanently blind. Trapped in a world of darkness—or thinking himself so—Roland would be vulnerable to the suicidal suggestion. The hypnotic instruction to kill himself piggybacked on the hypnotic illusion that he had lost his sight: both were triggered by the words over the phone."

At that moment, unnoticed by the detectives, a customer of the doggie barbershop exited the business, with a poodle in her arms—a poodle whose hair and nails had been trimmed much too short. Already the customer was composing the words of a poisoned-pen Google review.

A maroon minivan pulled into the parking lot of Tent's building across the street.

Tent fortified himself internally. "We must not disintegrate when met with the horrors of our enemy. We must persevere," he said. "The evil of Esperanza runs deeper than I could have ever imagined. He has taken on the guise of a woman—or maybe he was one all along. He has taken up residence inside the walls of my own headquarters. Imagine that. My walls breached, my defenses bypassed. Not by cannon or rifle. But by the unassuming demeanor of a middle-aged blond woman. All she had to do was sign a lease. The campaign has gone on for months; and I was powerless to fight back, because I didn't see the attack happening. Did she poison me? Rig a gargoyle to land on my head? No, not this time. This time Esperanza plays a different game. She complains about my noise levels to the landlord. She accidentally receives my mail and takes an inappropriate amount of time to get it to me. She changes our shared thermostat."

The driver's side door of the maroon minivan was now opening. A middle-aged blond woman in scrubs got out. Tent's voice had risen to a shout. "She parks in my parking space!" yelled Tent. Adam recognized the lady, from his first time visiting Tent's office, when she had been carrying a bag of fast food to the dentist's office area.

"The lady that works in the dentist's office?" Adam asked.

"The lady dentist!" yelled Tent. "I give you the dastardliness of Malcom Esperanza in full bloom. He lurks like a shadow, and moves like the wind. He is the twinkle in the eye of the stranger who wishes you ill. And he is the emptiness of the starry sky at night, mocking you with its godlessness. And now… now…" He reached into the back seat, retrieved his wool fedora, and placed it on his head, as if receiving power from it. "Now he is the lady dentist."

The older blond woman pressed a button on her key fob, to lock her minivan's doors, and a chirp from the vehicle signaled her success. She began walking from the minivan toward the front door of the office building, holding a large Styrofoam cup, with a plastic lid and straw. She had only made it a few steps, when Douglas Tent leaned briefly, but hard, onto the horn of the surveillance station wagon, causing a loud brittle honk to strike out at the woman from across the street. The woman's body jumped and did an instinctive jerking turn toward the sound, while her hand released the Styrofoam cup, sending it colliding into the ground, its lid flying off, and the ice and fluid within it cascading out across the parking lot.

Tent and Adam, like children, instinctively fell down behind the dashboard of the station wagon to hide themselves. They could hear the woman shouting toward them from the parking lot across the street, "I see you, you assholes! I see you!" Maintaining their crouched down position, Tent turned to Adam. "Now that I suddenly reconsider it," he whispered. "The lady dentist isn't Malcom Esperanza."

8

Discovery

It was the next day—a Sunday afternoon—at a time which Adam had calculated would fall between church services, when he found himself driving toward Last Baptist Church, thinking about God. As an atheist, Adam had always resented the suggestion that nature is less lovely to an atheist. He assured himself, at the time, that water was as wet to the unbeliever, the sky just as blue. But, driving now through San Antonio, taking in nature through the windows of his car, in the grip of his newfound belief in God, he knew it wasn't true—it never had been. Water was wetter now, the sky was bluer. The whole natural world was no longer a thing unto itself. It was a rich, spectacular expression of God's mind, and his love for man— for Adam personally. Meaning popped out of it everywhere, the visible proclaiming invisible grandeur. Adam drove on, and felt the warmth in his heart expand and glow. It was an emotional connection to God's presence, that he could feel whenever he wanted to now. Whenever he remembered to do it.

As he looked upon creation out the window, among the rolling, tree-toped hills in the distance, a yellow, layered cliff face appeared, as he rounded a high bend. Adam thought about the layers of it, and wondered how old Pastor Lacuna thought the world was. He wondered if the Pastor thought that earth was six-thousand-years old, as he'd heard certain wackos proclaim on the internet. A refreshing electricity went through his heart, at the thought of the earth actually being so young. The bodies of the many dead buried around San Antonio came to Adam's mind. All the former people, having lived their former lives, in the fashions of their day. The whole human drama of history seemed more real, more close, when Adam considered that it had only started six-thousand years ago. The obvious miracle of existence—as Pastor Lacuna would say—seemed more obvious—more miraculous—when Adam considered such an earth, so new and tailored to man: filled with fist fights and farming, as opposed to evolution's timeline wasted almost entirely on bacteria waiting for impossible math.

Adam's pulse quickened as he mentally rehearsed the words he would use, when sharing his conversion to belief in God with Pastor Lacuna in his office. Would the pastor be very surprised? Would he give him a hug? Would he try to make him come to church? That gave Adam pause. The out-of-doors, in the midst of God's handiwork, felt like church to Adam. The idea of being shut in a room, to worship God: it didn't make sense. It was in nature—with the big Texas sky rising above him—that Adam's access to the feeling of the presence of God within him felt the strongest. Adam wondered if this was incorrect. Another thing concerned him. What was the place of Jesus the Son of God in the whole affair? Adam was now convinced that God existed, and it made sense, and felt true to him, that the Christian God was the right one—for some reason. But it didn't seem to Adam that it was the presence of Jesus that he felt in his heart. He would say it was God the Father that he felt in there —but nothing about Jesus seemed to have taken up residence in his chest. Was something missing? Adam resolved to ask Pastor Lacuna about this, when he got to church. He hoped he would catch the pastor in between responsibilities, with time to talk. There were important things to say.

As Adam pulled into the large church parking lot, he noticed sparse smatterings of vehicles lingering here and there —giving the air of being temporarily abandoned, since no persons were walking about. In a singular instant of time, Adam's consciousness zeroed in on a particular car, parked on the outskirts of the parking lot, near the road, seemingly parked as remotely as possible, as if to avoid attention. It was a crimson Nissan Versa. Adam's mind tossed around within itself, wanting to think of the detectively thing to do, and think of it quickly. Did this look like the specific Nissan Versa he was on the look out for? How many such cars were there in San Antonio? Thousands? Had it been here on his previous visits? A really observant detective would know: Douglas Tent would know, Adam told himself.

He considered parking near the car, and looking through its windows, but worried that someone, perhaps watching him from inside the church, would notice and be suspicious. He decided to casually drive by the back of the vehicle, to get a look at its license plate. But his journey past it ended up being so nonchalant and naturalistic that he didn't get a good look at the plate. He got a few of the first numbers, but then quickly forgot them. Pull yourself together, he told himself. Be a detective. He remembered that his pocket notepad was in his jeans, and wished he had thought to use it. A security guard should be better at this. Finally—as if in over-reaction—he parked far away from the car of interest, settling on a spot up close to the entrance of the building. Adam resolved to use what he hoped were interview skills that exceeded the poor showing of surveillance skills he'd just demonstrated—to inquire of Pastor Lacuna whose car the crimson Nissan Versa in the parking lot might be. The odds are, Adam reminded himself, that the car was not the potentially criminal one he'd seen on the video tape.

Adam found Pastor Lacuna in his usual place: in his untidy office. His white hair combed into its usual impenetrable style. His suit well kept, but inexpensive. His necktie a carefree mixture of pink and purple. His bright, elderly eyes looking through his black thick-rimmed glasses—at the moment onto the screen of a laptop opened and sitting on a clear space among the piles on his old wooden desk, as he typed with concentration—putting the finishing touches on a thoughtful sermon, Adam assumed.

"Oh, hello, Adam," the pastor said, as he saw Adam in the doorway to his office. He quickly stood, shook Adam's hand, and quickly returned to his place at the laptop. "I'm sorry, but you have caught me at a busy time. I hope you'll attend tonight's service."

"Yeah," said Adam, and then trailed off.

"Oh, but that reminds me," said Pastor Lacuna, "I do have a present for you. I left it in my car. One second; I'll be right back." The pastor politely slid past Adam, and out of the office, removing his car keys as he went, and breezing through the front doors of the lobby vestibule, and into the parking lot. Out of the small window of Moses Lacuna's office, Adam happened to notice the crimson Nissan Versa, on the far side of the parking lot. Adam was planning out the words he would use, to ask the pastor about that vehicle, and then politely excuse himself and avoid church, when he made the amazing realization that Pastor Lacuna's trajectory of walking was taking him directly to the mysterious car itself. Adam watched with disbelief as the pastor's path went further and further past other possible cars, and it seemed to become certain that the far-flung Nissan Versa was his destination.

Adam went into frantic detective mode again. What should he do? And how quickly and competently could he do it? Suddenly, with a fateful sense of purpose in his heart, Adam's eyes landed on the laptop on Lacuna's desk. This was it. This was how detectives acted. He had to be intrusive and fearless in his hunt for information—for clues—clues, the spiritual food of the detective's soul. Adam sat down in Pastor Lacuna's chair, which made a friendly creaking sound, and suggested by its loose resistance that he lean back and enjoy himself. Instead, Adam leaned forward inspecting the laptop's screen. Thankfully, the computer had not had time to lock itself. On Pastor Lacuna's web browser, multiple tabs were open, all of them typical of a pastor preparing a sermon: a website that searches Bible verses on one; a map of the Middle East on another; etc. For a second Adam felt bad about this breach of privacy, but pushed forward mentally. He opened a new tab. He typed "www" into the new tab's address bar, to see which frequently visited sites would be suggested. One that came up seemed relevant to clue gathering: a cell phone service provider. Adam clicked on that address, and found, once he'd arrived at the website, that Pastor Lacuna's username and password had been remembered by the webpage, and so were already filled in, in the login fields.

Stifling another pang of guilt, Adam clicked the Login button, to sign into the website as Pastor Lacuna. It was a different company than Adam used, and so navigation of the website was not immediately obvious. Adam glanced up and through the office window, to find that Pastor Lacuna had retrieved his target object from the car—which appeared to be a book—and was now walking back toward the church. A few loose hairs on the pastor's otherwise perfectly preserved white hairdo blew in the wind, as did his pink and purple necktie—while he traversed the asphalt. Adam's heart felt hollow, and he imagined the pastor's disappointment and hurt—or maybe just confusion—upon discovering Adam behind his desk, rifling through his electronic workspace. Adam found a button on the website that promised to display a log of recent calls. Adam clicked on it, and was taken to a long list of phone numbers, next to matching dates and times. Adam scrolled down, until he came to the section that would contain information for the previous Sunday night, in the hours shortly after midnight—which was when Roland shot himself. He found a singular entry within this window of intertest. A number that was called by Pastor Lacuna, at 2:32 am that night. This time Adam remembered his pocket notepad, pulled it out with its pen, flipped to a blank page, and wrote the phone number down.

Adam glanced out the office window again. Pastor Lacuna was gone. Suddenly the sound of the lobby door, just feet away, sounded out. Adam quickly closed the tab he was on, and swung his body around the desk, to land in the chair he had begun in. At just that moment Pastor Lacuna reentered his office.

"I know we've mostly been speaking about broader philosophical topics," the pastor started to say. "But, you know, eventually, the specific text of the Christian Bible must be considered. If you want to know the whole Christian story." Pastor Lacuna sat down in his chair, that had only a brief second ago been occupied by Adam and his machinations. Would the pastor notice that his computer's screen was on, and not asleep? Could he feel unexpected warmth in his chair? Would an entry in the browser's history, or some other electronic record give Adam away? He tried not to look nervous, or sweaty. Adam was not a natural at lying. The pastor glanced for a brief second at his computer screen, before returning his eyes to Adam. Adam had no idea if he was on to him or not.

Pastor Lacuna extended a hand, holding the book across his desk to Adam. In order to be able to grasp it, Adam left his chair and stood in front of Pastor Lacuna's desk, taking the book from him. It was a medium-sized book, slightly heavy, with a soft, fake-leather cover—on which appeared, in gold letters, the title "Holy Bible."

"Why, thank you, Pastor Lacuna… I—"

"This is the ESV translation. I don't know if you know anything about translations of the bible."

"I just remember you said before, that there are multiple ones. And I think you said, some are good and some are bad," said Adam.

"Yes, there are several good ones in English. I like the ESV, because it is a good balance of literal translation from the original languages and readability."

"Oh, I see. Thank you."

"It was nice to see you. And I hope you'll read your bible. The Book of John is a good place to start, to learn about the life of Jesus. All four gospels—Matthew, Mark, Luke, and John—tell the story of his life."

"Yes."

"And I do hope you'll come to church tonight, to hear a sermon. And sing the good old fashioned hymns with us. You'll notice, in my sermons, I still use the King James Version. Which is the original one in English."

"Oh," said Adam. "Why do you use that version for your sermons?"

"Well," said Pastor Lacuna, "It's sort of a tradition among fundamental Baptists. The old-timers like it. So does my daughter."

"You have a daughter?"

"Yes. I'm sorry, Adam, but I must get back to my preparation here." He gestured to his laptop. "But I do hope I'll see you at this evening's service."

Adam knew that he wouldn't. "I'd like to... Actually, I have to see my detective friend tonight. But I'll definitely come some other time." It wasn't true that Adam had an appointment with Douglas Tent tonight. But, in light of the events of the last few minutes, it was definitely true that Adam was going straight to Douglas Tent's office, to try to tell him about the new clues.

"Well, we'd love to have you," said Pastor Lacuna, a sincere smile overtaking his aged face. Adam thanked Pastor Lacuna for the bible, shook the pastor's hand, and, as casually as he could manage, walked out of the church building and to his car. Once in his car, he felt that his escape from the situation was almost complete. He immediately started the engine, and drove away from the parking lot, to put additional distance between himself and the scene of his espionage. Only once he felt he was a comfortable distance away, did he pull into a gas station, and take out his cell phone. He also took out his pocket notebook and opened it to the phone number he'd retrieved from Pastor Lacuna's call log. Adam had Roland Bellwether's phone number in his phone's contact list—not because he had ever called Roland for personal reasons, but simply in case he needed to ask him to cover a shift at work. Adam looked around, through the windows on either side of his car. No sign of counter-espionage. He brought up Roland's number and compared it to the number written in his little, unassuming pocket notepad. They matched.

Adam felt the blood retreating from the skin all over his body, as the grandeur of the clue before him spread like a dead expanse of tundra within his emotional landscape. Was it Pastor Lacuna's car, that had been parked outside the perimeter fence at work, on that deadly night? Was it Pastor Lacuna who had implanted the evil hypnotic suggestions into Roland, and then triggered them, with the fateful phone call? Did this mean that Pastor Lacuna was Malcom Esperanza? Or, maybe he was an employee of the criminal mastermind?

    Adam rotated, within his mind, sitting in shock at the gas station, the idea of Pastor Lacuna actually being the nefarious genius Malcom Esperanza. It could make sense. Afterall, Pastor Lacuna's look, perhaps it was a little too perfectly pastoral. Perhaps, his white hair and glasses, and feminine neckties, were a disguise. What better place for a criminal to hide, than within the sheep's clothing of a pastor? Tent said that Esperanza was a master hypnotist. Had Adam himself been hypnotized? Suddenly, a deeper more disturbing question occurred to Adam. Had his conversion to belief in God been some kind of physiological manipulation, used by Esperanza against him? What would be the point? Surely, Esperanza—whoever he really was—would know that Adam was on the case, despite Tent's best efforts not to involve him in any danger. Maybe Esperanza, as Lacuna, was brainwashing Adam into becoming a Christian, in order to— what? Adam didn't know what to think.

    Adam's new theistic world seemed to spin around him, and be in danger of shattering. Tent would say that religion of every kind is a type of hypnosis. How fitting then that Adam had been so thoroughly sucked into belief in God, by the verbal hypnotism of Malcom Esperanza posing as a pastor. Adam grabbed a hold of himself mentally. A detective shouldn't overreact. He would simply follow the clues wherever they led. But what of the clues about God? Was Adam mistaken about where they led? He reminded himself that a good lie is 90-percent truth. Even if Pastor Lacuna turned out to be the devil himself, he would still speak the truth, most of the time—only corrupted by that ten percent of lies, which leads the hearer to hell.

    In the long, dark daytime he drove through toward

home, Adam came to the realization that the arguments Lacuna gave for God's existence making sense still made sense, whatever bad reasons the man might have had for sharing them. Adam grasped for the feeling of the presence of God in his heart, and found it was still there, glowing like a fireplace amidst Adam's winter of doubt. Adam resolved to investigate the pastor, and follow the clues wherever they led. But the clues about God, Adam decided, showed God's presence to be real and immediate. Adam also continued to desire to find out more about Jesus Christ, and figure out what his relationship to God exactly was. Things didn't look good for the innocence of Pastor Lacuna. In fact, things might be the very definition of bad. But, at that moment, Adam resolved in his soul, however this adventure ended: he would trust God, rather than man.

9

Employment

Despite a shielding cover of clouds, the sultry southern air embraced the citizens of San Antonio. The Sunday sun had crossed the height of its apogee in the sky, and was making its way through the late afternoon hours, when Adam entered the dentist's office building that was home to Douglas Tent's detective agency, and stood fruitlessly looking through the cloudy glass of his office door. No shapes or motions betraying life or light were detectible in the window. Adam detected the suggestion of cigarette smoke, leaking transgressively through the door as the tinkle of the entryway's fountain provided an eerie contrast with whatever in the name of all that's holy Douglas Tent was liable to be getting up to in his office of a Sunday afternoon. He tried the handle, and activated the door's chime as he entered into Douglas Tent's waiting room, and closed the door behind him.

    Immediately upon becoming aware of the room's condition, he knew that there was something more disheveled about the room's baseline mess. A tincture of light casting geometric shadows crept in from the building's tall windows, through Douglas Tent's personal office door to Adam's left. The cigarette-smoke smell was overpowering, and was now mixed with the scent of alcohol, sweat, and perhaps a hint of vomit. Adam reached behind himself and flipped up a light switch, banishing the low dimness and shadows of the room, and bringing its skewed cacophony—books knocked off the bookshelf, files fallen off the table and spilled across the floor, a wastepaper basket lying on its side, its balled-up papers strewn forth—into glaring clarity.

Suddenly detective Douglas Tent entered the room, from the hallway opposite his personal office door, wearing his blue, kimono-style bathrobe. His green eyes glared with the intensity of his usual genius, mixed with the dulling agent of sleep deprivation and drug use. He held a mug of coffee in one hand, and two mugs of coffee in the other, steam gently rising from within their brims.

"Well, it is good to see you again, my friend," said Tent, reassuringly English and patrician in the accent of his voice. "Inspector Bethany and I were just recovering from a harrowing investigation conducted last night, with extreme subterfuge and vigor."

"Inspector Bethany?" Adam asked.

A thud rang out from underneath the waiting room's unemployed receptionist desk, followed by a human clamor, after which the figure of Inspector Richard Bethany rose from behind the large, clutter-topped piece of furniture. He rubbed his balding, red-headed scalp on the spot where it had collided with the underside of the desk. "Where is my—?" said Inspector Bethany, looking at the ground around his feet. "Oh, there it is," said the police detective, as he bent down to pick something up, and then stood, returning his gun to his holster. Beneath the harness of the shoulder holster the detective wore a pink dress shirt, accompanied by a black necktie, loosened to hang beneath his unbuttoned collar. His shirt had become mostly untucked from his dress pants and undone belt, and his sleeves were rolled up to disturbingly asymmetrical heights.

Douglas Tent handed one of the hot mugs of coffee to Detective Bethany, who nodded a vote of thanks, took the cup, and tilted his face into the mothering intimacy of its vapor. Tent handed a second mug to Adam. Adam took it, in disbelief that Tent would know that a third coffee would be needed. "I expected that it was about time for you to visit again," explained detective Tent, explaining nothing. "Inspector Bethany and I were engaged last night in a prostitution sting. The operation was all the more challenging a display of law enforcement, since we were the only agents on the case, and the police department had no idea we were doing it."

Detective Bethany took his mug from his face, lowering it to his navel, but continuing to stare into it lost. "If I hurry I can still make it to evening church," he said out-loud but to himself.

"My sarcastic remarks, peppered throughout our conversation, by which I casually denigrate religion, do not seem to have yet had their intended consequence of causing detective Bethany to abandon the religion of his ancestors," said Douglas Tent. "I likewise was unsuccessful in my attempts to use the same method to convert Roland Bellwether to atheism. But, forsooth, he now is in a better place."

Bethany looked up at Tent, stirred out of his reverie, but still languid. "According to your atheism, Tent, the man is now engulfed in nothingness."

"Quite correct," said Douglas Tent. "But I stand by my assessment."

Bethany again brought his coffee to his mouth, placing his red mustache into its reviving ceramic mouth. Then he raised his face again from the cup. "What time is it?" asked Bethany, either not remembering or not caring that he was wearing a watch.

"It is four p.m." said the Englishman.

"There's something I've got to tell you," Adam injected eagerly to Tent. "I know who Malcom Esperanza is! I mean, I might know… I mean, can I talk to you about it… Sir?"

At the mention of Malcom Esperanza, Bethany looked up from his coffee—to which he had returned—and shot a glance between Adam and Tent, as if he knew the name in a starkly different context, and couldn't believe he was hearing it here.

"I know perfectly well whom you think that Malcom Esperanza is, and I know why," said Douglas Tent, holding his coffee cup exactly at chin level, and looking at Adam with focused intoxication. "But I still cannot let you work with me on this case." Tent put his cup down, on top of some file folders on the table, and picked up his wool fedora from a place it had been lying hidden on the floor. He began to pace around, in his dark-blue bathrobe, and gesture with his hands, one of which held his hat. He ran his free hand through his inky slicked-back hair, in order to begin.

"What do we know, and what do we not know? That is where a detective starts. And what do we think we know, that we really don't; and what do we know, that we don't know that we know? Aye, there's the rub. Detective Bethany is a professional lawman; you, Adam Hume, are an aspiring amateur. Neither of you has yet grasped the full enormity of the case of Roland Bellwether, or appreciated the relevance of certain —seemingly irrelevant—facts. For example, consider this: how does The Fluffy Bitch, a barbershop for dogs, located across the street from my office, stay in business, with such consistently heart-broken Google reviews? Are the owners unfamiliar with the existence of the internet?"

Adam held his hot coffee mug, precluded from drinking it by paralysis brought on by wondering what in the world Douglas Tent was talking about. Detective Bethany was drawn away from the gloom of his hangover, to join Adam in his paralyzed wonder.

"We know that the madman Dio Macina had escaped from a home for the criminally insane," Douglas Tent continued. "But who is ultimately responsible for that? Who, indeed, if not former President Ronald Reagan?" Tent paused in his pacing, for a second of silent contemplation, and then continued his circuit around the room. "The lady dentist is not the criminal genius I had originally suspected her of being. But, if not, then who is she really? I mean, really? But, and finally, gentlemen, let me come to the point." Bethany gave Adam a look, as if to say, "It's about time", but Adam was too distracted by Tent to notice.

"My point, gentlemen, is that there is less accidental about this entire case than meets the eye—our very presence on the case, the identity of the victim, and the context in which all of this is occurring in each of our lives. There are connections among all of these factors that—were they better understood—would paint a picture of a grand criminal plan which makes 9/11 look like shoplifting from work. In fact, 9/11 was part of it. Detective Bethany, please allow me to speak to Adam in private. As you say, there might still be time to make it to that second Presbyterian church service.

Bethany muttered, "It's just as well," with a few unintelligible words stuck on either side of it, picked up his suit jacket from its place on the floor, left his coffee mug in a hole in the mess on the desk, and left the waiting room clumsily tucking his shirt into his pants. When he was gone, Douglas Tent said to Adam, "There's something I need to show you. Come with me." And he walked toward the hallway opposite Tent's personal office, which Adam had never gone down, that led away from the waiting room. Upon turning the corner, Adam noticed that the short hallway terminated in a wall covered by a bookshelf, which, like Tent's other bookshelves, seemed to be crowded with books on crime, books on Texas law, and the publications of various investigational trade organizations. To Adam's left of the bookshelf looked to be a room that contained two cubicle-type desks, each with its own office chair, but an empty space where a computer, or other work paraphernalia, might be expected to be. Adam wondered if these desks had once belonged to employees, at some earlier time, when Tent's business was more than a sole proprietorship. No mention of such a time had ever been made in the stories.

To Adam's right of the bookshelf was a breakroom-type nook, that contained a refrigerator and counter space. Tent put his coffee and his fedora on a countertop in the break nook, and, looking behind himself suspiciously before beginning, grabbed one end of the hallway bookshelf and began to drag it into the break area. He was making slow progress, despite a blustering effort, and so Adam began to assist him. With Adam's help the task became swift, and the bookcase was moved entirely into the adjacent space, revealing that behind it was hidden a wooden door rickety with age.

"Wow," said Adam. "This reminds me of one of your cases."

"Which one?" inquired Tent quizzically.

"*The Case of the Hidden Door.*"

"Of course."

Against the wooden door Adam noticed an old leather-bound book was leaning. The book seemed familiar. Suddenly Adam remembered that it was the treatise on atheism—an only existent copy—that Tent had been using to hypnotize himself, because the words of the tome had the power to put the hearer of them—when read out-loud—into a trance. Tent put his fedora triumphantly onto his head, took a pack of cigarettes and a lighter out of his bathrobe's slack, blue pocket, and provided his mouth a lit cigarette to affectionately hold while he picked up the book and admired it knowingly.

"My experiments in self-hypnosis have deepened in scope and power," Detective Tent said, glancing from the book to Adam and back. "This is how I will defeat Malcom Esperanza. Perhaps he is more intelligent than even I, perhaps he is more healthy." He took a long drag on the cigarette, with an expression of mock pain on his face. "Therefore, if I am to beat him, it will be through a greater tenacity of will, and by a willingness to take a greater risk in committing myself to unconventional weapons. Spiritual weapons, my boy, for lack of a more scientific word."

Adam noticed the oldness of the book, the oldness of the door, and something ancient in the zealousness in Tent's green eyes, piercing hopefully through his manmade haze of smoke.

"My self-hypnosis," continued Tent, "has progressed to a point, that I don't even remember what it is, exactly, that I'm saying to myself during the self-hypnosis sessions. I begin to read to myself out of this book, and then I come to an hour or so later, only aware that I've been speaking to myself, without knowing what exactly I've said. But, I am aware that, generally, I am programming myself to have an ever stronger will, to win my fight against the criminal Esperanza. There is, Adam Hume, in the heart of every human being, a throne on which our evolutionary past has programmed us to want to place some kind of God. Instead, I place myself upon this throne. This is the goal of my self-hypnosis. This is how I will defeat the genius who opposes me."

Tent placed the book on the bookshelf in the break nook behind them, and gazed at Adam, while taking a few more drags on his cigarette—not to stare at Adam, so much as to have something to look at, while allowing the full gravity and brilliance of what he had just said to sink into his own consciousness.

"Once I have sufficiently programmed the requisite power of will into myself through self-hypnosis, then I enter my thinking closet. This, as you can probably guess," said Tent gesturing with one thumb to the rickety door, "is my thinking closet. You must tell no one about it. It is my most well-kept secret. No one but the two of us—now—knows of its existence. I am trusting you to keep its existence unknown, even upon pain of torture or death. The fate of the human race may very well depend on it. I give you, the inner sanctuary of my deepest genius."

With that, Tent flung open the door to the closet, and pulled the chain to a naked light bulb, hanging from the ceiling, causing it to come on, and displace the darkness of the closet's interior. Adam immediately became aware of a woman in Daisy Duke's, holding her knees, while sitting casually in the bottom of the closet. She wore a purple t-shirt, with a red dress shirt tied around her waist, matching her heavy red and purple eye makeup. Despite looking up at the men with big, innocent eyes, she gave the distinct impression of being a prostitute.

"Am I under arrest or what?" the young woman said petulantly, while chewing gum.

"Be out of there, woman!" commanded Douglas Tent. "And never defile my inner sanctuary with your presence again!"

"Whatever," said the woman, standing. She regarded Tent with a belittling look and exaggerated chewing of her gum, then turned and walked away. A few seconds later, the chime of the front door declared her exit from the detective agency.

"I'm sorry about that," said Tent. "That's Babby. She is a confidential informant."

"Baby?" asked Adam.

"No, Babby. Her street name. Never mind about her. I'm sure she wouldn't understand anything she might have seen in the closet."

"Unless she's Malcom Esperanza," offered Adam, not sure himself if he was kidding.

"Yeah," said Tent, laughing to himself. Then his eyes became serious, and he retrieved his pocket notebook and pencil from his blue bathrobe's pocket. He quickly jotted something down, then returned to the issue at hand.

"What do you learn from considering the closet?" Tent asked Adam.

For the first time, Adam noticed the interior of the closet. It was big enough for, perhaps, two grown men to squeeze themselves into. It contained no shelves, or any other items one might expect inside a closet. Instead, its three interior walls, from average knee to average a-foot-or-so-over head height, was covered in newspaper articles, notebook pages, maps, photographs, etc., all plastered onto the walls, like a kind of insane wallpaper. Thin red yarn ran from various points in the display to various other points, affixed by push pins, presumably to indicate informational connections between various items, in a grand overarching conspiracy. The yarn was affixed in such a way that it followed the bends in the corners of the walls, rather than running across the interior space of the closet and blocking the standing room.

Adam's eyes landed on a particular piece of paper, among the confusion of sights within the closet: a small scrap, apparently from a piece of lined notebook paper. On it was written —in Douglas Tent's handwriting, Adam assumed—"Who is Malcom Esperanza?" Beneath this question a few small photos were stuck: one was of Ronald Reagan; one was of the lady dentist; to Adam's amazement, one was of Pastor Lacuna (taken, it seemed, from his website); almost as amazingly, a fourth photo was of Detective Bethany.

"I'm showing you this, Adam," said Douglas Tent, "Because I am impressed by the work you've done on this case."

"How do you—?" Adam began.

"Never mind how," interrupted Tent, and took a drag of his cigarette. "The fact is, you're doing good work. Better than I expected you'd do. But, if we are to work together on this case, no one can know—not even Inspector Bethany.

"This case is big," said Tent, pointing his cigarette at Adam. "It is the very definition of big," he continued, returning the cigarette to his mouth. "Demons and angels have been banished from the world, Adam, and we see now existence for what it is: the result of an intractable web of accidents that didn't have us in mind, and doesn't care that we're here. But this uncaring, mindless force made one mistake, Adam: it made us caring and mindful. Malcom Esperanza: he is the embodiment of chaos and murderous blindness. And I am the man whom evolution has mindlessly created to stop him. Bertrand Russell said, that the first sign of an impending nervous breakdown is the feeling that one's work is terribly important," said Tent, and took a hard drag. "But mine really is," he added, exhaling smoke with the words.

"Of course," agreed Adam, happy to be vouchsafed such things from Tent.

"Sexism, racism, homophobia: these are the only real evils in the world," Tent continued. "But why do they persist? Man is perfectible—by nature, instilled with sympathy. Poverty and war are states that must be imposed on him by force. The source of all of these things—of all bigotry and capitalism —I am convinced, is the international underground network of evil run by Malcom Esperanza. A network that has had a series of heads, since the dawn of the industrial revolution. Each one has gone by the name Esperanza, and each has acted as a kind of Satan on earth, preventing the spontaneous outbreak of peace and equality that human nature would have otherwise caused to occur all over the planet. Stop him, Adam, and we can have the heaven that has been promised by religion's lies throughout the world.

"I'm going to need you to keep investigating Pastor Lacuna. I can't tell you where it's headed, or what exactly you're looking for. I must leave town, to pursue the more esoteric aspects of this case, in far flung locales. It will require my mastery of disguise, my knowledge of obscure Eastern European languages, and will test my karate to its berserker outer limits. You will have no contact with me. But I will communicate with you through letters. I can't know ahead of time when I will return."

Adam looked at Tent with a trembling bravery in his eyes.

"Are you ready to save the world, Adam? If we don't play God no one will."

Adam considered the betrayal he felt from Pastor Lacuna. He also considered the feeling of the presence of God in his heart, and his childhood dream of being a real detective. He nodded his head, that he was ready.

"Very good, Adam," said Tent. "You're hired."

10

Tent's First Letter

Over the course of the next two days—days which happened to correspond to Adam's two days off of work that week—Adam attempted to organize a plan, for the execution of his further investigation into the dastardly murder of mildly beloved co-worker Roland Bellwether. There was a lot of pressure. As he was up against an unparalleled criminal super-villain, his plan would have to be subtle, yet preposterous—barely held together with the chicken wire of daring conceptual ingenuity and unfathomable luck—with a surprising ending in which everything unexpectedly comes together from behind, to spring an iron-clad trap that would wipe the grin off the ghoulish, unknown face of Malcom Esperanza.

The problem, however, that Adam gradually became certain that he was having, was that he found himself—exactly at this most inopportune time—to be suffering from detective's block. This problem, as far as Adam knew, had been christened "detective's block" by him over the course of these first, harrowing forty-eight hours, but he imagined—hoped—that other, perfectly legitimate detectives had suffered it in the past. The symptoms of this malady were: a complete inability to come up with theories about his present case, or to think of any kind of strategy to go about the finding of more clues—despite many diagrams and lists scribbled across a rambling procession of pieces of lined notebook paper, before being balled up and tossed toward a wall in frustration.

Desperate, he decided to go back to his former inspirations. He watched all four *Lethal Weapon* movies; he reviewed his favorite cases of Detective Tent's—as recorded in back issues of *Detective Stories Magazine*, that were well preserved in a place of honor in a corner of a closet in Adam's apartment; and, finally, he set up the pieces, cards, and playing surface to the board game *Clue*, and tried to figure out how to play against himself. When all of this failed, he put some clothes on and exited his apartment complex onto the sidewalk outside, for a walk and some fresh air.

It was a clear, relatively cool day, as Adam beheld the four-lane road before him, that stretched east-to-west, as he stood outside the gated entrance which led to the Western-themed white-rock buildings, surrounding the ranch-like office of Adam's thoroughly Texan apartment complex. A pleasant breeze welcomed Adam to the out-of-doors, and many and sundry vehicles zoomed past in all directions, contributing, each in its own special way, to the loud blur of sound radiating from the road. Adam wondered, as he often did, where everybody was going in the middle of the day. Surely they weren't all overnight security guards. Shouldn't they be at work?

This reoccurring quandary barely had time to do its usual routine upon the stage of Adam's mind, when it was suddenly ushered off, by a faint buzzing sensation in Adam's pocket. He retrieved his cell phone to discover a text from an unknown number. It read:

"Bus stop just east of your apartment complex. Message under bench."

Adam's pulse quickened. The game would appear to be afoot. Unless this was some kind of prank. Maybe it was a test from Tent. Maybe it was an assassination attempt by confederates of Malcom Esperanza. Adam looked down at his body, and regretted that he would have to face the gravity of this situation in a t-shirt and swim trunks.

Adam turned to his right, and was jarringly reminded of the existence of a fully canopied bus stop, a few feet away. It was empty. Adam regarded it with a frozen apprehension, one might say, a lethargic panic, which Adam had long considered his trademark move as a security guard. It prevented him from acting quickly, but, crucially, it prevented him from acting rashly. Over the course of his security guard career, he would occasionally find himself in situations requiring a real-time judgment call, at which point he knew to use soothing self-talk to remind himself to be calm and observe all relevant facts. Such facts would then be jotted down in his pocket notebook, to be included later in a report that no one would read.

On this particular occasion, as no recording of facts seemed appropriate, Adam took two full minutes visually scanning the bus stop's bench, its surrounding canopy, and everything nearby that he could think to look at—a fast-food chicken restaurant, an oil-change place, a thrift store, sundry other businesses lining both sides of the road, the many cars streaming to-and-fro. Finally, Adam said a silent prayer to God the Father in his heart, felt a soaring jolt of excitement in his chest, approached the bench, and sat on it. He found himself being surprised, that the weight of his butt on the hard metal of the bench triggered no immediate homicidal explosion.

Feeling resigned now to whatever fate had in store for him, he started to reach under the bench, then stopped himself. Thinking better of it, he got low on all fours, and twisted his face and shoulders upward, in order to look at the underside of the bench. Stuck securely to it was a letter-sized manila-yellow envelope, attached with a single rectangle of duct tape. Adam swallowed hard, noticed the dryness in his mouth, then reached for the envelope, freeing it in one motion. Sitting back down on the bench, Adam tore the yellow paper flap, to discover inside the multiple pages of a handwritten letter. He turned his head right, then left, to observe the length of the sidewalk disappearing unoccupied into the daylit distance in both of its opposite ways. He straightened the folds of the pages, to read the first sheet. This is what the letter said.

"My friend and partner,

"Please forgive the surreptitious method by way of which this letter reaches you. It was necessary to activate my network of spies that I employ among the pauper class of San Antonio. For a hot meal, any one of them—man, woman, or child—will, I find, brave harrowing straits, to find a clue, or deliver a message. (And, by "hot meal", in the previous sentence, I mean to say: cocaine.) It is a sad reflection on the deep alienation caused by these, the late stages of capitalism that we find ourselves in, that such unfortunate people would be so invisible to society that I should be able to use them in this way. But it does work splendidly for my purposes, in many cases.

"I am not presently in Texas. But I feel it is necessary to reveal to you certain facts that will prove extremely relevant for the case for which I have agreed to employ you. (If I didn't mention it before, I, regrettably, cannot afford to pay you for your work. But you will be paid in priceless knowledge of the art of crime solving—a reward more to be cherished than gold—or even Bolivian gold, if you know what I mean.)

"I will now relate to you the facts of a case that came to my attention last month. I now believe that our adversary's murder of our late mutual friend may have been, in part, to distract me from this other case. This other case, if solved, I do believe will lay bare the clandestine source of our adversary's power, leaving him vulnerable to destruction. But, be warned: the solution to this mystery may very well lay bare the nature of our physical reality itself.

"Last month, I was contacted by a high-priced law firm in New York City, that arranged a private jet to fly me to a private airport, from which I was driven to the Four Seasons in lower Manhattan. A man met me in my room. He was a well-dressed, gray-haired, muscular man, perhaps in his early sixties. Despite identifying himself as a lawyer representing clients looking to hire me, there was a resigned fierceness and wisdom in his aged eyes, that put me in mind of a government hitman I once knew.

"Perhaps, my boy, you will remember the deaths reported, in close temporal proximity earlier this year, of New

York City's two richest billionaires? One an executive vice president of his family's oil refining company, the other: founder of a financial media empire. I learned from my meeting in the hotel room that, while both men were reported in the press to have died of natural causes—a likely story, given their advanced age—the true nature of their deaths has been covered up—using the money and influence of their families' vast fortunes.

"In order to attempt to persuade me to take the case, the man I met with—a legal representative for both families in this regard—revealed to me—under the upmost secrecy (and having me sign a legal agreement to secure my silence)—revealed that the men were in reality murdered, and in such a manner that has baffled the New York City homicide detectives, and every other advisor who's been unlucky enough to investigate the case.

"While my companion began to relate the mystifying circumstances of the murders, I concocted a series of libations from my room's smashingly appointed mini-bar, and wondered to myself whether cigarette smoking was allowed in the hotel's third-floor spa. The man sat on a chair by a couch and table, that comprised the room's business area. At his side was an aluminum attaché case, that he had come in with, but as of yet had made no mention of. I made note of all relevant physical characteristics of the room, and of my and my visitor's bodies, in case, by chance, the case contained a gun, requiring me to preserve my life through some gymnastic feat of violence.

"My visitor informed me that both billionaires had been killed by an injection in the neck, the syringes, in both cases having been found still inside the dead men's necks, as they lay inside their respective residences. The vice president of the oil company had been found on the roof deck of his seven-story town house in Chelsea. It was a 20-million dollar property with an in-ground pool on one of the floors. The billionaire hardly ever stayed there, except to throw parties, and occasionally to host his grandchildren, who would occupy the fourth floor —a floor taken entirely up by four children's bedroom areas.

The townhouse's fifth floor—of seven—was actually still empty and unused—such was the excess of wealth in the man's life— who died, literally, and figuratively, looking down on the little people, as they passed below him, on the streets of Chelsea—his avaricious mind snuffed out by a sudden, deep, painful sensation in his neck.

"The billionaire media mogul, likewise, was found dead and alone, with a syringe in his neck, and at a great height above the masses. He was found in his 20-million-dollar high-rise apartment. A miracle of opulence floating in the clouds above downtown Manhattan. From his bathtub, from every room, he could look down on New York, with such an elevated, panoramic view, it was like living in a glass elevator stuck halfway up to heaven.

"The clues, my boy, the clues: both men were found dead on the same day. Neither had had their expensive security systems, or other security measures interfered with. No one was seen by witnesses or cameras entering or leaving either crime scene. In both cases, nothing from among either man's panoply of priceless objects was apparently stolen. The killer seemed to pass through locked doors, past doormen and video cameras, as if a ghost. However, DNA and fingerprints were found on and around both bodies that indentified the same man as the killer: a New York resident living at the time as homeless on the streets of the city.

"He was a man who had been a physics professor at Columbia University, before having his tenure revoked for unorthodox theories about quantum mechanics, and an incorrigible penchant for lecturing in his underwear. After being thrown out of Columbia, in disgrace, he spurned offers of help from his friends and family, and embraced the life of a vagrant, begging on the street and shouting his theories about dark matter at families walking to dinner, before collapsing for the night on a cardboard bed, clutching his meth pipe, shoeless and unshaven. (As you may have noticed, I am embellishing the original narrative given by my visitor, with additional facts that I would learn later, in the course of my investigation.)

"What is fascinating about the homeless physics professor as a suspect is that he has an airtight alibi. He was in NYPD lockup at the time of the murders, under arrest for drug intoxication in public. The chemicals used to kill the billionaires would have been available at the chemistry department at Columbia, and the syringes used to do the killing match, down to their serial numbers, two syringes at the Columbia chemistry lab. But, inexplicably, the two Columbia chemistry-lab syringes are still at Columbia! And no chemicals appear to be missing.

"And so we have a suspect who would have had to be in three places at once, to do the crimes. And we have two murder weapons that are in two places at once as we speak. It is quite the tidy little problem. But a solution will be found: have no doubt. Inevitably, detective Bethany, and the rest of the chattering Calvinists down at the Presbyterian Church, or even our own late Roland Bellwether, when he was in a Baptist mood, would likely entertain the possibility of something supernatural at play, in the circumstances of the case I have just described. Perhaps some kind of demonic force at work. But, hopefully, as my pupil, you and I both know better than to seek after such fictional causes. As a reader of Roland's stories about me, you will no doubt know my motto, which he was fond of quoting me as saying: 'When you have eliminated the unscientific, whatever remains, however stupid, must be the truth.'

"Of course, I have yet to explain how all of this relates to our ultimate adversary, and how it may well open for us a window—of a precious and fragile sort—through which his ultimate unmasking and defeat is, at last, possible. That I will have to keep for another letter. When I have written it, when my circumstances in the field require me to contact you again, I will once more make use of my system of street urchins to message you in this same sort of way.

"Until then, however, I have an assignment for you. It is both an attempt to make headway on your end of the case, and also an educational exercise of your abilities. A good professional detective will tell you that a private investigator does not break the law. A truly great private investigator will tell you that the first guy is being a pussy. Therefore, it is time to earn your first merit badge: Breaking and Entering. Legal disclaimer: I'm only kidding. (I'm not really kidding.) Go to the church of the preacher you are investigating, when it is closed, and no one is there. Beforehand, you will need to have acquired all appropriate keys, to unlock the pastor's office and any drawers or file cabinets of possible interest. If you get arrested, this counts as points off of your score. The assignment will require steely nerves, and foolhardy nosiness. This job called private investigation requires a detective, for success, to possess four things: observation, imagination, moxie, and finesse. Let these be the light that illuminates your path.

"Good Luck,

"D.T.

"P.S.—My visitor's aluminum attaché case was full of hundreds of thousands of dollars, to pay my retainer. I love this job! Burn this letter."

Back in his apartment, Adam stood in the darkness of his room, splotches of orange light flickering on his face. Feeling a youthful mix of fear and determination about the thing he knew he was going to do, he let the flaming letter fall, gliding down into the metal trash can on his floor.

11

Hannah

As Adam drove once more toward Last Baptist Church on Backwoods road—towards its next-door barn and horses, towards its holy parking lot—his palms were clammy; his neck was red in patches. He wasn't cut out for undercover work he confessed to himself: he didn't like lying, interacting with people under false pretenses, and he didn't think he was any good at it. He had done dramatic acting, at an amateur level on a few occasions during life and enjoyed it; but that's different he realized, turning the topic over in his mind —when you're acting, your fellow performers and the audience are in on the game; it's imaginative, philosophical, not inclined to make its perpetrator feel a kind of mud had been smeared all over his ethical spirit and left to dry and harden into painful, ugly chips of dirt—the way Adam felt right now.

His plan was to visit Pastor Lacuna, and do some reconnaissance—to case the joint. He figured he could use his profession of security guard to justify the sprinkling in of casual questions about the keys to this or that door, and whether or not the church had a burglar alarm, without sounding very suspicious. All last night, and into this morning, while driving the electric security cart around the property he had been entrusted to be a watchman over, donning his watchman's uniform in the night, the cart's electric motor propelling him from fence to parking lot, he had been rehearsing in his head the various ways his conversation with the pastor might go—in furtherance of the crime at hand—what the pastor would likely say, and Adam's artful response. Finally Adam had given up, exhausted from the ever-branching possibilities of permutation, and decided he was sufficiently prepared to improvise in the moment.

    It took Adam twenty-five minutes to get from his place to the church. From anywhere to anywhere takes twenty-five minutes driving in San Antonio, and involves a highway. The august forefathers and accidents of time that made the city's shape made it so that its most prominent highways create a wagon-wheel on the map of Texas—with 410 making a circle around downtown—the hub of the wheel—and the 1604 loop making a larger circle around the wheel's outer rim—encircling San Antonio proper. The most salient of the wheel's spokes being highway I-35, which runs from southwest to northeast in a grand act of diagonal bisection. And thusly does the city, home of the Alamo, sit like a wooden wagon wheel on the sun-dried ground of a Texas prairie, its citizens ants, running tirelessly along its circles and lines.

    And so it was on a Wednesday afternoon that Adam stood before the exterior glass doors, beneath the entranceway portico of the church's front façade, and gathered his nerve, face-to-face with his own uncertain reflection in the glass. When he thought he was no longer red and sweating like a whore in a Baptist church, he entered and glided into the small outer office area that he had so often passed through, on his way to Pastor Lacuna's office within. But, this time, he was immediately aware of the surprising fact that the pastor's door was closed, and he was even more immediately aware of the even more surprising fact that someone was sitting in the receptionist's desk in the small outer office. His plan was off to a rocky start, and he began to use all of his will to suppress the panic building within him.

    From behind the front desk, a young woman looked up from what she was doing and regarded Adam pleasantly. She had golden brown hair, and blue eyes, and didn't seem older than a recent college graduate. There was an old-fashioned wholesomeness to her energy, and intelligence, and perhaps a slight frustration and sadness in her eyes. She seemed to have been doing something clerical, in regard to a folder of papers opened on the desk before her, and other similar folders of papers that were stuck into a black plastic file sorter at the corner of the desk. At the moment of Adam's entrance she apparently had been distracted from her clerical task, as her elbows were on the desktop, and one hand was doing something with a small metal nail clippers, to another hand, the long fingernails of both hands being adorned with red nail polish. On one side of the desk was a brown leather purse next to a pile of books.

"Hello," she said, placing the fingernail clippers onto the desk beside the open folder. There was a pause in which Adam thought he detected a slight widening of the girl's eyes, as if she liked the look of him. "Pastor Lacuna isn't here right now; is there something I can help you with?"

Adam's courage seemed to have found its sea legs, and his body's physiological revolt was for the moment mostly quelled. "Oh... um... yes, I was just— there was something I wanted to talk to the pastor about."

"Well, I'm actually the only one here right now. Our evening service is at 7 pm." She looked at a small watch on her wrist, with a pink leather band. "Pastor Lacuna, or one of the assistant pastors should be here within the next two hours. I was just about to take these books to the book nook, and lock up," she said, gesturing to the pile of books on the corner of the desk.

There was another pause, in which she looked at him in an unbroken way, not wanting the exchange to end. Adam lingered in the moment, not knowing what to do. Finally, she said, "You could come with me to take the books back, if you wanted to. Have you seen the book nook?"

"I have not," said Adam, and smiled with one side of his mouth.

"Okay, follow me. One second." She stood and closed the file folder in front of her, and put it in the plastic divider on top of the others. Then she looked at the folders disapprovingly for a second, took them all back up again into her hand, then with her other hand she fished a keychain out of her purse, with a small golden-cross fob dangling from it. With one hand, she worked a small key between her thumb and forefinger and turned to the wall behind her desk, against which stood two vertical black metal file cabinets. She slid the little key into a little keyhole at the top right-hand corner of one of the file cabinet's faces, opened a drawer, deposited the files, closed the drawer, returned the keys to her purse, lifted the books into the crook of one arm, put her purse around the shoulder of her other arm, and, looking at Adam, said, "Shall we?"

"Yes, of course," said Adam, remembering what planet he was on. He held open the door of the outer office for her to pass through, despite it already being held open by a door stop. He followed her into the lobby, at which point she turned and said to him, "I'm Hannah, by the way."

"Oh, I'm Adam. It's nice to meet you, Hannah." They shook hands, despite Hannah's lopsided posture, unbalanced by the books in her arm. She walked to the wooden doors leading into the sanctuary, and reached out an arm to open one of them, but was stymied by her purse wanting to fall down her arm. She hiked up her shoulder, trying to get the strap of her purse back into position.

"Let me get those," offered Adam, and, in a fit of chivalry, began taking the books from her, before she had decided whether she wanted him to or not. After the burden had been transferred to Adam, who held the books in front of him with both hands, she decided that she was glad he'd done it. Empowered by the success, Adam's chivalry flirted with absurdity, when he shifted the books to his side, holding them against his hip with one arm, so he could open the door to the sanctuary for her to walk through.

"Thank you," she said, giving him a compassionate look of concern. "Oh," she blurted out, suddenly remembering something. She walked over to the four glass double doors at the entrance of the lobby. Adam heard the rattle of keys, and then a metal pop, as Hannah, her back to Adam, moved from door to door, the metallic pop, in each case, indicating the locking of the doors. She returned to Adam, who was still dutifully holding the door to the sanctuary open, and with a smile, returning her keys to her purse, she passed on through.

They walked together through the aisle behind the last row of pews, from one end of the sanctuary to the other. Adam again felt a spiritual lightness that he'd first felt upon first visiting the church, as if things were somehow in soft-focus—like a dream about heaven. Many lights, high above in a circular array, were positioned to shine down upon the stage from every angle. The pregnant emptiness of the auditorium fascinated Adam. He looked beyond the many rows of pews that wrapped around the room—probably eight-hundred people's worth—past them to the wood-floored stage and pulpit, behind which was a space for a choir, and beyond that to the baptismal pool, situated in a raised central spot, cut out of the back wall. He imagined the experience of being up there, behind the stage and above it, standing hip deep in religious water, Pastor Lacuna placing a leaderly hand on his back, in anticipation of his submersion beneath the cool, renewing waters. He imagined coming up out of the waters again, sight and sound returning with a jolt, a chill on his skin, and the sound of a thunder of Christian applause.

Adam's daydream was interrupted by his and Hannah's emerging from the sanctuary, to the space on the other side.

"This is the book nook," Hannah said, gesturing to four five-foot high book shelves standing next to each other on the church's ever-present green carpet. To Adam's left was a men's and a women's bathroom. At the far end of the space was the beginning of a staircase disappearing down into a lower level. Above that were large windows, allowing sunlight to stream pleasantly in. The book nook featured two leather armchairs, with an end table between them—for comfortable reading experiences, next to the book shelves—and a matching leather couch. To the right of the shelves were various displays with newer books, and an unmanned glass counter, in which still more new books were displayed. Around the corner from all of this, to Adam's right, was a green-carpeted hall, leading back along the exterior of the sanctuary, and eventually to an exit, in the direction from which they'd come.

"The books on the shelves are for borrowing. The newer ones are to buy," Hannah said. "But there's no one to give the money to right now. You can put those wherever," Hannah said, referring to the armful of books Adam was still carrying. He placed them as gingerly as possible onto the book nook's couch. In front of the couch, between it and the leather chairs, stood a coffee table, on which Hannah deposited her purse.

"So, I get the feeling you aren't a member here at Last Baptist Church," she said, taking a few of the books from the couch, and beginning to place them back into their rightful places on the shelves, according to whatever alphabetical scheme.

"No, I— I've been meeting with Pastor Lacuna in his office. He's been counseling me, you might say, on spiritual matters. I was an atheist at the beginning of last week."

"You don't say."

"I initially came in—well—someone I knew had died, and I was asking Pastor Lacuna some questions. He was telling me arguments for the existence of God."

"He's very knowledgeable about that kind of thing. Did you find the arguments convincing?"

"I actually did eventually. I decided that I believe that God exists. Which is funny, because I'd been having this sense of panic for days—since my...coworker had died—and I found that when I gave in, when I gave in to the sense that I had already previously had—the sense of the presence of God—and when I started believing—the panic disappeared."

"It sounds like you're on the right track," Hannah said. She gathered some more books from the couch and took them to the book nook's shelves.

"Yes, the right track. But then, I suppose that implies that I'm still not at my destination...spiritually."

"Do you feel that you are?" Hannah asked, looking up from her task to regard him with unfeigned curiosity.

"Well," said Adam, "No. I feel this connection to God now.

But Pastor Lacuna was also explaining to me about the Trinity: that there's the Father, the Son, and the Holy Ghost—that it's one God in three persons."

"Yes that's a deep one," said Hannah, sliding a book into its place.

"But the way he explained it actually made sense. But, when I think of Jesus. Well, I don't think that I have with Jesus whatever it is that Christians are supposed to have with him."

There was a silence, in which Hannah paused from her re-shelving, and wondered what to say.

"Have you gone to this church for a very long time?" Adam asked.

"My whole life," said Hannah.

"Oh."

"I'm Pastor Lacuna's daughter."

If Adam had still been holding books, he might have dropped them. For a second his lungs struggled to expand, the air in them suddenly heavy with thickening plot.

"I'm his youngest daughter. I wasn't there when they took the photo on the internet."

"Oh," said Adam, "Then maybe you can help me."

"How do you mean?"

"I just mean, Pastor Lacuna isn't here, but maybe you can help me better understand—understand what's missing still with me—spiritually."

"You don't want my help," said Hannah matter-of-factly and retrieved the last portion of wayward books.

"Why don't I want your help?"

"I'm not a very good Christian," said Hannah not looking up from her place at the shelves.

"Oh." Adam considered his next words, and then disappointed himself by coming up with: "You seem nice."

"Thank you," said Hannah. "But you don't really know me, you know? Looks can be deceiving. I mean, how would you characterize a person, who was the daughter of a Baptist preacher, who rebelled against him in her teens? And, sure, all teenagers do that, right? But then, let's say this daughter graduated from college, and didn't go to church very often, and didn't preach the gospel to the lost. You know, and that's what's really bad about her: because she knows the truth. She knows the gospel of Christ, and that people are dying and going to hell, but she still has never taken the Bible, and opened it up, and shown someone how to get to heaven. Never in all her twenty-five years. And why doesn't she? Because she's afraid to, I suppose. She doesn't feel like God can use her. Of course, God can use anybody. But still—she's afraid."

By the conclusion of her words, Hannah had put all of the books but one in order, and was now facing Adam, in an accidental posture of open-armed defiance, a single book in her right hand, as if it were her palm, flung open in exasperation.

"What would you say about such a girl?" Hannah finally asked.

Adam again struggled to come up with something wise, and again landed helplessly among clichés.

"It sounds like she's doing the best that she can."

Hannah gave him a look of wounded resignation, and found an empty place in which to entrust the final hardback.

"But you know."

"What's that?" asked Hannah.

"You said that you know—that you know the truth," said Adam. "And so, perhaps you can help me."

Hannah sat down on the nook's leather couch. Adam sat beside her. A visceral excitement stirred in him, being that close to her, and he tried not to be distracted by it. He was here to figure out how to break into this church, he reminded himself. But, at that moment, the thing he most wanted from Hannah was to ask her about Jesus.

"I've heard the term 'the gospel' but I suppose I'm not exactly sure what it means. Your father, Pastor Lacuna, explained to me about the Trinity, but I don't believe he mentioned what exactly a person has to do, to go to heaven when they die."

"The gospel," said Hannah, "is the good news. It's what you have to believe, in order to go to heaven when you die."

"What's the good news?"

"I can tell you," Hannah said.

12

The Keys

"The gospel, the Apostle Paul says, is the death, burial, and resurrection of Jesus," Hannah began, sitting with Adam on the book nook's leather couch.

"Well, let me start somewhere else." She went to one of the shelves of used books for borrowing, and returned to the couch, with a battle-worn bible, with a black-leather cover, creased and cracked from use. Along the edges of its pages the gold paint was faded and scratched. Hannah turned—the bible on her knees—toward Adam, to address him more formally.

"Pastor Lacuna gave me a bible. I haven't managed to start reading it yet. An English Standard Version, he said it was."

"Okay, this is an issue on which my father and I strongly disagree. The issue of bible translations."

"He told me that your church uses the King James in sermons, but that he personally uses the ESV."

"Yes, I strongly disagree with that."

"Why?" asked Adam.

"Well, it has to do with what a person believes about preservation," Hannah said. "Theologically conservative Christians—Fundamentalist Baptists, like us—will all tell you that the bible is the word of God, and that God has preserved it for us, so that we can have confidence in the book. It's not the opinions of the men who wrote it, and its meaning hasn't been lost with copying over time. The bible says about itself that 'no prophecy of the scripture is of any private interpretation. For the prophecy came not in old time by the will of man: but holy men of God spake as they were moved by the Holy Ghost.'"

"Okay," said Adam.

"But the disagreement comes about the nature of the preservation. A lot of people, like my dad, want to say that the exact words of the original autographs—what the writers originally wrote down—was perfect, in the original languages, but that there are various English versions today that all do an equally good job of translating the original manuscripts into English. That's what they see as preservation."

"Sounds reasonable."

"But it isn't."

"Why not?" asked Adam.

"Because the bible says elsewhere, about itself, 'The words of the Lord are pure words: as silver tried in a furnace of earth, purified seven times. Thou shalt keep them, O Lord, thou shalt preserve them from this generation for ever.' So, it's the words themselves that God promises to preserve, not just the ideas. Jesus said, 'Man shall not live by bread alone, but by *every word* that proceedeth out of the mouth of God.' So, people that believe like me—people who subscribe to the position called King James Only—believe that, for the bible's promises about itself to be true, for the words to truly be preserved unto this current generation, there must be a word-for-word perfect translation, in a modern language. Because, if we had to learn ancient Greek—the language of the New Testament—to read God's word, that's not preservation. English is the common language of the world today—as Greek was in the time of Jesus—so it makes sense to us that God would preserve his word perfectly in English today. The King James was the English version of the bible that came out just as English as a language was first taking shape in the early 17th century, and it's the version of the bible that has had the greatest spiritual influence on the world since then, by far. So, we believe that the King James is the perfect, preserved word of God in English today."

Adam looked up, and to one side, thinking. Then his eyes returned to Hannah's. "That makes sense", he said. "But your father doesn't agree with you?"

"No," said Hannah. "He and my mother used to fight about it at home, I remember. That's how I was exposed to both sides. My father doesn't take a public position on the issue from behind the pulpit, so as not to alienate any church members. But, privately, he believes—well, he believes as he told you."

"I saw your mom in the picture on the internet that you weren't in. She looks like a good lady."

"She passed away earlier this year," said Hannah, a stifled jolt of pain appearing in her eyes.

"I'm sorry to hear that," said Adam.

"My parents also disagreed about the gospel itself actually. They would get into impassioned disagreements about it. I take my mother's side on that issue also."

"What did they disagree about concerning the gospel?"

"First I should explain the gospel to you," Hannah said, "So you can understand. It'll be good for you," she said and playfully slapped Adam on his upper arm. She opened the bible on her knees, and began excitedly leafing through its tracing-paper-thin, gold-edged pages.

"Okay, this is the first verse," said Hannah looking down at the bible on her knees, happy to be sharing the word of God. "What I am going to show you is called the Roman's Road—it's just a few verses, from the letter that the Apostle Paul wrote to the people in Rome, which, taken together, tell a person how to get to heaven. The same message is taught literally everywhere in the bible. But the Roman's Road is a convenient way of presenting it, that Baptists have come up with."

"Okay," said Adam, the openness of his heart readable on his face.

"The first verse says—" Hannah lifted the bible, to point the pages at Adam, and trace her finger presentationally along the bottom of the verse with a finger as she read. "It says, 'As it is written, There is none righteous, no, not one,' and—" She pointed to another verse in the same chapter, "For all have sinned, and come short of the glory of God'. That makes sense, right?" she asked Adam. "God has a perfect law, made up of all the commandments in the bible—thou shalt do this, and shalt not do that—and all of us, at one point or another, have broken one of his laws. Therefore, we are sinners. It's in our nature."

"That makes sense," said Adam. He thought of the physical violation of the church building he had planned, and felt a pang of guilt, and worry.

"The next verse on the Roman's Road," said Hannah, turning the pages, while keeping the book open to Adam's view, "is this: 'For the wages of sin is death; but the gift of God is eternal life through Jesus Christ our Lord.' So, there is a punishment—a wage—that we have earned, for sinning, that is called 'death'. But this is actually a spiritual death, which is what leads to hell. The first time you sinned, when you knew what you were doing, your spirit died. And it's been dead ever since. But, if you die physically in that spiritual condition—that's when it is too late. Then you are what the bible calls 'twice dead', and doomed to be punished for your sins forever in hell."

"Okay, that's not good. I'd like to avoid that," said Adam sincerely.

"Good. But that's where the second half of this verse comes in. That's the good news. '...the wages of sin is death; *but* the gift of God is eternal life through Jesus Christ our Lord.' What we've earned is death and hell. But there is a gift that God wants to give us, which is the gift of 'eternal life'. Just as spiritual death takes a soul to hell, spiritual life is the ticket into heaven. Receiving the gift of eternal life is called being born again, being justified in the eyes of God, being saved."

"So how does a person do that?" asked Adam.

"Well, like it says: it's a gift. It can't be earned, because none of us are good enough to earn it. We're all sinners."

"Sure."

"So, it can only be received as a free gift, through believing. Through faith. The word 'grace' in the bible refers to God's generosity, to him giving us something that we don't deserve, that we haven't earned. And the bible says, 'For by grace are ye saved through faith; and that not of yourselves: it is the gift of God: Not of works, lest any man should boast.' The gift of eternal life—of salvation from hell—is freely offered by God's grace, and it is received by faith—by believing. The people that are going to end up in hell are those that are trusting in their own goodness to save them, trusting in the good works they have done, be they the Muslim works, or the Mormon works, the Jewish works, the Roman Catholic works, or whatever. Whereas, those that are going to heaven will just be those that get there only through faith—through believing the right thing. '…by grace are ye saved through faith…Not of works'."

"So what's the thing you have to believe?"

"Well, that's where Jesus comes in," said Hannah, "and his death on the cross. The next verse on the Romans Road says," she pointed again, "'But God commendeth his love toward us, in that, while we were yet sinners, Christ died for us.' So, that's how the gift of eternal life was paid for, and that's what you have to believe to be saved: that Jesus Christ was God in the flesh come to earth as a man—"

"Yes, Pastor Lacuna mentioned that."

"—that he was God in the flesh," Hannah continued, "that he lived a sinless life, died on the cross for our sins, was buried and rose again. That's the gospel."

"I see," said Adam.

"It's important that he was God in the flesh, because only God in the flesh could live a sinless life, and only a sinless man could be sacrificed to pay the penalty for all of our sins. It's important that he was buried for three days, because that's when the price was being paid. The bible actually says that while his body was in the grave for three days and three nights, his soul was in hell."

"Really?"

"Yes. Because you see he was twice dead. He had to be, to pay the penalty that we all deserve—which is death and hell. And, in those three days and three nights, miraculously, he was able to experience however many thousands of years-worth of hell it is that is deserved, to pay for all the sins that have ever been sinned, and ever will be on earth. And, it's important that he rose from the dead. Because that proves that the payment is finished. He paid it all, and rose again. And that's why the gift is free, to all who will simply believe."

"Hmm." said Adam.

"The bible says," continued Hannah, turning a few pages and pointing to another verse, "'For whosoever shall call upon the name of the Lord shall be saved,' and—," pointing to another verse in the same chapter, "—That if thou shalt confess with thy mouth the Lord Jesus, and shalt believe in thine heart that God hath raised him from the dead, thou shalt be saved. For with the heart man believeth unto righteousness; and with the mouth confession is made unto salvation.' In these verses the bible is making the point that when a person really believes something, it's a natural, automatic thing, that you verbalize it at some point. So, for example, if my favorite movie is Casablanca, there comes a point—perhaps after wondering and considering what my favorite movie really is—when I eventually say to myself, 'You know what? My favorite movie *is* Casablanca.' Or I could say it to myself in my heart. That's confessing it, in bible terms. Or a person can call out to God, and say it—which would be calling on the name of the Lord, asking for salvation. Either way, through internal or external confession, or through crying out to God, asking him to save you, you are taking a step—from unbelief to belief—by a verbal act. That's what those verses are about."

"Interesting," said Adam, feeling on the brink of completely understanding.

"Lastly," said Hannah, "and this is really the final part of it—is the issue of the term *eternal life*. We saw in this verse—," she turned to a previous verse, "'the gift of God is eternal life through Jesus Christ our Lord.' Elsewhere, Jesus says, 'He that believeth on me hath everlasting life.' And he said, 'I give unto them eternal life'. John 3:16 says of believers, that they have 'everlasting life'. So, think about this: if a person hears the gospel, and believes it, then, according to the bible, that person has salvation from God, through Jesus, which is called eternal life. Could such a person then, for any reason, lose their salvation, and end up in hell, after all?"

"Well—" said Adam, and looked into the middle distance. "Could they?"

"They couldn't, you see," said Hannah, "Because if you could lose it, tomorrow or a million years from now, then it never was eternal life, and God was lying when he called it that. Because that's what 'eternal' means—that it never ends."

"That makes sense," said Adam.

"And this is very important to understand," said Hannah, "because it goes back to understanding that salvation is a gift, and not produced by the good works of the man. Because it's two sides of the same coin—"; she closed her bible, and turned it over, to represent one side of the coin; "Just as there is nothing we can do to earn salvation"; she flipped her bible over, to represent the coin's other side; "likewise, there is nothing we need to do to stay saved. If there were, then we'd be back to earning our own salvation, instead of it just being accomplished by the work of Christ, in his death, burial, and resurrection."

"That makes sense," said Adam.

"And so that's the gospel," said Hannah. "That's what I would say, if I were to give the gospel to someone."

"Well, you know," said Adam, "I think you just did."

Hannah smiled, her eyes darting with enjoyment around various parts of Adam's face. "I suppose I did. Do you believe it?"

"I think I've got to think about it. But I wonder, what's the part of the gospel that you and your father disagree about?"

"Oh that. Well, it's a theological issue among Baptists today, and, I suppose, among people since the beginning of time. There's a side of the debate called Lordship Salvation, and there's a side that's sometimes called the Free Grace position—or what I would just call the bible's position. Lordship Salvation people—including famous preachers today like John MacArthur (it seems to be a position that has infected the Baptist church from Calvinism)—anyway, the Lordship Salvation people basically say that believing in the gospel—believing that Jesus was God in the flesh and died for your sins, and that you have eternal life thereby—believing that is not enough to save you—you also have to 'turn from your sins', or, as it's sometimes said, 'repent of your sins'."

"By which, they mean what?" Adam asked.

"Well, different ones of them define it in different ways: some say you have to stop sinning, some say you have to 'be willing to stop sinning'. But, the point is: sin is the transgression of the law, according to the bible. Therefore, turning from sin, by definition, means following the law. And the bible, as we have just seen, couldn't be more clear that following the law can't save you—only faith can. In fact, in the book of Galatians, Paul says to the Galatians, who are trying to be saved by faith plus works, that 'Christ is become of no effect unto you, whosoever of you are justified by the law; ye are fallen from grace.' And he says, 'by the works of the law shall no flesh be justified'. In his letter to the Romans—where we just were—Paul says, 'Therefore we conclude that a man is justified by faith without the deeds of the law.' And he says, of salvation from hell, that 'if by grace, then is it no more of works: otherwise grace is no more grace.' In other words, the two are mutually exclusive: either we are saved by grace through faith, or we are saved by works: but it cannot be both.

"As I explained just now, a person has to understand that he is a sinner, and therefore in need of salvation, in order to call upon the Lord, and be saved. But that's different from 'repenting of your sins'. Repenting of your sins, in one way or another, means to stop sinning. And that's works. Therefore, these Lordship salvations people aren't just misspeaking, they're teaching a works-based gospel message, that, according to the bible, can't save anyone. As Paul said to the Galatians, Christ is become of no effect unto them. Not because they've lost their salvation. (As we saw, a truly saved person can never lose his salvation.) But Christ is become of no effect unto them because, instead of teaching a biblical gospel, they've twisted it into a gospel that cannot save."

"So, it doesn't say in the bible that a person has to repent of his sins to be saved?"

"Not in the King James, I can tell you that. Who knows what some of these new, wacky translations say. The bible does use the word 'repent' in connection with salvation. But, in the bible—if you let the context in which words are used define them—then you see that 'repent' just means 'to turn', to change one's mind about something. So, someone could repent of sins, or repent of anything. For salvation, a person has to repent of not believing the gospel, and believe it. That's why Jesus himself said, 'repent ye, and believe the gospel,' meaning, 'turn from not believing the gospel, to believing it'. He never says, 'repent of your sins to be saved'."

"I see. So, then, your father believes that a person must repent of his sins to be saved?"

"Yes. Like I said, he and my mother would get into impassioned arguments about it, which led to me becoming very familiar with both sides of the issue. While she was alive, he didn't preach 'repent of your sins to be saved', from behind the pulpit, even though he believed it. But since she died, he has been—despite my objections."

"But, based on what you've said, you seem to imply that your father isn't saved."

A far-away look came over Hannah's eyes. "No, he isn't," Hannah said gravely.

Adam looked at the bible on Hannah's lap, then back up to her eyes. "Thank you for sharing that with me," he said.

"I can relate to you, Adam," Hannah said. I had a friend die recently too. He and I, we—well. I should tell you that salvation is by grace through faith alone, and therefore, of course a believer cannot lose his or her salvation—he will go to heaven no matter what his behavior is on earth. But the bible does promise that there is punishment in this life for a believer who sins. It says, 'whom the Lord loveth he chasteneth, and scourgeth every son whom he receiveth.' A scourging or a chastening being a corrective punishment, like a father for a son."

"Yes."

"That's what I believe my friend's death was. It was punishment from the Lord for sin. Because he and I, we were—" Hannah looked at Adam woundedly. "We were sinning together."

A surge of sympathy for Hannah welled up in Adam's heart.

"I told you I wasn't a very good Christian," she said.

Adam thought for a moment about all she had said, and, then, to change the subject, and wanting dearly to know more about her, he asked, "What did you study in college?"

"I studied psychology," Hannah said. She placed the bible on the coffee table, reached into her purse, and retrieved her key chain—as if to indicate that it was time for her to lock up and leave now. "My favorite thing to study was hypnotism."

13

Tent's Second Letter

Adam attempted to constrain his face from displaying the vague but paralyzing shock he felt at Hannah's uttering of the word, "hypnosis". Suddenly he wondered if she knew everything, and was taunting him for his ignorance, as she stood, and walked behind the couch, his countenance temporarily safe from her view.

"We can go out this way," Hannah said, gesturing to the carpeted hallway that led back around the sanctuary to the church's front parking lot—defaulting to a casual tone of voice, despite the depth of the conversation they had just had. She adjusted the strap of her purse on her shoulder, and caused a tinkling of her keys as she fiddled with them, while waiting for Adam to come along.

"Yes," said Adam, standing, taking one last look around the book nook, as if to thank it for its hospitality, and joined Hannah where she was standing. His thoughts abandoned any meditation on the theological issues they had been discussing, and he frantically cast around in his mind for some plan to get Hannah's keys away from her, before she got in her car, and he in his, and they both drove away from each other, his chance to fulfill his detective hero's assignment hopelessly lost for who knows how long. What would Douglas Tent do? And where would Adam get crack to smoke on such short notice?

But, seriously, he said to himself, as he and Hannah drifted slowly, inevitably, down the hallway and toward the light shining through the glass of the metal double doors at the hallway's end, toward the horrible failure represented by the otherwise pleasant and sunny parking lot beyond. Time slowed down, but with each step Adam was getting closer to it being too late. His thoughts, in their hurry, stumbled into each other, and collapsed into a pretzel of impotently tangled attempts to succeed.

When they got to the door, Hannah started to press against one of the horizontal panic bars that ran across the middle of both doors and the door began to open. "Oh, I've still got to lock this," said Hannah. Letting the door fall closed again, she selected what looked like a straight Allen wrench which came to a loop on one end—by which it was attached to the keychain—inserted it into a little hole in the middle of the panic bar, and turned the wrench. There was a metallic pop, and the front of the bar sprang forward, indicating that the door was now locked from the outside, but could still be opened from inside, by pressing on the bar.

Adam considered pretending to need to use the restroom, to stall for time, but found himself not acting on this thought. Then, suddenly, when all seemed lost, as if a gift from above—or from somewhere—Adam's panicked mind burped forth an idea.

"The office door," Adam said, a little too enthusiastically.

"What's that?" asked Hannah, her hand on the door, ready to pass through it.

"The door to the office area. I sort of held the door open when we were leaving it. Is that supposed to be locked too?"

Hannah considered for a second, then looked at Adam with recognition. "Yeah," she said. "I should probably lock that". Hannah started to let go of the door and walk back into the hall, when Adam stopped her.

"No—no, I'll do it! Let me. Just give me the keys, and I'll run back there, and lock it, and bring you back the keys." He started to reach for the keychain.

"No," said Hannah. "I can do it. We can walk back together. It's my responsibility."

"Trust me," said Adam. "I'm a security guard. It'll make me feel useful. Locking doors is my calling in life."

Hannah raised her eyebrows in friendly resignation. "You should cut back through the sanctuary. The doors to the lobby are already locked." She extended the keychain, and Adam grasped it in his hand; what felt like literal electricity shot up his spine. "Be right back" he said, and affected a brisk, but—he hoped—not-at-all-suspicious gait back down the hall. Along the hall were doors, granting access into the sanctuary. He ducked into the nearest one, and jogged through the sanctuary to the main lobby. He closed the office door, glancing first at the file cabinets within—the targets of his intrigue—making sure that they hadn't popped out of existence since he had last seen them, and triple checked that the office door was definitely not locked.

He stepped back into the sanctuary, to be out of view of the windows in the lobby doors. He found the key he needed on the key chain—the little one that Hannah had used to open one of the filing cabinets. Those filing cabinets, Adam's detective instinct was telling him, in the heat of his detectively roguishness, were where Pastor Lacuna's skeletons were hidden. He worked the little key off of the chain—a task slightly prolonged by Adam's frantic hands. He slipped the key into his pants, examined its former companions, and decided the little one wouldn't be missed among the mess of others.

Adam pushed a few beads of sweat on his upper forehead into his hairline with the edge of one hand. He took a few deep breaths, then emerged into the hallway, to find with horror that Hannah was gone. Then, with relief, he saw that she was standing just outside the door, enjoying the air and sun. She waved at him with warmth and—Adam thought—the slight awkwardness of desire.

Adam emerged from the church building, careful not to let the door fall closed. "It's all good?" Hannah asked.

"In my professional opinion," said Adam, "Your office door is safe and secure. I didn't lock your father's door though."

"That's okay," said Hannah.

With great care, but trying to look as naturalistic as possible, Adam began to close the panic-bar door. He knew that if the latch snapped into place, he wouldn't be able to get back in, and use his cabinet key. Like a surgeon working with high stakes, and no time to lose, he felt the latch of the door get as close as it seemed it possibly could to snapping into position, without actually doing so.

"You have to make sure that closes all the way," said Hannah, her arms crossed in front of her innocently, standing a few feet away, shifting her weight absent-mindedly from one foot flat on the ground to another on tip-toe. "It has a problem, where sometimes it doesn't."

Adam pretended to pull on the door, as if testing its closedness, terrified that he would accidently pull the unsecured door open. "Safe and secure," said Adam.

Hannah turned and began walking to her car: a white Honda civic, that looked to be about eighteen-years-old. Adam followed, and she unlocked her car door and opened it, turning to face him, standing between the door and her car.

"It was nice to meet you, Adam," said Hannah Lacuna.

"Did you remember to arm the burglar alarm?"

"As far as I know, we don't have one of those," said Hannah. Adam was suddenly struck by a strong sense of déjà vu—as if he'd said goodbye to her before, or hello, in a parking lot such as this. But, of course, that was impossible—they had never met.

They faced each other for a long instant. She glanced at his mouth, then back up to his eyes; a slight ripple moved through her lips; because she wanted to kiss him, but she didn't know it.

"I'll see you around, Adam," she said.

"It was nice to meet you, Hannah." As Hannah lowered herself into her driver's seat, Adam noticed a few un-Baptist seeming books strewn about the backseat of her car: one on eastern philosophy, and another about the science of evolution.

Adam lingered in the spot where she'd said goodbye to him, watching her car travel toward the parking lot's exit, and feeling a sense of good auspices about having met Hannah, mixed with a sense of impending doom, about the betrayal of her that he would now perpetrate. He started walking toward his car, in case she could still see him. Then when she was thoroughly gone, and when he had scanned around, and found no one to observe him, he turned and walked back to the church.

Back in the office area, standing in front of Hannah's desk —having let himself back in the church, and having securely closed the double door behind him, and having walked with guilt back through the holiness of the sanctuary—Adam now stood and glared at the two black vertical file cabinets standing in a corner, against the room's back wall: his enemies.

He fished the little file-cabinet key out of his pocket, and approached the first file cabinet—the one he'd seen Hannah open. He inserted the key, turned it, and rifled through the contents of each of the cabinet's drawers in turn. He found various folders, full of various things: financial records, personnel records, records of donations and tithes given to the church, church members' contact information—but nothing that seemed suspicious. A thought occurred to him: this file cabinet, the one that Hannah was working out of, wouldn't be where the pastor's dark secrets would be kept. He inserted the key into the second black file cabinet, and—just as Adam suspected—it didn't work. He hadn't noticed any other file-cabinet keys on the chain. Hannah didn't have access to this one. This had to be the one that contained the clues that Adam was after.

Adam went into the pastor's office, opened and closed all the drawers of his desk, examined his bookshelves, and every other object. All he was able to find was a normal, expectable mix of order and disorder, and the accoutrements of a Baptist pastor. The pastor's laptop wasn't there. He found no second file-cabinet key.

Adam re-entered the outer office, and glared with hate at the second file cabinet, which blackly mocked him with its impenetrable criminality. Anything could be in there: perhaps all the secrets of Malcom Esperanza's grand, final, world-ending scheme. It was so sturdy, so heavy-looking. He probably couldn't even move it alone.

Then, with an involuntary sort of wisdom, Adam's eyes landed on the desk where Hannah had been sitting, and his consciousness was filled with a triumphant presence, there, alone and little, on an empty expanse of desk: Hannah's nail clippers. The flat, little rectangular bit of metal, crisscrossed with grooves and coming to a slightly hooked point, to allow it to act as a nail file, was still extended from the clippers, attached to them by its hinge. Adam took up the clippers, gripping them so as to hold the little nail file like a key. He went to the second file cabinet, a resigned determination in his heart. He thought about the assistant pastors, the ones that Hannah had mentioned were on their way. He began to insert the small nail file into the lock on the file cabinet's upper righthand corner. He had to jiggle it, to work it in, and then, as the file slid the last part of its length into the slot, Adam felt a change inside the lock, and before he knew it, the lock was turning with a satisfying hallow thud, announcing the file cabinet's inglorious defeat.

Looking through the drawers of the cabinet, Adam found them all to be empty, except for the bottommost one, which contained a single folder—which, to the endless thrill of Adam's detective soul, was actually, honestly labeled "SECRET". Within the folder was a single page—what looked to be a digital photograph, that had been printed on a black-and-white printer—which gave the picture's contents all-the-more a cloak-and-dagger atmosphere. The paper was labeled "Surveillance"—the word written above the photo on the page's white boarder, in handwriting with a black ink pen. What the photo pictured was a woman, standing between the door and driver's-side seat of her car, saying goodbye to a man, in a parking lot. The picture was taken through a chain-link fence—the pieces of the fence blurred into obscurity, the moment between the man and the woman inside the fence in privacy-invading focus. The man held the woman's face—he looking down at her, and she looking up at him, with playful love in their eyes. It seemed he was about to kiss her, or just had.

    The woman was Hannah Lacuna. The man was Roland Bellwether.

    Back in his car, in the parking lot, Adam felt secure that his break-in of the church was finished—and the pastors had not arrived; he had not been found out. His mind swam, attempting to sort out the kaleidoscopic implications of the photo he had seen. In his haste—in the greenness of his detective skills—he had not taken a photo of the picture, or copied it with what must have been a working copier somewhere in the office. That would have been smart. But the picture was seared into his detective brain. Roland and Hannah, in a romantic embrace. What did it mean? Most intriguing was the context of the photo. It seemed to clearly have been taken by someone spying on the lovers—presumably Pastor Lacuna. Had the pastor killed Roland, because of their sinful affair? Perhaps Hannah had killed him, for the same reason. And how did any of this relate to Malcom Esperanza, and the two dead billionaires in New York City? At that moment, as if in answer to the very thought, a text message registered, with a soothing buzz of Adam's phone within his pants. Retrieving his phone, and perusing the screen, Adam saw the message.

    "Look in your trunk."

    It was from an unknown number, which made Adam suspect it was Tent alerting him of another furtive correspondence. But the bluntness of it made it sound like some kind of threat. As Adam popped his trunk, exited his car, and stood above the lid of the trunk, while it stood suspensefully ajar, he had a vision of a body being in it—a message of terror from Malcom Esperanza. He exhaled with relief, when the trunk proved to be its usual, empty self. Then Adam noticed another manila-yellow letter-sized envelope affixed with a single square of duct tape, this time stuck to the inside of his car's trunk lid. Adam removed and opened it. Despite the possible tactical unwiseness of continuing to stand there, at the scene of his crime, with the assistant pastors on their way, Adam couldn't help but read the letter, not even sitting back down in his car seat first. This is what the letter said.

"Adam,

"I have uncovered him. I've found him out! The dark turns that the case of the murdered New York billionaires has taken, my boy, have shaken my adventure-tossed consciousness.

"It is a truism I have long observed, during my storied investigational career, that the secondary tragedy of murder inevitably has—discoverable beneath however many earthen layers of time and secrecy—an initial, primary tragedy at its root. The story of the solving of a mystery, then, is the story of putting together the pieces of that foundational tragedy, from which the eventual, consequential tragedy of murder doth spring—like maggots springing from rotten meat.

"My investigation has led me to become aware of an exclusive cigar bar in New York City—in fact, so exclusive that it only has three members, secrecy surrounding its exact location. The cigar lounge employs a single worker, who makes a generous salary, to be constantly on call, to wait on the three club members, whenever they might decide to meet—this employee being an elderly African American man, with a humble disposition—all of which no doubt appeals to the virulent racism deep within these three men's souls. (With the profound criminality no doubt overheard on occasion, by this cigar bar worker, he is lucky to still be alive.) The men meet to discuss money, business, and the perpetration of awesome evil.

"It was during one such meeting, during the winter of this year, that the men were assembled, cigars nestled in their mouths, tumblers of fine whiskey resting in their hands, relaxing against their leather armchairs, and surrounded by antique wooden furniture, and bookshelves lined with aged volumes, that a dastardly scheme was conceived—one more dastardly than their usual attempts to entertain their opulent, blackened hearts. There is an undeniable thrill, to be sure, that comes with ruthless money-making on the global stage—so they agreed in their cozy room, illuminated by the warm, orange light of a small chandelier hanging lowly overhead—but there is another, more visceral thrill that comes from evil done face to face. The men had together planned and carried out murders in the past, and rapes followed by murder. They had drunk the blood of babies. But always, in the past, a certain care was taken not to get caught. Victim and witness would not be left alive.

"But that night's idea was more daring. The men decided that they would take a drive out into the city, pick up a homeless man, and take him back to one of their mansions. Then they would take turns raping him. They would drug him beforehand, it was decided—not enough to remove his memories of the attack, but just enough to give the memories a dream-like quality befitting a nightmare he would want to pretend had never really happened, and could blanket unsuccessfully over with denial. The men did not consider themselves homosexual, but found that homosexual rape seemed more transgressive, and therefore more fun.

"The appeal, the pizazz of this idea, for the men, was that they would not try not to get caught. This time they would leave their victim alive. They would take no heroic efforts to cover their tracks: they would casually go about their business and then be done with it, relying thereafter on the skill of their lawyers, and the public's reluctance to believe accusations against rich, successful men, to protect them. That would be the exercise, the experiment. They could maintain whatever position or office they now occupied, they reasoned, and they would face no consequences. The homeless man's story would not be believed, if it was even ever heard. That would be the really satisfying thing of it.

"This plan and subsequent crime of these men, by its nature, could not be found out about directly. I had to deduce it from other facts. The most surprising thing, the thing I was not expecting to uncover, was the true identity of the third man.

Two of the cigar-bar bons vivants, you may have guessed, were the two murdered billionaires, whose murder I am in the process of solving. (And, as you may have also guessed, their victim, selected at random on the night of the crime turned out, unfortunately, to be the homeless former professor, whose DNA was found at the scene of both murders—during which he was impossibly locked away in police custody.) The third man—the owner of the bar—was another billionaire, who is still alive. His name is known to New Yorkers, and to the whole country. What is not known to the whole country is that this third man is Malcom Esperanza.

"Devastated, suicidal, the once brilliant physicist—after the men's attack on him was ruefully complete—at first threw himself into the drugs and debauchery of his homeless milieu. As the evil men had counted on, he despaired of any hope of finding justice against his victimizers in our country's courts-of-law. Finally, one night, on the verge of death from starvation and chemical self-abuse, an amber of resolute hatred flared up within the man, saving the smoldering fire of his soul from blinking out into a heap of cold ash. He opened his eyes, feeling the wet cold pavement of the alley he was sleeping in against his tattered clothing, as if for the first time. A plan flared like lightning across the remnants of his mind. He remembered his denigrated theories about quantum mechanics and the nature of time and space, for which—among other things—he had been unceremoniously drummed out of university. In that dying moment of renewed rage, a final puzzle piece fell into place, and the homeless scientist finally realized what his theory had been missing. It was clear to him now. He could do it. He could return to his work, and by it summon a power from the laws of physics that humankind had heretofore never known; he could summon it, and use it to destroy his attackers more totally than they could ever expect.

"The man stole new clothes. He showered at the YMCA. He relied on an old friend from his professorial days, to give him a guest room to sleep in, and a garage in which to continue the experiments he had abandoned years ago. With a swiftness that the man could only suspect was due to a kind of providence of fate, the man constructed a device and turned it on. It worked, and the man was able to use it to murder the two men from the cigar club, with impunity. For reasons that I do not yet understand, the third man—Esperanza—has escaped him. You might have noticed that I said that the fateful meeting in the cigar lounge occurred in the winter of this year—a season that this year has not yet experienced. Because, you see, the man was able to kill his attackers before the attack took place. He had invented a time machine.

"Yours in Crime Solving,
"D. T."

14

Whiskey and Religion

Then it was night, and Adam was in his apartment, the patter of rain percussively babbling through his roof and walls. It wasn't that his existential dread had fully returned, but something like it. He felt manhandled by confusion. Could Douglas Tent really be serious that the men in New York had been murdered by a homeless physicist with a time machine? Was such a thing possible? Or was this some type of test from Tent? Adam, he was surprised to find himself thinking, tended to believe that the time machine was real. After all, ever since last week, the unreal seemed to be coming true. Douglas Tent was real—even if Lucy Truthteller had, in the stories, concealed the degree to which the real man's genius shaded into seemingly true insanity. Malcom Esperanza was apparently real —even if amorphous and as evanescent as a ghost.

But the real unreality of the last ten days had been of a biblical sort. Adam now truly believed that there was an infinite, all-knowing, all-loving, omnipresent mind, that created the universe, and knew the future and his very thoughts. Not only that, but, according to the beautiful and paradoxical Hannah of Last Baptist Church on Backwoods Road, things only get more uncanny from there. There is a real hell, she would have him believe, hot and sulfuric, beneath his feet—beneath everybody's feet—as we go about our trips to the mall. And then there is a heaven, presumably involving clouds and bright, joyful light. Could this be true too? Did the blood of Christ really trickle down his broken body, did he really descend into the depths of damnation, to buy forgiveness for Adam for the laws of God that he had broken? Adam saw the logic of it. But somehow, in his heart, he didn't quite believe that he himself was on his way to hell, and therefore in need of salvation—surely not him. He was a security guard. He'd drunk too much in his twenties; he had been careless with the hearts of some of his fellow creations of God—the female ones. He had transgressed what he assumed the biblical ethic of sex was—he'd never been married, but he wasn't a virgin. But still: hell? Him? Adam Hume? And what of the millions, or however many, of his fellow human beings, already burning—as he stood that very night in the dimness of his one-bedroom dwelling—those at that moment crying in agony, and tormented in flames, right now, and forever? Could it be true?

    As the appointed time for Adam to arrive at his security-guard job drew nearer, he stood in his bedroom, looking into his small walk-in closet, at his security-guard uniform's shirt hanging and crisp and white and ready—but also aged with use. He looked at it and wondered what side of the battle of good-vs-evil he was on. He yearned for goodness, but felt lost. He picked up his cell phone, and—affecting a voice that he hoped was raspy enough to be believable, without sounding overdone—he called into work, saying he was sick. And it was true. But it was a spiritual sickness. He needed to think. For the first time, in a long time, he noticed a two-thirds-full bottle of whiskey, tucked behind sundry papers and books and DVDs and his high school yearbook—on his closet's upper shelf. He repositioned himself, to get a better look at it, ensconced among his memories and mementos, standing above his head. It took on a sudden salience, as if bidding him hello. Next to it was a shot glass, that he'd totally forgotten was there.

    Adam carried the whiskey bottle and shot glass into his apartment's front room, his socks pressing into the softness of his carpet as he walked, he in his underwear, strings of water flowing down the glass of his second-story dwelling's balcony door, a bolt of thunder resounding distantly outdoors. He placed the bottle and the shot glass on the peninsula of countertop that separated his apartment's sitting room—and the sliding glass door leading to the balcony on the far end of it—from the kitchen area on the other side. There was a cast-iron bar stool, with a wicker seat, standing on the sitting-room side of the counter top, and its twin stood at the countertop's head. Adam sat on the sitting-room barstool, and regarded the inanimate whiskey bottle and shot glass with suspicion, inquiring with his eyes whether or not their intentions toward him tonight were honorable. Then a flash of lightning, then a crash of thunder. Then a knock came at the door.

Adam looked at his watch. It was 11:30 pm. He had been silently interrogating the whiskey bottle longer than he thought. Who in the world could be at his door?

He half staggered and half crept to the door, to carefully peer through the peep hole. Standing there, on the other side of his door, was Hannah—wearing a white trench coat and white sneakers, a mostly closed compact pink umbrella in one hand, and a book in the other. His heart stopped beating for a few seconds. He blurted out, "Just a second," then ran to his bedroom, collected his jeans from the floor, a clean black t-shirt from his dresser, threw them on, ran a toothbrush across his teeth in the bathroom, then peered again through his front door's peephole, to convince himself she was really there, before opening the door, and looking at her, with pleasant solicitude.

"I'm sorry if I woke you up or anything," said Hannah. "It's just that, you said you were a security guard, and I know that security guards are sometimes nocturnal, and I found out that you live near me, and I saw that the light that seemed to correspond to your place was on, and I just was worried that you'd be up tonight, alone, thinking about what we talked about today. And I just wanted you to have a bible to read, while you thought about it. I felt bad when I realized that I hadn't given you one. So, I brought you one now. I'm sorry if that's strange. But I felt, as we say, that the Spirit was leading me to do it."

She offered the book in her hand to him. It was a formidable, but portable size—brown faux leather cover, gold paint on the edges of the pages, "Holy Bible" written in gold letters on the cover.

"It's a King James version. I didn't want you to be here, considering the afterlife alone, and relegated to reading the ESV," said Hannah.

"Thank you," said Adam, and he took the bible from her. "How did you know where I live?"

"I know where a lot of people live," she said. "Recently, as an exercise in finding things out, I asked the San Antonio Voter Registration Office to give me the names and addresses of everyone who voted in the last presidential election. It cost me thirty dollars."

"And they just give that kind of information out?"

"They're legally obligated to. As part of the Texas freedom-of-information act. The legal theory being, if your tax dollars have gone to the creation of a document—any state-produced document—then you have a right to read it."

"Wow. Good detective thinking."

"Well," said Hannah, "I'll leave you to your thoughts." She gave him a casual wave of her hand, then started to fiddle with her pink umbrella.

"Wait," said Adam. "I was just… I mean, I have some more questions."

"You do?"

"Yes, and I—Well, I think I was about to take a shot of whiskey. Do Baptists believe in taking shots of whiskey?"

"We do not," said Hannah, and looked at him lingeringly.

"Do *you* believe in taking shots of whiskey?" Adam asked.

"I've been known to in the past," said Hannah.

A quintessentially human atmosphere passed between them. Nobody knew what he or she wanted; but they wanted it strenuously.

"Would you sit with me, then, while I have one, in the kitchen here? And I'll tell you what I've been thinking about—about what you told me this afternoon."

"I shouldn't," she said, "It wouldn't look right," her blue

eyes glimmering with happy indecision, as she rocked playfully from side-to-side, as if subconsciously attempting to gain momentum to propel herself—either toward leaving, or toward staying.

"Okay, one shot," said Hannah, and stepped across the threshold of Adam's apartment. Adam closed the door behind her, as she undid the sash of her white trench coat, which Adam took from her, and hung in the coat closet in the corner of his kitchen space, along with her compact pink umbrella.

Adam gestured to the bar stool at the head of the counter at the kitchen's border, and she sat on it, while he sat next to her, across the counter's corner, his back to the sitting room, its singularly lit lamp casting sparse light into the apartment, the dull but near sound of storm still roiling beyond his balcony's sliding glass door. Hannah wore a red dress, with short sleeves, and a high neckline, and small white polka dots all over it. Her lips were the red of her dress. Her earrings were small golden crosses, dangling meekly on either side of her face.

"Why don't Baptists believe in drinking?" Adam asked, and poured himself a shot.

"It's been called the 'two-wine' theory," said Hannah. "The times when the bible is saying bad things about wine, Baptists take it to be that alcoholic wine is being discussed, whereas, when the bible says good things about wine—which it does plenty—then Baptists take it that the word 'wine' is referring to grape juice."

"Interesting," said Adam, and downed his whiskey in a single gulp, tilting his head back to do so, then resting his gaze back upon Hannah, his face contorting slightly, his eyes widening and watering slightly, as he struggled not to react to the pleasant but overpowering burn spreading inside of his throat. It'd been a while.

"The alternative theory, of course," Hannah continued, "is that wine is just wine, and that it's overdoing it that makes it bad—that drunkenness is the sin, not drinking. That's what I believe. But I wouldn't openly oppose my church's teaching on the issue. It's not a major theological point, and fewer people drinking isn't the worst thing in the world. I also like the idea that my church is stricter than I am, when it comes to standards of behavior. The way I see it, if you had a bodyguard, you'd want him to be more, not less, paranoid than you are. That's his job."

"That makes sense," said Adam, and poured another shot. "What would your church say about two unmarried people such as us, alone in my apartment together, this late at night?"

"They'd be against it," said Hannah.

"But you don't think it's wrong?"

"No," said Hannah, "I agree with them on that one." She took Adam's shot glass in her hand, and downed the whiskey within, placing the glass back down on the counter with a thud, and wiping one corner of her mouth with the middle knuckle of an index finger. Adam was speechless for a few seconds.

"I've been thinking about what you said," he said. "About heaven and hell—the afterlife. I wonder about hell. Do most people end up there? Forever?"

"Yes," said Hannah. "Jesus is specifically asked that in the bible, if there be few that are saved. That's when he said that, 'strait is the gate, and narrow is the way, which leadeth unto life, and few there be that find it.' Not that it's hard to get into heaven —it isn't: you just have to believe. But few will do it, because it takes humility to put one's faith in Christ alone, rather than trying to earn it through good works. Most will try to earn it, hence, all the religions of the world, that aren't biblical Christianity."

"Still," said Adam, "it seems like a harsh state of affairs, for a loving God to create—most people that have ever lived suffering in hell for eternity."

"Look at it from God's perspective," said Hannah. "He didn't create the world to make us happy—he did it to express himself; and he is loving and forgiving, but he is also just and holy. That's why Jesus had to die. If punishment wasn't exacted for sin, God wouldn't be taking his own law seriously, his law being an expression of his holiness. The bible says that God is the potter, and we are his clay. Some are formed to be vessels of wrath, and some to be vessels of mercy. Those of us that choose to accept the gift of eternal life, through faith in the death, burial, and resurrection of Christ, will end up honoring God, by showing forth his mercy by being with him in heaven. Those that do not will honor God, by showing forth his power and justice and wrath—by burning in hell forever. Either way, God is honored, and his creation expresses him."

Adam poured another shot. He rolled the small round bottom edge of the glass in a circle on the counter. The babble of rain continued around them. Thunder crashed a mile away.

"Before my father convinced you of the existence of God, were you always an atheist?" Hannah asked Adam. Adam told her of his childhood, of attending a Presbyterian church, where he didn't remember ever being presented with the gospel clearly. He told her of his childhood conviction that he should be a preacher or a detective, and that a detective was what he had wanted to be. He told her of drifting into atheism, and of his encounter with God, camping that night in the woods, staring alone up at the moon. He told her of the existential dread he had felt, since the recent death of a coworker, and how it had been cured by his newfound belief in the existence of God, inspired by Pastor Lacuna. He didn't mention where he worked, or when exactly his coworker had died. He also left out the part where his interest in becoming a detective was renewed by Roland Bellwether's murder, or the part where he was currently working with Douglas Tent to investigate her father.

He had taken a second drink midway through his monologue, and he punctuated the conclusion of it by shooting a third. He felt the warmness in his belly, and a dizzy euphoria swam through his head. He felt the closing of his mind to theological thoughts. He regretted having had three drinks so quickly. He looked at Hannah and yearned for her, for her youth and beauty. He perceived that a dark part of him was feeling contempt for a lighter part; a voice within him told him that his childlike groping after comfort in religion was pusillanimous and sad. He poured another drink. He listened to hear if the storm was still storming. It was.

"Have you always been a believer?" he asked her.

"No one is born a believer," she said. "But I remember being saved, when I was five years old. I remember my mother, in my room, tucking me in to go to sleep. But first she read me a bible verse to teach me the gospel, which she tells me she'd done many times before. But this time, I understood. It was John 5:24. 'He that heareth my word, and believeth on him that sent me, hath everlasting life'. I understood it all—not perfectly, not every detail. But I understood, even as a child, that I was in trouble with God, because of disobedience, and that Jesus had died to save me. So I believed.

"And I went to church; I love my church. I liked to be the pastor's daughter. My brothers and sisters were all already in high school or college or older, when I was born. It felt like being an only child, with many young, cool aunts and uncles. I had a lot of friends, and did a lot of things. I worked at bible camp. I worked on the school buses that the church uses to pick up children in poor neighborhoods, to take them to church every Sunday."

"They do that?"

"They do. In my teens, I was rebellious. I would fight with my father. I'd try to stay out past my curfew. I smoked a cigarette. But I always believed in the rules, even when I was breaking them. It wasn't until my mother died, at the beginning of this year, that I, for some reason, started questioning some of the rules more. I didn't question the bible, mind you—I've never stopped believing in the King James Bible, as the perfect word of God on earth. But, I started to question some of my church's interpretations about what the bible is actually saying about a few things."

"What kind of things?" asked Adam, and absent-mindedly poured a shot.

"About personal behavior. And then about politics. Maybe it was because my mother had disagreed with my father about salvation, and about the King James Bible, and she was right. And now my father was teaching a false gospel from the pulpit, and I realized that he wasn't even saved. So I naturally began to wonder what else he was wrong about. The atheist philosopher Bertrand Russell once said, 'All movements go too far.'"

"You're the second person who's quoted Bertrand Russell to me lately."

"He's in hell now. But, my point is, I went too far in my rebellion. I read books that argued for the other side of things. I went so far as to become ideologically aligned with the Democratic Party for a month and a half—economically, not on abortion."

"That is a pretty far swing, from what I imagine are the standard politics of a fundamentalist Baptist," said Adam. "But you got over it?"

"Thankfully, yes," said Hannah. "When everything had settled, I was back to being a political conservative, and an Independent Fundamental Baptist. And my confidence in my beliefs was strengthened, and my understanding of them, by my period of examination and skepticism. But I did end up retaining a few minor disagreements with our side."

"Like about drinking?" said Adam.

"About drinking," said Hannah. "And playing cards, and rock 'n' roll."

"Do you believe that the earth is six-thousand years old?" asked Adam.

"I do," said Hannah.

"Why?"

"Because it is."

Adam laughed. Hannah took the shot glass from him, and swallowed its contents whole. The sirens of emergency vehicles screamed by at a near remove.

"But, along the way, along the way of rebellion," continued Hannah, "I met a friend—a guy who sometimes attended our church: the one who recently died. As I found out, he wasn't saved. But he did believe in God, like you." Hannah glanced at Adam, then returned to looking at her memories, as they floated around the kitchen. "He and I," she said, "used to drink alone in his apartment. He's in hell now. There's nothing I could do to save him." She considered the totality of everything and then concluded, "Belief is the currency of adventure."

"What does that mean?"

"I don't know exactly," said Hannah. "It just occurred to me to say it. But I suppose it means that it's what we choose to believe that determines the path we take in life, and gives the path its meaning."

"You used to drink alone with him in his apartment, you and your friend that died?" asked Adam.

"Yes," said Hannah.

"How did that go?"

"Well," said Hannah, "as I mentioned before, we ended up sinning together."

Hannah looked at Adam, an intangible frankness passing between them.

"You are a security guard?" asked Hannah finally. "And your friend who died was also a guard?"

"Yes."

"When did he die?"

"He died at work. A week before last Sunday."

Hannah hid her face from Adam, by gliding off of her stool, and hurriedly retrieving her trench coat from the closet. Before Adam could react, she had it on, and was holding her umbrella by the door.

"I'd better go," she said, her eyes wet, a tremble in her voice. She fiddled with her pink umbrella, preparing it to function when she needed it outside.

"Hannah," said Adam, stepping off of his stool, and standing to face her, "Maybe you shouldn't drive. You could sleep here."

"Thank you," said Hannah. "But this has gone along far enough. But tell me something before I go," said Hannah, looking down at the umbrella in her hand.

"What's that?" asked Adam. The sweet smell of fruit from her shampoo was in his nose. He noticed the streams and curls of her hair, like the flows and eddies in a river of hot caramel.

"Why did you steal the file cabinet key from off of my keychain?" she asked, her blue eyes looking suddenly up at him.

The muscles in Adam's face loosened with intoxication and shock. Hannah looked at him like a starving person, looking at a giver of food, submissively begging for mercy.

He stepped in close to her, and kissed the redness of her lips. Lightning lit the darkness; a peal of thunder quaked through the room. Hannah stood there, and melted, and kissed him back.

15

Looking

Adam awoke, and it was early, and he hadn't slept enough. There was a terrible dryness in his eyes and in his brain; his skull was fragile and sore. The events of the previous night came to him in a rush, the later ones seen through a fog of whiskey. He saw the uncovered secrets of Hannah's body, and her intimate reactions, to their intimate deeds. He gently maneuvered himself out of the queen-sized mattress, that resided on the carpet in a corner of his sparsely adorned bedroom, and sat in the chair facing his desk, next to the mess of blankets and consequences which his bed on the floor contained.

He looked at Hannah, who lay unclothed upon his mattress, sleeping, facing the wall and its large window, curtains drawn against the harsh beginnings of day—her form beneath the sheet a curved half of an hourglass, from shoulder to hip to thigh, casually announcing the majesty of womanhood throughout the room. Adam looked at this ancient line of her, and was moved by it—feeling the presence of a treasure. He saw that the bible Hannah had given him was sitting next to his closed laptop on his desk, but he didn't remember putting it there. Lights were off in the room, but a diffused illumination crept in around the corners of the window curtains. Adam felt profound guilt in his soul, but sexual satisfaction in his body—mixed with his hangover's wounded moan.

He quietly placed the Bible on his lap in the chair, and opened it to a random place. Before him were black letters on white pages. He remembered that the words of Christ were sometimes printed red in bibles. He flipped forward, towards the New Testament, looking for letters of red. In the book of Matthew, his eyes landing on a particular verse in red, in the middle of other red verses. It turned out not to be the comforting message of open-mindedness he was hoping for from Christ. He read—in Matthew 5, 27 and 28:

"Ye have heard that it was said by them of old time, Thou shalt not commit adultery: But I say unto you, That whosoever looketh on a woman to lust after her hath committed adultery with her already in his heart."

He continued—in verse 29 and 30:

"And if thy right eye offend thee, pluck it out, and cast it from thee: for it is profitable for thee that one of thy members should perish, and not that thy whole body should be cast into hell. And if thy right hand offend thee, cut it off, and cast it from thee: for it is profitable for thee that one of thy members should perish, and not that thy whole body should be cast into hell."

Guilt squirmed beneath Adam's skin, and he considered the concept of hell. He imagined, for example, hypothetically, knowing he would always feel hungover, always feel his current state of malaise. What if he could never leave the chair he sat in now? He imagined a simple torment—say, waiting for a bus, in cold weather, with no gloves on—the frigid numbing air burning against one's fingers. What if the bus never came? What if a person were made, by supernatural means, to stand on that cold sidewalk waiting, literally forever?—never mind being always on fire, and covered in worms, or whatever it is that happens in hell. Adam was dizzy from the vertigo of looking into eternity.

A thought appeared in Adam's mind, like a bird landing brightly on a high branch. He remembered that Hannah had shown him, that salvation from hell comes only from believing that Jesus died for one's sins, and never from good behavior. So then, in this red-lettered verse, Jesus couldn't be saying, that looking at a woman, and having dirty thoughts, sends a person to hell. The thought that had come into Adam's bruised mind was this: the woman, then, in verse 28—the one being lusted after—wasn't only a literal woman: she represented wrong belief. Jesus was saying, not to want the alluring woman of a religious untruth. Not with your eyes. Not with your hands. She will take you to hell. Trust instead the woman of truth.

Adam looked at Hannah, still asleep in the dimness of their early-morning crime scene. Adam's stomach began the first faint twitch of hunger, but a whine of pain in his temples disagreed. He flipped forward through New Testament pages; his eyes happened to land on a verse in the gospel of John, again in red letters, among a sizable section of red.

"Verily, verily, I say unto you, He that heareth my word, and believeth on him that sent me, hath everlasting life, and shall not come into condemnation; but is passed from death unto life."

John 5, verse 24: Adam remembered Hannah telling him that it was this verse that her mother had read to her, when she was five-years-old, that had caused her to understand God's love, and plan of salvation—had caused her to become a little Christian believer. And now Adam had found it, here, now, with Hannah sleeping in his bed. Instead of dwelling on this chance occurrence, Adam rose, and shambled into his kitchen, carefully closing his bedroom door behind him.

In the kitchen Adam saw a remnant of old coffee—from however many days ago—languishing in his coffee pot. He retrieved two coffee mugs, deciding he would heat himself one up, and one for Hannah.

Adam noticed a small collection of dirty dishes in his sink, that had been there already when Hannah had come over in the night. They made him remember a previous encounter, in his 20s, when he had gone home with some strange lovely girl from the bar—of a handful of times that that had happened—and they had done what people sometimes do. He remembered, in the morning, when he had taken a drink of water from her kitchen sink, before escaping away, into the accusatory light of dawn—he remembered noticing her dirty dishes in her sink, among all other foreign things in the otherness of the unknown place. His attention had focused on her dishes in her sink, on their shape and color, on the miniscule fragments of food, floating in the pools of water they contained. Her dishes were a part of the quotidian movements of a life of which he was not a part.

He remembered that there was always an undeniable feeling of emotional emptiness to those encounters, that had, in a way, contributed to their melancholy poetry. He thought of Hannah, that he didn't know her favorite movie, didn't know her middle name. In his conscience was a nagging announcement that the laws of God were broken by such actions, but he didn't allow himself to put this feeling into very many words of thought.

Standing among the parking spaces, outside of Adam's building—half an hour later—within the wooden fence that surrounded his affordable gated community, Hannah stood in her bright red dress—its brightness somehow dulled with a morning-after wrinkle. The occasional tree, rising stalwartly from among the parked cars, was beginning to possess that tincture of fiery colors, mixed in with their green—announcing the arriving of a Texan fall.

Adam stood facing Hannah, both of them in the space between her open driver's-side door, and the driver's seat of her very-used Honda Civic—its white paint dutifully maintaining a freshness of attitude, despite its sundry scars of travel. There, within the shielding wing of Hannah's departing coach, the man and the woman were saying a layered goodbye. At the end he kissed her, her lips tugging on his heart. It felt like a purloined thing, like stealing the offering money at church.

As she lowered herself into the car, and as Adam closed her door—attempting to affect a smile as he did—he suddenly felt old déjà vu. He remembered the picture of Roland Bellwether, kissing Hannah goodbye—in just the way that he just had, and just before his murder. He was walking in a dead man's steps.

As Hannah pulled out of her space, and drove away, toward the apartment complex's gate, which opened automatically to allow her out—a horrible thought occurred to Adam, and he was suddenly afraid, that if he turned around, he would discover Pastor Lacuna's crimson Nissan Versa parked somewhere on the edge of view, watching what he'd done. With ice in his veins, he turned around, and scanned the rows of cars and trucks, on either side of the drive that curved away into a combination of circles, around which the apartment buildings were placed. His body tense from not wanting, but needing to do it, he looked for the Nissan, and—to the everlasting chill of his guilt-ridden blood—he found it.

The Nissan was just close enough to not be hidden by the curve of the drive and the vehicles in between them. It was under a canopied set of spaces, that apartment residents paid extra to park in—a first class section of parking. If it was the Pastor's vehicle, it had managed to park in a restricted spot, without getting towed. Adam wondered if the car was, in fact, occupied, and as soon as he did, it pulled out and drove away, around the bend, in a hurried fashion.

Adam, though barely dressed for polite society—his hair, his unbathed person projecting the aura of a hungover sinner—he nevertheless realized that his car keys were in a pocket of the swim trunks he was wearing, and he darted toward his car, parked a few feet away, to pursue the escaping intruder. He caught up with his target, as it was passing through the opening apartment-complex's gate, having taken the long way around. He attempted to recall the things that Douglas Tent had told him and shown him about following someone with a car, during their day of surveillance training together.

The reality of actually following a person landed on Adam like a blanket of cold water, and his heartrate sped, as he took the turn out of his complex and onto the four-lane street which flowed past—the Nissan Versa traveling in front of him. Looking at his car's clock, he saw that it was 7:45, being of a Thursday morning. The traffic was thick and fast-moving. Adam remembered Tent telling him about the use of a "cover car", by which a mobile surveiller follows his subject, with a car between them, to hide his presence. As the surrounding vehicles come and go, and as the target takes his turns, the surveiller can employ more or fewer cover cars, sometimes finding himself right behind his subject, in which case he should keep his distance.

Adam, as he followed the Nissan Versa, found himself—before he knew it—disastrously right behind his target, stopped at a light. He remembered Tent telling him that, in such a situation, it is best for the surveiller to position his car jogged a little to the passenger side of the car in front of him. This prevents the target from seeing his pursuer in his driver's-side mirror. Overhead the San Antonio sky was a ceiling of clouds with grey and black bottoms, and bright white sides—as if a layer of darkness was struggling to conceal the lightness and bright blueness above. Even the sun was thusly obscured. The ground here and there retained dampness from the storm of the previous night. In the dimness of the morning—and in Adam's fear of looking too closely and thereby betraying the truth of his sleazy, foolhardy endeavor—he could not tell if it was Pastor Lacuna that drove the car he was following. He could see the vehicle's license plate, and again was disappointed in himself for not recording the pastor's plate when he had had the chance.

As the chase continued, Adam sometimes felt he was too close to the Nissan, sometimes too far, and in danger of losing it among the jigsaw puzzle of moving metal boxes. He remembered Tent telling him that, besides taking cover, the other most important thing to be aware of was the rhythm of the traffic lights—aware not even so much of the next light, so much as the one after that. At one point, the Nissan was stopped at the next light further down, but Adam, stopped at his light, still had full view of it. When a green light has been green a while, "an old green", it should be approached speedily, lest it turn suddenly red. Once it is within striking distance, the surveiller can slow down again. At one point, in the pursuit, Adam was stopped by a red light, and separated from his prey. He turned right onto the perpendicular street, then cut left through a gas station on the corner, to get back on the original path again, bypassing the stoplight's forbidding demand.

The game and dance of stoplights and distance continued for a few miles, straight down Thousand Oaks Drive with no turning—passing over some train tracks, passing under the foreboding sky. Finally, the crimson Nissan took a right onto the access road of I-35 South, but it didn't merge onto the highway. When the car turned off of the access road, and into the parking lot of a smut shop called the Adult Complex, Adam began to strongly suspect that he had not been following Pastor Lacuna all along, but that he'd been following one of his neighbors, ultimately into a porn store, that surely wouldn't be open right now?

The cloudy daytime mixed with the uninviting emptiness of the store's parking area made for a deserted loneliness. The Nissan took a turn around the far corner of the forlorn store and disappeared into another part of the lot. Adam slowed down to a crawl, in epic danger now of his pursuit becoming obvious—if it was not already. There was no way out, except the way he'd come in. High above the access road, stood the adult store's sign: "Adult Complex" it read—bordered by a circular red neon bulb that was not lit. Along the bottom of the sign was written "Exit Starlight" which was either a reference to nearby Starlight Terrace, or else was a very short poem about lost hope.

Adam drove slowly past the front of the store, approaching the corner his subject had gone around. The entrance door was next to a window of cloudy textured glass, behind which were more turned-off neon lights. The building had no other windows. Before rounding the corner, Adam stopped and looked behind himself. He saw that a billboard faced the Complex sign, from across the turn-in to the store. It therefore wouldn't be readily visible to motorists passing by, but only to those in the porn store's parking lot. On the billboard, high above, was written the question, "Where will you go when you die?" Beneath this question, on the left, were clouds rendered in soothing blue tones, to symbolize heaven. On the sign's right was a picture of fire, orange and bursting with violence.

As Adam pulled further in, he noticed that a fence ran all the way around the parking lot. Across the fence to the right looked to be some kind of business with a collection of RVs. To the parking lot's left was a grimy Day's Inn. Adam noticed two small dumpsters in a far corner of the fenced-in lot, and shuddered to think what might be in them. As he took the turn left, around the corner of the building—the one the Nissan had taken—he finally saw the Nissan parked facing the side of the store, against the far fence—with the Day's Inn beyond. Along the porn store's fenced border with the Day's Inn was a long canopy beneath which stood two freight shipping containers, impenetrably holding the store's backroom of filth.

Adam instinctively parked in a space next to the Nissan, two spaces away. It didn't make logical sense to him, but it seemed like the thing to do. He got out of his car, not knowing what he would say to the pastor—or to whatever random neighbor he had actually been following—upon encountering them. In the moment, he had only a vague strategy of acting personable and confused. Perhaps he would ask when the porn store opens, act informed by the response, and leave.

As Adam approached the crimson Nissan Versa, he saw that it was empty, He scanned around himself, along the perimeter of parking lot fence—no one. Looking at the side of the store, he saw that there was a small space, between the fence and the store's back wall. He approached it slowly—feeling the possibility of an ambush. Who parks at a closed porn store, and then lurks around the back side of it? Someone looking for a place to attack the guy who was following them?

Adam started coming around the corner. Beyond the store's back fence, and beyond the Days Inn's entrance, I-35 rose into the sky, on metal and stone pillars, in a grand arch in the daytime air—emitting the whiz of passing traffic. Powerlines ran along the outside of the back fence, with wires streaming down into a box at the top of the store's back wall—powering the electric hypnosis of porn. When Adam was all the way around the corner, when he started to think he was going to look completely upon an unoccupied emptiness behind the store, then suddenly a figure was before him, and angry hands grabbed him, and slammed him against the porn shop's back wall.

"Why the fuck are you following me?!" the figure demanded, grinding his fists into Adam's chest—gripping handfuls of Adam's shirt with powerful rage. The figure was Pastor Lacuna.

"Why are you following me? I said!" The pastor demanded again. The grooves in the wrinkles of his face were deep with tension, and crowding together toward his wide thickly bespectacled eyes. Adam said nothing, and the pastor threw him down to the ground.

Adam looked up at the pastor, noticing the old age of the man, somehow exacerbated but also put aside by the animating spirit of his obsessive glare and posture toward Adam. A gust of breeze agitated the pastor's necktie. He reached inside his suit jacket and pulled a thing out, that had been tucked inside of his waist. It was a handgun. A revolver. He didn't point it at Adam, but he continued to stare down at him enraged, the handgun at his side. Adam rested on his elbows, looking up at the pastor, speechless.

"Did Roland tell you that my daughter was easy? Is that what happened? Is it?" the pastor shouted.

Adam didn't respond.

"She made the mistake once. I won't let her make it again."

Traffic whizzed by. Behind the porn store, the pastor and the amateur detective were alone and undetected. Grey clouds floated on, blocking the sun.

"Is that why you killed him?" Adam asked, looking defiantly upward.

Pastor Lacuna raised his gun, pointing it down at Adam.

16

Tent's Third Letter

Adam lay there on his back, propped up on his elbows, in the surprisingly clean and uncluttered alley between the porn store's back wall and the fence that stood close behind it. A breeze caused the few errant hairs of Pastor Lacuna's otherwise solid white hairdo to dance, but did not alter the rictus of wounded rage upon the wrinkles of his face. Lacuna held his arm defiantly extended toward Adam lying at his feet, the black mid-caliber revolver's wooden grip clutched in the bones of his thin-skinned hand—pointed at Adam's face.

Adam unthinkingly looked down the barrel of the gun, then looked away, the blackness in the little perfect circle of the barrel's end whispering horrors at him, from a distance on the other side of death. Adam heard the click of the gun being cocked, and he turned his head to the side, his eyes closed, cringing in the muscles of his face. His body was rigid all over. His thoughts had slammed to a halt and begun to crash into one another like the boxcars of a train. Then Adam heard the subsequent click of the gun's hammer slamming home, and he knew that he was dead.

An abbreviated version of his life passed through his mind. He saw an image of a little girl, who'd been his classmate in the second grade. And he remembered being eight-years-old, and riding his bicycle alone at dusk, in the suburbs he grew up in, while in his little mind he thought of his female classmate, knowing nothing yet of sex, but in the grip of a romantic reverie, feeling—inspired no doubt by 80s love songs—that the connection between a male and a female in love must be the meaning of life. He thought of the innocence and drowning elementary-school intensity of that feeling, of its openhearted search for meaning. And then—in that frozen instant of his death—that original amorous experience was juxtaposed with his final sexual encounter—last night with the preacher's daughter. It too, he knew, was a desperate groping after the meaning of life, but it was not innocent. Rather, somehow, it'd been a crime.

The frozen timeless moment of death continued and Adam saw the bible Hannah had given him, sitting on his bedroom's desk, he oblivious to it, his conscience doing him no good, as the bible looked down on the tangle of sheets and bodies, an overlooking observer, silently judging and convicting. Adam, in that moment, knew that the smirk and charm with which he had navigated the emptiness of his life till now—and all of its melancholy poetry—would not protect him from the crushing of the steely laws of God. He knew the answer to the question posed by the corny religious billboard above them in the sky. He knew that, if he were really, truly dead, the demons would be there any second, to drag his soul to hell.

But he was not dead—not his body. There had been no bang of a gun's report, no fire, no smoke. The pastor had dry-fired an empty pistol at him. Adam rolled languidly onto his stomach, his weight still on his elbows, his face in his hands. He felt warm tears streaming down his cheeks—not from grief or shock, so much as from a sudden surging of stress, now suddenly released and overflowing his emotions. With its flow it brought along residual stress from the entire past two weeks of confusion and detection. He didn't know how much was there, until he felt it flowing out of him, childlike, lying in the invisible filth behind the unopened porn store, the shadows of the pallid morning hanging all around him and the violent preacher standing by.

Pastor Lacuna let his arm drop to his side with resignation. "I didn't kill Roland Bellwether," he said. "I knew he was having an affair with my daughter. I followed them. I took a picture of them together, and I was going to confront her about it. But... I couldn't. I wanted to. I just couldn't bring myself to speak the words, to tell her that I knew. I didn't want for it to be real. I knew she had drifted in some ways, over the years..."

Adam was brought out of his introspective flood by the pastor's candid revelations. The detective in him was piqued at the chance for information. He quickly worked to pull himself together internally. He lifted his shoulders, his face rising out of his hands.

"I was following them the night that Roland died," the pastor continued to say, to Adam's back on the ground, and to the air in front of him. "I was there, at the place where you work —parked outside. But I didn't kill him. I could have, yes—if hatred could kill a person, he'd have been dead already. I shouldn't hate. I am a man of God. I'm sorry that you've seen this side of me, Adam. But I do hate fornication. It is an ugly thing. I don't apologize for that."

Pastor Lacuna placed his gun back into his waistband, far enough around to his side for the front of his jacket to conceal it again, as it fell against his belt.

"You called him that night, pastor. Your phone called Rolland Bellwether seconds before he died. Why?" Adam asked, still prone and speaking toward the ground, his face still hot, his eyes still wet from crying.

"Maybe my phone called him, Adam," Pastor Lacuna said. "But I didn't. My phone was stolen, by a police detective."

"What?"

"A police detective came to my house. He told me his name, showed me his badge. He asked about my phone, and asked to see it, as it had been involved in some kind of crime. I showed it to him. He ended up walking off with it, against my protest."

"It *was* involved in a crime," said Adam. "It was involved in the murder of Roland Bellwether."

"No, I mean, this was before. Roland was killed the Sunday before last. The police detective stole my phone the day before the murder. It was Saturday afternoon. I remember, I was working on my sermon for Sunday morning. I called the police station later, and asked if there was any detective with the same number on his badge and name as the one who'd come to my house. They said that there was."

"Did you report the stolen phone, or tell them what had happened?"

"No. It seemed awkward, to report to the police that the police had stolen my phone. I wasn't sure what to do. I've been using my wife's phone, until I get a new one."

"Was your phone password protected?"

"It was," said Pastor Lacuna. "But the detective had me put my password in, so he could look at whatever it was that he was looking at, to investigate whatever it was. He basically was vague and insistent, and talked me into letting him walk away with my phone without much protest."

"What was the detective's name?" asked Adam, still on the ground, but his blood beginning to move again.

"He had a red mustache," said pastor Lacuna. "His name was Richard Bethany."

Adam was speechless. Pastor Lacuna waited for a response, and when he didn't get any he said, "Please come to my office sometime, and we can speak about this further. Stay away from my daughter."

He walked to his car. Adam heard the pastor's car door open and shut with a creak and a slam, and the roar of the engine coming to life, and the sound of the tires, and all of it fading with distance, until only the aggregated whine of the highway was left. Adam felt the prickle of the pavement under his arms, and saw the monotonous concrete in front of his face—a symbol for the hard facts that surrounded him, and their impenetrable mystery.

As Adam finally stood, a rush of blood and confusion swirling through his head—just then—his phone in his pants buzzed to life, declaring a text message's arrival. Bringing his phone from his pants pocket to check its screen, Adam had a premonition who it would be. It was another text from Tent.

Adam felt weariness together with a strength of will which told him that the ship of his soul could brave more storms before sinking. The text message read,

"Left porn store dumpster, inside left fork pocket."

Adam had never heard the expression "fork pocket" before, but its use—in relation to a dumpster—made its meaning immediately clear to him. Adam looked toward the small twin dumpsters, on the far end of the empty parking lot from him, ensconced in the rectangle of fence that tightly sheltered them. They took on an ominous aura, now that Adam's life was headed to them.

Before crossing the parking lot, Adam considered the suspiciousness of what he was going to do—and of what he had been doing. He glanced around his situation's stark panorama. He noticed, perched atop the porn store—above the corner he had rounded before encountering the pastor—a white bullet camera. He was relieved to notice that it was not pointed at the rear of the store, and thus would not have captured his and Lacuna's confrontation. Instead it was pointed at the long shipping containers housed along the fence—guarding against whatever ghouls would attempt to penetrate the containers' two-inch steel doors, to get at the trove of indecency inside. The camera stood high on the wall, keeping guard, and high above Adam saw again the billboard about the afterlife; and high above that hung still the grey sky, beyond which, Adam mused, were the billions of light-years of twinkling blackness that stand between the earth and God.

Steadying himself, in his fire and his fog, he strode toward the sturdy receptacles of trash. Arriving at the dugout of fence around the dumpsters, he saw that its front side was two closed gates tied together with a padlocked chain. Looking closer, he realized with relief that the padlock was not completely closed, but merely brought the chain's two ends together, within its unclasped shackle. Adam was familiar with this move from security-guarding. It was common in his experience for gates in facilities where he had worked to be secured this way: sometimes a padlock's key was missing; sometimes a guard couldn't be bothered to continuously lock and unlock the thing; in either case, the false appearance of impenetrability was considered deterrence enough.

Unlatching the padlock from one side of the chain, and opening one side of the gate just enough to squeeze into the square of fence, Adam stood uncomfortably close to the left-hand dumpster. Like the passageway behind the store, the pavement around the dumpsters was not dirty, did not display in physicality the spiritual feeling of grime that stuck to the surface of one's skin here. Adam was happy that he wouldn't be opening the dumpsters themselves. He beheld before him the thing that he assumed Tent was referring to, in his text, as the left dumpster's left "fork pocket": one of the deep loops of steel, welded to either side of the trash receptacle, by which it would be lifted and emptied by a garbage truck.

Adam didn't discern a letter within the shadow-darkened interior of the fork pocket. He slowly began to slip his hand inside. He felt that he was penetrating deeper into the sleaze of the porn environment, achieving a deeper dirtiness. He wished he were wearing gloves. He shuddered to touch either side of the inside of the steel loop, his fingers grazing as lightly as possible, looking for a letter—afraid of what macroscopic or microscopic refuse or vermin his fingertips might brush across. Finally, pressing far inside, he felt the familiar crispness of a paper envelope. He pulled it out, turning it over to see if it was infected with stains or wetness. It looked okay.

Adam emerged from the dugout, and reconstructed the chain-and-padlock ruse. He considered sitting in his car, or driving all the way home, before opening the letter. However, his curiosity was too great, his mind too beaten down, to wait. He tore the letter open, and straightened its folds. This is what it said.

"My Dearest Adam,

"Since last we corresponded, the case of the murdered billionaires has taken many amazing turns. I dare say, the game has never been more afoot: the game is so afoot it's a leg. I write this letter from a position more penetrated into the worldwide criminal organization of Malcom Esperanza than any crimefighter has ever ventured. All I had predicted, through my battle-hardened detective's intuition, about this case's consequences for crime, politics, and the nature of reality itself, has come crashingly, gloriously to pass.

"When writing my first letter to you, it was my tentative theory, that Malcom Esperanza was—somehow—the perpetrator of the billionaire murders, and either framing the homeless physicist, or else assisting him in his reality-bending crime. Then, as my second letter related, once I had uncovered the existence of the secretive billionaire trio of violent, evil cigar-bar comrades, I realized that Esperanza was not the homeless man's accomplice, but—in fact—one of his intended victims. I have now detected the entire epic story, and I can tell you why the time-traveling assassin was unsuccessful in the killing of Malcom Esperanza. And, my friend, the answer does no less than reveal the source of Esperanza's black power—revealing him truly to be the Satan of our world.

"Malcom Esperanza's true identity now known to me, I had set about to infiltrate the staff at Malcom Esperanza's multi-million dollar mansion in Westchester, New York. Employing an unparalleled mastery of disguise—for which I am renowned—I got hired as a house servant on the estate, posing as an illegal Mexican immigrant named Diego Tienda. Not only would this give me undercover access to Esperanza's estate—under his very nose—but it would also allow me to witness his corrupt, racist business practices.

"You'll be interested to note, that it is a condition of employment at his estate, that all servants must undergo an interview with Esperanza himself. Esperanza uses this meeting as an opportunity to thoroughly hypnotize each person, implanting in them trigger words, which he and his criminal underlings can then later use to manipulate the employees, and erase their memories. In this regard, my regimen of self-hypnosis proved invaluable: not only was I able to maintain my psychological integrity—pretending to be under his spell—but, by doing so, I was also able to learn his implanted codewords, which would give me control over his other servants.

"Utilizing my knowledge of the trigger words, I was able to obtain all needed information from hypnotized members of his security staff, to allow me access to the most top secret rooms in his mansion's hidden subbasement. The subbasement is shockingly advanced in its accommodations for scientific research and labs—the most important area of which is dedicated to literature and technology related to advanced study of the nature of time and space. It was in this room—deep below the 19th century gilded opulence and rolling acres of verdant hills of the estate above—that I found the homeless man's quaintly hobbled together time machine.

"It had the appearance of a metallic egg, jury-rigged together, just large enough for a human adult male to squeeze into. It would seem to be of less sophisticated technology than some of the industrially constructed instruments around it—including the pedestal and short set of stairs that Esperanza had placed it on—but appearances would be deceiving. What the device lacks in crafted finish, it makes up for in the ingenious grace of the ideas of its design. I, myself, only know of quantum mechanics, general relativity theory, and particle physics what I have gleaned from independent study in my spare time; however, I consider myself to have achieved the equivalent of a triple PhD in these topics.

"Therefore, I was able to read through the homeless man's notes and papers, which Esperanza had in the room—which the inventor must have taken with him from his timeline. Space prevents me from going into the science of it, but—like so many breakthroughs in the history of science—the idea, once understood, is so simple, yet so counterintuitive, that its beauty overwhelms the comprehender of it. Yes, I'll take Einstein over the bible any day.

"It was suddenly clear to me what must have happened. The mystery—as it always eventually is, my friend—has finally been laid bare. In an alternative timeline to our own, the homeless former physicist—he of the outré theories about time and quantum mechanics—was raped by the cadre of bloodthirsty billionaires. This, in a moment of fiery determination, inspired him to return to his theoretical work—thereby happening him upon the long-sought-after secret of time travel—the secret which I was privileged to read in Malcom Esperanza's underground hideaway.

"Hobbling together the needed materials, working with the ardor of a man possessed, the physicist was able to construct the history-shattering devise, and use it. He used it to kill one billionaire, and then the second. But, when he made the third trip—the one intended to put an end to Malcom Esperanza—a snag was hit. Somehow, Esperanza—wily demon that he is—was able to foil his own assassination and take the homeless man's time machine from him. (In the common musing, that is often had, about going back in time to kill a monster, it is never considered that the monster might prevail, and thereby become a monster with a time machine.)

"In reading the brilliant man's theories about time—which led to his construction of the machine—it was further revealed to me how, in the changing of the past, a time paradox is prevented. Apparently, what happens is, upon returning to the newly created timeline, the time traveler's previous timeline no longer exists, except for whatever effects it's had on the newly canonical time, and its continued existence in the memory of the returning time-traveler. There would now be two versions of the traveler in the newly created present: the one who went back, changed things, and remembers the way things were before; and a version of the same person, who never went back in time, because there was no need to—from his point of view. I do not know what happened to the version of the homeless physicist whose time machine Esperanza stole. Probably Esperanza murdered him. But the version of the man that was in police custody while the murders were happening was never raped, and will never build a time machine. He will go on being homeless and uninspired.

"What is really important to understand, for our purposes, is that Malcom Esperanza has a time machine. And now, from the standpoint of the helpless history of humankind, it's as if he's always had one. All his former incarnations, throughout time, were set up by him—may have literally been him. The machine has given him power to erect his criminal conspiracy for thousands of years—obliterating any foe, changing any circumstance, traveling back from our present to do so. We are only allowed by him to exist, because he has not yet enacted his final plan for us. There is no devil, no hell, no metaphysical evil, Adam: there is only Malcom Esperanza.

"People of good conscience in our day—not Republicans and capitalists, but all good people—feel in their hearts, that there is a virulent stream of racism, of sexism, of classism, of homophobia, that has run through history, that should not be there. It is an affront to human decency. It is a black cloud, a rotting stain upon the world. Why is it there? We now can say. The natural state of our world, of humankind—a state of peace, a state of acceptance toward every people group, toward every kind of love—this beautiful default state has been systematically dismantled by Malcom Esperanza's time machine. Traveling back into the past, he has laid the seeds of hate, of bigotry, acting as the spiritual poisoner of our collective mind —over and over again. It was he that founded the Ku Klux Klan, that assassinated JFK, that denigrated the religion of Islam with 9-11 and the cult of radical extremism. All that remains, of our original timeline—of the timeline of political and social Eden that we originally had—is a heartbroken wisp of its memory subconsciously situated in the emotions of the present's left-wing liberals. And we ache for its return. Before Malcom Esperanza's meddling, white people were a powerless minority, homosexuality was the norm, gender conformity did not exist. He has remade the world in his image, by an infernal misuse of science!

"I must now tell you, Adam, of another room I found, in Esperanza's basement. It too was stocked with technology and files full of notes—but not this time in regard to the study of the laws of physics; this room was medical in its purpose. All the accoutrements of a theater of surgery were arrayed within the space—the bed, the lights, the anesthesia, the tools, and everything else, in cool, medical sterility and baby blue hues. I read through the notes, and papers, and was alarmed to discover that the operating room was preparing to operate on me. A plastic surgeon from Thailand, and his team of nurses, were staying in the mansion, and preparing a multiplicity of reconstructions, to be done to me against my will, once Esperanza has succeeded in my capture. The operating bed, and a nearby wheelchair, were both fitted with wrist and ankle constraints.

"The nature of the surgeries planned by Esperanza for me are these: facial feminization surgery, breast implants, and vaginoplasty—a fascinating procedure whereby a man's penis and scrotum are turned inside out, to construct a vagina where his male organs once had been. He also plans to change my race: included in the papers is the description of a treatment, whereby the patient's skin and facial features are altered, to transition from white to black. At the end of the hours-long battery of surgeries, and a lengthy period of healing, I would be an African American woman.

"The twisted psychology of Esperanza's plan is obvious. He has taken great pains to use his time machine to turn the world into one suffering under the groaning domination of straight, white, men—because he is one, and because he loves himself with a narcissism unparalleled in humanity. Because he hates all those things that are not him. Therefore, the very worst thing he can think to do to me is to turn me into everything he despises—a racial, gender, and even sexual minority (because I'll be a lesbian)—and then let me go. But, in the fervor of his rage, he has miscalculated badly. He has not counted on the goodness of those that are not like him. I have decided, Adam, that I will turn myself in, and submit to his surgeries. I will not flee from this exciting opportunity. He has laid the seeds of his ultimate undoing at my hands. The road will not be without its difficulties. There will be weeks of soreness, swelling, and discharge. I won't be able to smoke crack or cigarettes while I'm healing, because it constricts blood flow, and could lead to necrosis. I will need to take estrogen treatments for the rest of my life, and—on a regular basis—dilate my new vagina, to prevent it from healing shut, like the massive wound that it technically is. But, the payoff, the glorious payoff, my friend, will be that—when I finally bring Malcom Esperanza to justice—it will be as the greatest black, female, lesbian, transgender detective that the world has ever known.

"In closing, in regard to the murder of Roland Bellwether, I believe that Roland was hypnotized by Esperanza himself—appearing to his victim through some deceptive guise—and that the trigger words, which brought about his suicide, were delivered by a plant, whom Roland knew but never suspected. It could have been the preacher. But it may also have been someone else. Suspect everyone.

"As always: yours in crimefighting,
"Denise Tent"

17

The Mountain Top

Comanche Lookout hill, in Comanche Lookout park, at 1,340 feet, is the fourth highest point of elevation in Bexar County. Adam had passed it before, driving along Nacogdoches Road, near his apartment, as it stood like a giant, slumbering, tree-covered mass of earth by the road. On the morning after Adam's clash with Pastor Lacuna at the smut shop—and the receipt of the most astounding letter from detective Douglas Tent—Adam was still in his security-guard uniform (shirt still tucked in, his subconscious still on the lookout for wrongdoing) as he drove home from work. It was a chilly morning, and the sun was just coming up. Instead of proceeding directly home, he turned onto Nacogdoches Road, and drove toward Comanche Lookout hill, which beckoned to him, from its ancient, American past. He'd been instructed in a dream last night to do so.

Adam parked, and was the only car, the only soul in sight. He walked up the main path, assuming that the main path, inclining ever upward, would take him to the summit. The paved path cut through the tall woods covering the hill, as if a steam roller had been driven through a forest—leaving a corridor of sky carved out of the canopy of green. On either side of Adam as he walked, were trees and brush, extending to his left and right forever. Occasionally, along the path, would be a steel park bench, installed upon a square of concrete, facing the path, its back to the line of the woods. Within the woods, on either side, was the sporadic rustling of invisible animals—and then silence. In some places, Adam could see past the verdant façade of the line of the woods on either side, and into a thick expanse of tangled, leafless branches—some so small, so densely packed together, that it made Adam think of it as the dead inside of a massive wooden brain.

Adam persevered, onward and upward. He began to notice cracks in the pavement of the trail, with black coloring along the length of them—indicating where fissures had been mended with tar, and overcome their mending—baking in the Texas sun. Almost at the top, Adam passed a four-story stone tower, enclosed in a green metal fence, with no gate, and spearhead finials. Each floor with a vertical slit for a window, and a rickety door hanging in the air, it seemed like a tower where prisoners would be kept, in the Middle Ages.

At the apex of the mount was a clearing of rock floor, that extended down the south side of the hill—a barren patch in the hill's otherwise billowing cover of trees—providing a vantage point, that one who'd reached the top of the hill could look out from, enjoying a bird's eye view of the town below, all the way to the distant horizon: Nacogdoches Road blazing a path past the hill's base, lined with its stores, motorists flowing by in both directions; other stores and residential homes stretching forth, living in between the trees; and then, further away, a treeless area of industry; and then the dull blue line of the dawn sky meeting planet earth.

In the clearing were three park benches: one facing the main view to the south, and two other ones, pointed to the west and east, their three proud backs to each other, across the square area in between—keeping their empty watch on the world from above. As Adam surmounted the hill, and came into the clearing, clouds were stacked suspended in the great dome of the sky: frozen, out-of-focus cotton. He thought at first that the benches were unoccupied, that he was alone—assuming it before he perceived that he was wrong. There, in the middle of the main, south-facing bench, sitting slightly to one side, was the distinctive, lovely back of the wayward Christian Hannah Lacuna. She did not turn around as he approached, his feet making scraping sounds in the dirt and pebbles.

Adam stood beside her, as she continued looking forward, beautiful and lost in thought. At last she turned her head to see him, a wisp of a startle in her eyes.

"Adam Hume," she said, doubt clearing from her face, being replaced by a knowing smile.

Adam sat down on the bench beside her.

"How did you—? Do you come here often?" Adam asked.

"No, I never do. Do you?"

"No, never." said Adam.

There was a pause and Adam looked around at the heady scene and circumstances, at the clues in nature's plan.

"Then why are we here?" he asked.

"I had a dream," said Hannah, checking his eyes for skepticism, finding instead a deeper attention.

"I had a dream, too." said Adam plainly.

"In my dream," said Hannah, "Roland and I were on this hill, on this bench—as you and I are now. So, that's why I came."

"In my dream," said Adam (showing no surprise at Hannah's use of Roland's name), "I was on this bench with a private detective named Douglas Tent. It was sunrise, like now. He was saying that I've almost figured everything out. There was tremendous hope and meaning. Like, he didn't just mean I'd figure out the murder case, but also life in general."

"It was sunrise in mine too."

"What did Roland tell you in your dream?" Adam asked.

Hannah looked forward at the far-away world beyond. She swallowed, and a mist came to her eyes. Her eyebrows tensed, holding in pain.

"He said I was forgiven. For not saving his soul."

Adam looked at her, wanting to comfort her, wanting to kiss her. He suddenly became aware of another person in the clearing. At the edge of the stony ground were six large stone bricks, embedded like a retaining wall, beyond which the ground turned downward, becoming a steeply sloped trail into the trees beneath. Upon the wall, Adam realized, was a youth of cryptic gender, in a hoodie and grey shorts. The person was holding a phone while seeing the sight of the city below, clamorous music being played into the air, showing no knowledge of the concept of headphones.

Adam had never more strongly wanted someone to leave. As if perceiving the daggers that Adam was glowering into their neck, the person stood up and wandered around the wall, disappearing by descent along the far side's trail down the mount, leaving the hill's rocky bald spot, entering again its cloak of trunks and leaves—to find some other strangers somewhere, with whom to share non-consensual songs.

"We didn't speak about it the morning after," said Adam, "but it seemed that night, like you realized that my coworker who'd died, and your friend who'd died: that they're the same person. That it was, in fact, the death of Roland Bellwether, that led me to your church, and to speaking with your father."

"You said that your dream is to be a detective," said Hannah, wiping her eyes with her fingers and thumb.

"Yes," said Adam. "So, I'm investigating Roland's murder. I'm working for a famous private investigator named Douglas Tent—the man who was in my dream last night."

"So, you stole the filing cabinet key? To investigate? Because you think that my father had something to do with Roland's death? It wasn't suicide in your opinion?"

"I don't think that it was suicide. We—I believe that someone close to, someone he knew, forced him to shoot himself."

"Forced him?"

"I don't know if it was your father or not. His car was at our security-guard job site when Roland died. He told me that he was following Roland, but that he didn't kill him."

"Do you believe him?"

"I don't know."

They both looked forward nonplussed toward the vista conquering their eyes. But they did not see it. Instead, both of their minds reached out through their skins, meeting in the space between them on the bench.

"Your interest in Christianity, then," said Hannah, "is that real, or just part of going undercover to investigate?"

"Hannah, no—that's real. That's the realest thing about me right now."

Hannah looked into his eyes, satisfied that he spoke the truth.

"Roland and I didn't even see each other that often," she said. "We drank, we went to the movies. We listened to rock 'n' roll. He read me some poetry he'd written, that he'd never read to anyone before."

"Did you know that he was the author of the stories of Lucy Truthteller, which chronicle the adventures of the detective Douglas Tent?"

"Adam, I don't know who Douglas Tent is. I knew Roland was a security guard, and a poet. I knew that he hungered for the truth, but ultimately didn't find it."

"I find myself surprised by Roland," Adam said. "At work, I always thought he was an out-of-shape nerd. I read his stories, and I didn't even know they were his. But even more surprising to me—well..."

"You're surprised that I found him attractive?"

"Yes."

"For me," said Hannah, "it was hearing his poetry. I saw beauty beneath his surface. It seemed to me that he had it in his soul to be something great in the world. I longed for him to know the truth. In the end, all I did was give him pleasure on the way to his doom."

"He is in hell?"

Hannah looked at Adam, wounded and resigned. "I'm afraid so," she said.

"Why does it take forever?"

"What's that?"

"Hell," said Adam. "Surely whatever evil we do on earth is only ever finite evil. Even someone like Hitler. After however many thousands of years of being on fire, wouldn't the punishment be paid?"

"Here's how I think of it," said Hannah, her countenance brightening at the opportunity to talk theology. "The whole proposition of life on earth is that it's an arena in which we experience separation from God. That's the whole point."

"Okay."

"And the experiment is to see how we handle this separation. God is still everywhere, but there's a hiddenness to him, experienced by those on earth. So that we can be free to accept or reject him, without being forced to accept him by an overwhelming show of his presence."

"I see," said Adam.

"But the thing about physical death, then, is that that's when the hiddenness of God is taken away, because you've already made your decision by then, to receive Christ or not. And then a person is subject to an overwhelming show of God's presence forever after that.

"But the thing is, the saved and the unsaved experience God's direct presence in very different ways. If a person has been born again, by faith in the death, burial, and resurrection of Christ as the payment for their sins, then they are forgiven. And the way that this forgiveness is awarded is that the believer's spirit is changed, indwelled by the Holy Spirit, so that the person's reborn spirit is now incapable of sin."

"Even though a Christian on earth inevitably does sin," said Adam.

"Yes," said Hannah, "but that's only because the body is not yet redeemed, and therefore influences the believer to sin, despite his spirit not wanting him to. Which is why the apostle Paul commands us that we walk in the spirit, and not in the flesh, that we not fulfil the lusts thereof. But the body's sinful pulling on us will always win sometimes, as long as we live in this body of death."

"On earth."

"Yes. But when the body dies, if a person is saved, then they are released from the evil influence of the unsaved flesh—and are a sinless spirit in heaven."

"That sounds good."

"It is," said Hannah. "Because, to be in God's presence—as his sinless child—is heaven."

"But to stand before God, after physical death, as an unsaved spirit, who is still a sinful being—" said Adam.

"Is hell," said Hannah. "The sinner in hell has rejected the sacrifice: the death and suffering of the spotless lamb, who is Christ. Therefore, the only atonement for sin left to them is their own suffering: their own burning in hell. But they're an unworthy sacrifice: they are sinful rather than spotless. So they burn forever, fecklessly unable to remove a single blot from their accounts—each an eternal, fiery monument to man's proud farce of saving himself."

"Wow," said Adam. "So that's why it's eternal."

"Yes, that's eternal death. That's how I tend to think of it," said Hannah.

Adam looked away from Hannah, something in him stirred then soared.

"How do I do it?" he asked.

"Do what?" said Hannah.

"Put my faith in Jesus Christ, for the saving of my soul. I want to do it. I want to be a child of God, and stand before him, as a sinless being, when this body is gone."

Hannah looked at Adam, with a warrior's eyes.

"Let me ask you the questions," she said.

"Ask me," said Adam.

She reached to the far side of her, where her purse was resting, hidden against the bench. She opened it, and retrieved a small, nicely-bound bible. She faced Adam, holding it with both hands in her lap.

"Adam Hume, you've heard the verses, on a previous occasion. Do you believe the bible, when it says that all have sinned, that we've all broken God's perfect law?"

"Yes," said Adam.

"Do you believe, as the bible says, that, because of your sins, you would have to spend an eternity in hell, paying for your sins forever, unless you're saved, unless you're born again?"

"Yes," said Adam.

"And do you believe that Jesus Christ was God in the flesh; that he died for your sins, was buried, and rose again?"

"I do," said Adam.

"And do you believe that—because of Christ's sacrifice, and for no other reason—that you have eternal life, and will go to heaven when you die—that salvation can never be lost once it's given?"

Adam smiled. "I do," he said.

Hannah smiled back. "Then, according to the bible, my brother, today is the day of your salvation." She took his hands in hers, both resting on the bible in her lap, and she beamed at him, the joy of the moment more unreal than last night's dream.

She gave Adam a peck on his lips, and his smile broadened. Elsewhere in his body he had an involuntary reaction that he was sure was inappropriate to the current spiritual context.

To the east, a fruit-juice fire of orange spread its fingers between the horizon and a dark square cloud concealing the newly risen sun. Rays from the sun cut through the cloud in places, like swords of glass, like God's divine wisdom lighting down from heaven to man.

18

Revelation

After that lofty morning, on the hilltop with Hannah, Adam spent solitary hours in his apartment, and strolling thoughtfully through his apartment's walkways. He looked a lot at the sky, and was warmed in his heart by the scenery of creation. But sometimes his heart would speed with anxiety—as his thoughts recurringly turned to a meditation on the reality of hell. He knew he was free from it now, cleansed by the blood of Christ—but the idea of his friends, his family going there, or being there: it was an unbearable horror. He continued to stroll, and carried the worry with him, a singular weight upon his otherwise buoyantly new soul.

Perhaps it was divine intervention, he thought, but it was not until that evening—when it was Friday, and he was not assigned a security-guard shift—that it occurred to him to actually Google the name "Malcom Esperanza". Unsurprisingly, the vast majority of search results were in reference to the name as occurring in the detective stories of Lucy Truthteller, about the P.I. Douglas Tent. But then Adam had the idea of searching for the name, in the online card catalogue for the San Antonio public library. He was amazed to find that Malcom Esperanza had written a book, and a singular copy of it was available to rent, at the Central Library branch downtown.

The name of Malcom Esperanza's book was *Deadly Karate Moves*, and the dark blue cover was mostly filled with a black-and-white photograph, that looked like it was taken in 1985, which featured an actor in a gi, with the beginnings of a mullet, overdoing a dramatic portrayal of grabbing the throat of another actor in a gi, who possessed a more developed mullet and was overdoing a dramatic portrayal of having his throat grabbed.

On Saturday afternoon, Adam was in his car, traveling south on 281, toward the repository of literature that is the Central Library. As he drew near his destination, the earth tones, light blues, and green patinas of the heavenward climbing rectangles of the downtown San Antonio skyline appeared in the distance—a vista framed on either flank by roadside trees. Exiting the highway, and joining the casual traffic parade, he passed among towers brimming with business, and crossed the San Antonio river, its banks lined with shopping and the footfalls of tourism.

Finally, he pulled into the parking garage belonging to the library, took his ticket, and rode the concrete spiral up to the open air of the roof, where plenty of spaces remained available to park in. Exiting his car, and standing in the midst of the roof-top parking lot, Adam was at eye-level with the tops of some buildings adjacent to the garage, with the skyscrapers looming just beyond them. One corner of the roof was surrounded by a church next door, whose clocktower was topped with a steeple and cross, and whose steeply pitched roof was mounted by a weather vane and a seemingly inaccessible church bell under a canopy topped with a cross.

On one side the view was obscured by the imposing burnt-sienna square, peppered with a variety of windows, on the upper left-hand corner of which was written with silver letters "Central Library"—below which stood the upper beginnings of poles, bearing a Texan and an American flag. The middle of the parking-lot roof was bisected by a hollow space around which the angular spiral drive of the garage did wind, the deep space covered with a weathered canopy and bookended on either side by yellow-railed stair cases, whose concrete steps descended the two stories of concrete parking garage. Next to the staircase nearest the library was an elevator, rising out of the ground, protected by an offshoot of canopy.

Adam's mind was excitedly swimming, as he walked

briskly to the elevator, and pushed the button to call it forth. So excited was he, that he missed some important clues on the roof, that would have alerted him to the danger he was in of shortly being immersed in a coincidence: he did not notice a familiar car that was parked in the lot as he arrived; nor did he notice another car familiar to him, that pulled in to park just as the elevator swallowed him up.

Once inside the main library, Adam emerged onto the 2nd floor, and mistakenly turned to his left, to notice a white-haired black man, watching knowingly the words of a book, alone in the middle of a sea of shining tabletops. Adam then turned the other way, and found himself among a forest of metal bookshelves. Having acquired the call number of Malcom Esperanza's book, he finally found the bookshelf he needed, its paper label indicating it to be so. Turning down the corridor of books, the sense of silence and solitude that the shelves exuded was shattered, when Adam saw a person, situated at the far end of the pair of shelves that they were both between. The person didn't notice Adam. He was engrossed in a book, that he had allowed to fall open to a certain page, having laid it on a bare space of shelf, at chest level. The person was standing in a karate pose, and was practicing self-defense moves, the descriptions of which were written and pictured in the book, as he obliviously enacted them, kicking and judo chopping into the air. The person continued not to notice Adam. The person was Douglas Tent.

Adam spun backwards out of the aisle, and rested his back against the side of a shelf, barely concealing himself. What in the hell? Why was Douglas Tent at the San Antonio Public Library, and was he practicing karate moves out of Malcom Esperanza's book? Adam's heart raced, and tiny beads of sweat broke out instantly high on his brow. Then a realization so obvious he didn't grasp it till now presented itself to his mind: Douglas Tent was not an African American woman. He appeared in every way as Adam remembered him, and his front and side kicks, though not overpowering in their presentation, did not appear to be the work of a man who'd recently had his genitals turned inside out.

Adam considered starting back down the aisle, and casually greeting Tent as a friend—after all, that's what he was, wasn't he? But the shock of seeing him so unexpectedly, after the disturbing content of his letters, made Adam anxious about seeing him. Just as Tent had initially appeared to Adam like a character walking off of the page of a story, he now appeared as a character walking off of the pages of the bizarre story in his letters. He didn't know if this was all a part of Tent's plan somehow, or if confronting him now would ruin something Adam didn't fully understand. For a while he was lost in a maze of wondering; then a thought occurred to him: how long had he been standing with his back to the bookshelf? Was Douglas Tent still back there?

He rushed to the elevator, and pushed the call button with a jittery finger. Encased in the metallic insides of the elevator car, Adam repeatedly balled up and loosened his fists at his sides, trying to find comfort in repetition, while looking at the ceiling at an utter loss. Reaching the ground floor, Adam exited toward the parking garage, walking past the police officer stationed at a greeter's stand, in the library's foyer—turning Adam's thoughts vaguely to the morass of justice, crime, and law that he felt himself enmeshed in.

Eschewing the parking garage's elevator, Adam climbed the concrete stairs, from the ground floor, toward the parking on the roof, passing the lower levels, with their low, corrugated ceilings, held up by yellow pillars. He saw himself traversing the oil stains, and faded yellow lines of the roof's pavement, to find his car and make it safely home, from which vantage point he felt he could safely and calmly figure out what in the world was going on.

But at the top of the flight of stairs, he hesitated. Looking to his right, he noticed what he had failed to detect before. Douglas Tent's beaten-up golden station wagon was parked among the cars, on the garage's roof, and also among the cars was Pastor Lacuna's crimson Nissan Versa. Adam backed-up, lowering himself below the surface of the floor, down the stairs from which he'd just emerged. From this place of refuge, he continued glancing around the parking lot, bracing himself for the sight of either the preacher or the detective.

As if conjured by anticipation, just then, the door to the roof-top elevator sprang open, and Detective Douglas Tent walked right past the subterranean staircase Adam was hiding in, seemingly impossibly not noticing him lurking there. Tent continued on to his station wagon, with his usual gait of confidence, his usual fedora dedicated to his head. Adam's eyes peeked out, watching across the ground of the lot, his view level with the pavement, his vantage point partially concealed by cars parked between the detective and him.

Tent was wrapped in a tan trench coat which must have been put aside before, as he wasn't wearing it when Adam had observed him previously between the shelves. It's collar was up, and the wind fiddled with its various edges, and perturbed the brim of Tent's fedora as he swept toward his vehicle. He put a hand on his driver's side door, then suddenly turned around, his eyes drifting from side to side, observing the lot behind him, as if he'd heard a sound. He's seen my car, said Adam breathlessly in his mind. He knows I'm here. Then Tent opened the door to his station wagon, entered it, and drove away.

"Who is that man?" said a voice behind Adam. He jumped, and turned to see, standing close behind him on the steps, a friendly-faced Pastor Moses Lacuna.

"What are you doing here?" Adam asked.

"Following you, again. Obviously."

"Pastor, I—"

"Who was that man? In the trench coat and fedora? A detective?"

"Yes," said Adam. "That's Detective Douglas Tent. I mentioned to you in your office once a private investigator who's trying to solve the murder of Roland Bellwether. That's him."

"Why were you hiding from him?"

"I wasn't... I mean... Why are you following me?"

"The man I just saw getting into that car, who you say is Douglas Tent: that was the man with the red mustache, who stole my phone the afternoon before Roland was killed.

"What?"

"The man," said the pastor. "He had a red mustache, and said he was a police detective by the name of Richard Bethany. But that was him. Douglas Tent stole my telephone."

"What? Pastor—"

"It must have been a fake mustache. And a wig. Come to think of it, he was wearing a fedora that day too. There was red hair beneath it. I knew there was something artificial about him. It was the mustache and the hair: it was fake. But I'd remember those green eyes anywhere. That was him. He took the phone, Adam."

Adam didn't know what to say. He stood there looking at Pastor Lacuna, wondering what to believe. Beneath the stair steps they stood upon, were floors of metal, and concrete and paint, housing the cars of those seeking books, or working to provide them. Feet away from the pastor and Adam and the garage, the burnt sienna square of the Central Library branch building stood a stalwart against illiteracy: a faithful structure built out of matter, and out of words and knowing.

19

The Plan

Darkness had fallen: Friday evening having slipped into Friday night, as Adam sat, once again, in the work office of Pastor Lacuna, inside the small outer receptionist area, off of the lobby of Last Baptist Church on Backwoods Road, in San Antonio, Texas. It was strange to Adam, to be in church at night, and the stillness, the cloaked serenity of it, caused Adam to feel an electric foreboding. Probably it was also the other circumstances.

Adam sat facing the Pastor, who'd removed his jacket, and rolled up his sleeves, sitting in his place at the desk, his thick-rimmed glasses framing his look of concerned determination, his tie, busy with colors and shapes, dangling between his elbows as they pressed into the desk, his fingers interlaced and pressed against his mouth, as if in a subconscious gesture of prayer, as he considered what he wanted to say.

Next to Adam, also facing the pastor from the visiting side of the desk was Hannah Lacuna, sitting in a chair brought in from her usual place behind the desk in the receptionist area just outside the door. She wore her white trench coat, beneath which were form-fitting blue jeans, and a silky, green blouse, open at the sternum, revealing a small golden cross, on a thin golden chain, framed by the golden tresses of her hair, flowing into rippling curls on either side of her neckline; her bright blue eyes were troubled, but ready to fight.

"There are some things the three of us need to talk about, Adam," said pastor Lacuna. "First of all, my daughter tells me that you've made a profession of faith. That is a serious, and wonderful, and important thing."

"Yes, sir," said Adam.

"Now Adam, you know, as my unfortunate outburst made clear before, that I—let's say—have had great misgivings about approving of a relationship between you two."

"Yes, I understand that, sir," said Adam.

"But, the way that Hannah tells it, you've understood the gospel, and your belief—your conversion—is sincere." He gave Adam a serious, searching look. "But salvation is only the beginning of the Christian life. You and Hannah are adults, but Hannah still lives under my roof; and she is unmarried, and my daughter, so that makes me responsible for her biblically."

"Yes," said Hannah, agreeing carefully.

Lacuna put his hands on his desktop, and sat back in the chair, relaxing into an idea. "Forgiveness is a virtue, but so is discernment. Adam, in light of what Hannah tells me about your salvation, I am willing to approve of your and Hannah's seeing each other, contingent on some important conditions."

"Okay," said Adam.

"First, you've got to come to church on Sunday. A new Christian needs instruction. He needs to be taught the word of God, and fellowship with other believers—with his brothers and sisters in Christ. That's what church is for."

"Okay," said Adam. "I will."

"Very good," said the pastor. "The other thing is that there is a Christian way to date. You two should not be together alone, unsupervised. I have a pretty good idea about what you two must have gotten up to at your apartment, Wednesday night—"

"Father—" said Hannah.

"And you should know," the pastor continued, "that sex before marriage, Adam, is a serious sin."

"Yes," said Adam, "I actually had a chance to read a little about that, in the bible, Pastor. That lusting after a woman that one is not married to is a sin. According to Jesus."

"Yes," said the pastor. "And the bible plainly says, 'flee from sexual immorality.'"

"'Flee *fornication*,' it actually says," said Hannah.

"Okay," said Lacuna, "let's not debate translations right now."

Hannah crossed her arms and her legs, and then uncrossed them.

"The other thing that I wanted to say, to you both, is that I had nothing to do with the death of Roland Bellwether. It's unfortunate that he's dead, and it's unfortunate that he wasn't a believer. I'd appreciate it, Adam, if you'd tell Hannah what we discovered at the library today—that we have a suspect now in Roland's death. I think it exonerates me."

Adam's eyes went to the blackness between the blinds of the window. He looked at the pastor, then turned to Hannah.

"Well, the thing is—" He looked at the carpet, to see if the right words were lying there.

"You didn't know this, Hannah, but someone stole my cell phone," said the pastor, "the day before Roland died. Adam says that my stolen cell phone was involved somehow in Roland's death. What did you say it was, Adam?"

Adam looked at the pastor nonplussed, then turned back to Hannah. "It would appear that Roland was hypnotized. We, the detective I'm working with—Douglas Tent—and I, we think a hypnotic suggestion was implanted in Roland at some point, to be triggered latter by code words."

"Hypnotized?" said Hannah, her eyes lost, her mouth slightly agape.

"The code words," continued Adam, "once said, triggered Roland to believe that he had gone blind, and that he should therefore kill himself. He received the trigger words through a phone call, when he was at work and near our supply of security-guard firearms."

Hannah's gaze went from Lacuna to Adam and back again, as if to ask if this were some cruel joke.

"But, I've identified the man who stole my phone, Hannah," said Pastor Lacuna. "We saw him, Adam and I both did, when we were at the library this evening."

"You were at the library this evening. Together?"

"Yes," said the pastor.

"Why?"

"Well," said the pastor, then looked at Adam, as if for help.

"He was following me," said Adam, with casual accusation.

"Father!"

"Look," said Lacuna, "The point is: we have a good suspect, for the murder of Roland Bellwether."

"Which is who?" asked Hannah.

"I don't think we should jump to any hasty conclusions," said Adam.

"The detective that Adam is working with: Douglas Tent. That's who stole my phone."

Hannah looked at Adam with shock and disappointment. "You mean to tell me," she said to Adam, "that the detective who's working with you to try to solve the murder of Roland Bellwether is the one who killed him?"

"Again," said Adam, "I don't think that we should assume that. But, it does seem that the evidence, such as it currently appears—well… maybe."

"What other explanation is there?" demanded Hannah.

"Well—" said Adam. "Douglas Tent is a complicated man: full of puzzles. I honestly tend to think, at this point, that this is all a part of some greater ploy on Detective Tent's part, about which I am not privy, directed toward laying a cunning trap for Malcom Esperanza."

"Who the hell is Malcom Esperanza?" asked Hannah putting a hand defiantly on one of her knees.

"He's a criminal mastermind," said Adam.

Hannah's eyes narrowed looking through Adam.

"He's in the books," Adam explained, "the books that Roland wrote about the cases he solved with detective Tent. Esperanza is an elusive genius behind perhaps most evil in general in the world. No one knows what he looks like. His presence is merely subtly implied, as the intelligence behind the nefarious events in the world."

"He sounds like the devil," said Hannah.

"To Tent he is. A secular version of the devil."

"I take it that this detective Douglas Tent is not a Christian?" asked Hannah.

"No, very much to the contrary. He's a bombastic atheist."

"Would you say that he hates God?" asked Hannah.

"Well," said Adam, considering it. "Yes. I mean, he rails against religion every chance he gets. He thinks it's a fairy tale for the weak. He's very concerned about global warming. He smokes crack."

"He smokes crack!" exclaimed pastor Lacuna.

"It sounds bad, I know," said Adam defensively. "But, you have to understand: he's a crime-solving genius. He's really talented. It comes with eccentricities. But if you read the stories, he's a force for good."

"The man sounds like a reprobate," said Hannah. "You're a saved Christian now. You shouldn't be working with this guy."

"What's a reprobate?" asked Adam.

"I don't think we need to get into all that," said Pastor Lacuna.

"Please, father. I think it's relevant." Pastor Lacuna held his peace.

"A reprobate," Hannah explained, "is someone who has rejected God's gospel, his plan of salvation, long enough, and enthusiastically enough, that God decides to harden their heart, so that it is no longer possible for them to believe anymore. Such a person is spiritually doomed."

"Like the people in hell?" said Adam.

"Certainly, the people in hell are reprobates," said Hannah. "Because the bible says that whomsoever believes the gospel will be saved. So why don't the people in hell simply believe the gospel, accept Jesus as their savior, and go to heaven?"

"Why don't they?"

"Because," said Hannah, "they can't. They have turned from the truth so many times, that God has allowed their ability to believe to be lost. They can't believe it. Their heart is so hardened against it, that it is impossible, even to escape hell; they can't believe it."

"But, at that point, they know that God exists, right? Because he's put them in hell."

"They even know that Jesus is his Son. The Bible says that every knee will bow to Jesus, and every tongue will confess that he is Lord, even the people in hell. The problem, for them though, is that they will kneel, and call him Lord, but they still will not believe that they deserve condemnation—they will forever have too much pride. So they will never escape condemnation."

"That's one way to interpret what the bible says about reprobates," said pastor Lacuna pedantically.

"How would you interpret it?" asked Adam.

Pastor Lacuna tapped a pencil on his desk, made a sweepingly presentational gesture of resignation with the fingers of his other hand, and said, "Well... some other way."

"My point is," continued Hannah, "that there are people on earth whom, like the people in hell, God has given up on, and consigned to damnation. The bible calls these people reprobates, and sons of the devil. In the first chapter of the letter that Paul wrote to the Romans, a distinguishing characteristic of reprobate persons is given: that they engage in unnatural sexual acts. The specific example of homosexuality is given."

"Wait," said Adam. "Are you saying that a homosexual can't go to heaven?"

"The bible makes allowance, I believe, in 1st Corinthians, chapter 6," said Hannah, "that a person could do a homosexual act—out of confusion, perhaps, or intoxication, say. But, what I believe that Romans 1 is teaching—"

"What *you* believe," put in Pastor Lacuna.

"What I believe is taught," she continued, "based on what it says, is that a person who burns in lust for his or her same gender, as the bible puts it ('burned in their lust one toward another; men with men')—someone with a sincere craving for homosexuality, in other words, or, I would say, a sincere craving for any other 'vile affection' that is 'against nature'—to use Romans 1 terms—like, say, bestiality or pedophilia: such a person is a reprobate—not because those sins are unforgivable, but because only someone who has already had his or her heart hardened against salvation, only someone who has already become a reprobate, would be capable of having it in their heart in the first place, to do such unnatural sins—like being a serial killer or something. Regular, plain old lost people, like you and I used to be before we believed, we just had it in our hearts to do natural sins. In fact, we still do."

"Wow," said Adam, and glanced at Pastor Lacuna to see if the reference to natural sins had reminded him of Adam's recently having had sex with his daughter. Instead he found the pastor intently eyeing Hannah, with a look on his face that suggested her exegesis reminded him of a rotten smell.

"That's very interesting," said Adam.

"Is detective Tent sexually perverted?" asked Hannah.

"I don't know," said Adam. "There was this hooker, locked in—". Adam stopped himself, remembering that he had been sworn to the deepest secrecy about Tent's thinking closet. "I don't know," he said.

"Well, be on the lookout for it," Hannah suggested. "It could be another clue that he's a reprobate, along with hating God and committing murder."

"It doesn't make sense," said Adam. "Detective Tent has spoken warmly of Roland, and he's not given to speaking warmly of people. I think he even was crying once, about his death. Why would he kill his good friend?"

"A reprobate would kill his good friend," said Hannah.

Adam considered this, then said, "He has this old book." Adam paused, and during the pause, he noticed both Hannah and Pastor Lacuna sharpen in their attention toward him, wondering what in the world a book would have to do with this.

"It's this old book about atheism. He reads it to himself, because he says that, the way it's written, the sound of the words of the book hypnotize whomever hears them. So, he's on some kind of regimen of regularly hypnotizing himself, to have more confidence in his power over the world."

"My goodness," said Hannah. "I believe I told you before, Adam, that I went to college for psychology, and that hypnotism was a special area of interest for me."

"You did," said Adam.

"Based on what I know about it then, and based on what I know about the bible, I don't believe that what you are ascribing to hypnotism could be hypnotism alone."

"What do you mean?" asked Adam.

"I mean, the killing of Roland. I don't believe mere hypnotism could have done that. I believe this book—this book on atheism—is acting like the incantation of a spell. If it can put people into trances so easily, and if Tent used it to hypnotize Roland into killing himself when prompted, then the book is more than hypnotic. It must be an instrument of black magic, that allows its hearers to become demonically possessed."

"Wait," said Adam. "Are you saying that Tent used the book to hypnotize Roland, causing him to undergo a latent demonic possession, stole your father's phone, and then called Roland at work, issuing the code words that triggered the demon inside him to activate, causing Roland to take his own life?"

"Exactly," said Hannah.

"I didn't think of that."

There was a pause, in which Adam and Hannah exchanged a charged intensity, and Pastor Lacuna regretted the degree to which, he felt, this meeting he'd called in his office had gotten out of hand.

"So how are we going to stop him?" asked Hannah.

"Stop who?" said Adam.

"Detective Douglas Tent," said Hannah. "The reprobate with the magic book full of demons who's murdering people. We have to stop him. We need a gun."

"Hannah," said Pastor Lacuna, disapprovingly.

"Your father has a gun," said Adam. "He pointed it at me, the last time I saw him."

"Father!"

Pastor Lacuna put up his hands, in a fatherly call for decorum. "Look, Hannah, Adam," he said, "the take-away that I'm hoping for this meeting to impart is that I didn't kill Roland Bellwether."

"We know, father. Detective Douglas Tent did."

"I'm still not convinced of that," said Adam.

"Hey, I've got an idea," said Hannah. "Douglas Tent smokes crack. I assume he drinks, smokes cigarettes, everything."

"Yes," said Adam.

"What you do is," offered Hannah, "is go over there with a bottle of high-proof rum, like it's a present for him. He'll be excited to receive it. Then, when you get the opportunity, you douse his demonic book in rum, and light it ablaze. If he threatens you, you shoot him—with father's gun."

"Is that a serious plan?" asked Pastor Lacuna.

"It's just what occurred to me, off of the top of my head," said Hannah. "But I feel like, as a plan, it's very strong."

"It's just hard for me," said Adam, "to believe that detective Douglas Tent is evil. He is definitely strange. But he seems to me still, like he's a good guy."

"A person," said Hannah, "can be talented, and a nice guy, and still be evil. The bible says that 'Satan himself is transformed into an angel of light', and Jesus said, 'Judge not according to the appearance, but judge righteous judgment'."

"I believe it is very dangerous, and unloving," said Pastor Lacuna, "to consider anyone on earth to be beyond God's forgiveness."

Adam digested Hannah's words, and the words of her father. "I want to go see him first," he said. "Before I go trying to set books on fire, I'll go to go see him—and see if I can find some clue that Hannah's theory is correct."

"Be very, very careful," said Hannah, her young eyes full of love and hate.

20

Detective Douglas Tent

As Adam pulled into the parking lot of the dentist's-office-slash-detective agency, that housed Douglas Tent Investigations, he felt a foreboding sense of déjà vu. He exited the car, and walked toward the entrance, the building's tall row of unforgiving black windows clinically mirroring Adam's trepidatious approach. Once in the building's quaint entryway, he stood once again before the cloudy glass of the detective agency's mahogany door, and hesitated.

Hannah Lacuna had saved his soul, and he didn't want to believe her far-flung metaphysical condemnations of detective Tent—but in some dim covert of his spirit, they resounded with a forlorn ring of truth. Two weeks ago, he had inhabited such a different world: he had been content to sit in his solitary guard shack by night, in a world described entirely by the laws of science, occasionally getting drunk on a day off, and rarely achieving romantic interludes of varying degrees of tragedy. The only non-chemical magic in that world was the fantasy of detective stories starring Douglas Tent. And now, not only was the detective real, but so too was the world of angels and demons that the detective so aggressively does not believe in. The amazing thing being: the structures of Adam's world had not changed so much —the buildings, the cars, the air breathed in and out. But the invisible things behind and all around them—the facts and spirits —these things were a whole new country. "Belief is the currency of adventure," as Hannah had wisely said.

But, if Douglas Tent is a demon-possessed killer, then who is Malcom Esperanza? And what was to be made of the outlandish story in Tent's three letters? Adam decided to keep an open mind. Hannah was right about many big things, but even her father didn't agree with her on her more radical views; and her father, after all, is a pastor. Adam would talk to his friend Douglas Tent, and give him the benefit of the doubt. Still, Hannah's warning to be very careful lingered in his ears.

Adam opened the detective agency's door, and once again was in the familiar office space of detective Douglas Tent. But there was something less vibrant about it: the cloud of tobacco smoke was thinner than before, the piles of files less mountainous than before. There were no lights on, and a sickly chemical smell hung in the dim atmosphere—perhaps from some scientific experiment, Adam reasoned.

Tent appeared from his open office door, with seemingly no recognition of Adam in his glaring green eyes. He wore his familiar kimono-style blue bathrobe, but the man was changed. There was a deathly pallor upon his face, and the clammy moisture of a cold sweat upon his skin. His eyes were troubled, his stature stooped. He was thinner, and leaned upon an antique cane of either darkened metal or wood.

Suddenly the detective rushed—with a quickness that his anemic appearance would have suggested was impossible—toward Adam, shouting as he moved, "Who goes there? Friend or foe?" his formerly dapper English tones taking on an uncharacteristically frightened shrillness. Upon achieving an arm's-length nearness to Adam, Tent swung his cane forward, its end landing under Adam's chin, and pressing against his throat.

"I assure you, intruder," said Douglas Tent, "that this antique cane of mine is also a gun—loaded with a .410 shotgun slug." Adam saw Tent's grip tighten around the cane's talon-like brass handle, and Tent's finger rest upon a tiny trigger barely protruding from the junction of the handle and the upper end of the cane's shaft.

"I know," said Adam. "You acquired it on a case: *The Case of Too-Many Butlers*."

Tent's eyes narrowed, as if looking into abating fog. Then warmth and remembrance mixed with the detective's gaunt countenance. "My boy!" exclaimed Tent, lowering his cane-gun, "I apologize for that. I'm a bit under the weather. Let's have a drink." Tent turned and shuffled toward his office, his body still bent, as if from sharp, persistent pain in his viscera.

The men settled into Tent's office, its desk still a cluttered collection of papers and filled ashtrays, framed newspapers clippings of the detective's bygone acts of crime-stopping still decorating the walls, the tinted one-way glass still looking out on the office's parking lot—the tall windows comprising the wall to the men's immediate side, which Tent's desk and Adam's chair—facing one another—abutted close against. Adam sat in the chair facing the desk. Tent's attention went to the silver platter on the sideboard that lined the wall behind his desk—on it was a defeated panoply of used booze bottles, their glass bodies standing in a gaggle of emptiness. A lone bottle of gin remained half-full. Tent placed two ornate tumblers on his desk between them, and slopped a swallow of gin into each. Then he poured three or four more servings into his own glass. He picked up a lime wedge from somewhere, which looked like it had been bitten and sucked already; Tent demurred, and tossed it aside. Tent sat, and took up his beverage, motioning toward Adam with a toasting gesture. "To crime," he said, and took a long gulp of gin—not waiting for Adam's response.

Tent took the glass from his lips, and was struck with a coughing fit—the coughs becoming hacking and unhealthy sounding. Adam took the opportunity to wonder if the gin was poisoned or drugged, to wonder if it was best to take the drink, so as not to arouse suspicion.

"Phew, excuse me," said Tent. "As I said, I'm under the weather today, I'm afraid." His eyes were red and watering; his voice a hollow rasp. Adam, more out of inertia than logic, took the drink, and sipped it, the gin bitter and warm in his mouth.

"How is your investigation of the preacher going?" Tent asked, leaning back in his desk chair, crossing his robe-draped legs, and holding the gin in one hand.

"I, well—" Adam should have been prepared for the question. "Don't you know, sir? I mean, you seem to always know what I'm up to."

"I do," said Tent. "But I thought I'd ask anyway."

"Your letters," said Adam, "the letters you sent: that was such an amazing story—about finding the identity of Malcom Esperanza, about the time traveler failing to kill him, about his plan to turn you into a woman. Did you escape, after all, and not submit to the surgery?"

"Well," said Tent. He stood and turned to face the rear wall. "I must confess that the chronicle of my escapades, as represented by the reports in my letters, was not entirely truthful."

"How much of it was truthful?"

"Technically, none of it." There was a motion of Tent's right elbow, indicating the taking of a drink. He exhaled a thirst-quenched sigh of relief. "Except," said Tent, wandering to the other side of the small office, the side populated by a table flanked by two floor lamps, and a bookshelf against the far wall. "Except," said Tent, turning to point to Adam with a casual melodrama, the fingers of his other hand grasping his tumbler to his chest. "Except the bit where I found out the true identity of Malcom Esperanza. That part is magnificently true."

"Then who is Malcom Esperanza?" asked Adam sincerely.

Tent began to pace a circuit around the half of the room not taken up by Adam and the desk, limping and leaning on his deadly cane. He looked at his feet, and touched a bent index finger to his chin in contemplation, and occasionally glanced toward Adam for emphasis as he spoke, before returning to his meditational wandering of gaze, toward nothing in particular in the external world. His speech was as excitedly didactic and British as ever, but with an almost imperceptible slur at times, as if the gin had had a greater effect on him in his weakened state, or as if, perhaps, this had not been his first snort this Saturday afternoon. Sometimes in his route a pain would flare up in his body, and he would avail himself of a hand on the table or on the bookshelf, to steady himself, while continuing his address.

"I apologize," Tent began, "for not being truthful. But, I

was truthful, Adam. The facts were invented, but the message was true. I couldn't risk telling you what I was actually doing this week, lest you be in danger of capture and abuse at the hands of Malcom Esperanza. So, I told it in a kind of code."

Adam took another sip of gin, dumbstruck, but wanting to understand.

"In truth," continued Tent, "I have been spending last week uncovering the identity of Malcom Esperanza, an accomplishment unrivaled in the history of crime-fighting. And I have laid the seeds for his arrest, soon and at my very hands. I couldn't risk giving you the real information, you see? Except the truth was hinted at, and implied. In truth, it is *as if* the man Esperanza has indeed had a time machine, and it is *as if* he's used it to change the course of history for hundreds or thousands of years, making society racist, homophobic, and cavalier toward global warming. You see?"

The cloud in Adam's brain got thicker but not darker. He put his drink to his lips, but decided against it.

"Factually," Tent went on, "I've still no proof of Malcom Esperanza's crimes. I've circumstantial evidence, and a chain of brilliantly speculative deductions. What I've accomplished this week is: to set in motion a plan that will allow me, once and for all, to confront the man, and accuse him of his deeds, of his infinite and systematic evil. Do you know who Eugene Vidocq was?"

"I don't," said Adam.

"He was the inventor of our profession; the first private eye—in France in the early 19th century. He began as a criminal himself, and then was the first police detective—using his underworld connections to find out who had done which crime; after which, he opened the first private detective agency. He was the originator of emphasizing trace evidence, and of the keeping of criminal dossiers. He was also a master of confronting a doer of crime with the crime that they had done, and thereby causing a confession."

"You think that Malcom Esperanza will confess?"

"Not out of guilt, surly not. But perhaps out of pride. Failing that, I'll break him under torture."

Adam abandoned his tumbler, on the surface of Tent's sturdy desk. He felt drugged, but probably just from gin.

"Are you a homosexual?" he said.

Tent stiffened and froze, turning toward Adam, leaning on his cane with astute attention, as if he'd heard a gunshot. Then his demeanor relaxed, and he said, "Roland kept my sexual orientation out of the stories he wrote. I applaud him for it. It was irrelevant to the telling of a charming detective story."

"I always got the impression from the stories," said Adam, "that you were sort of asexual."

"Asexual? No, far from it, my boy. I am proud of my sexuality, but I don't advertise it. I am auto-sexual."

Adam recommitted to the drink he had abandoned on the desk, holding it solicitously against his chest, intuiting that he'd be needing a series of gulps. "Auto-sexual?" he asked.

"It is a relatively unknown, but perfectly normal variant in the rainbow of human sexual natures. It simply means that I am only attracted, sexually, to one person on earth—and that person is me."

"You mean, masturbation?"

"Not quite, Adam. Masturbation, as it is normally conceived of, is the act of a person touching him-or-herself, while fantasizing about having sex with another person. For me, fantasy doesn't enter into it: I am merely relishing the moment of experiencing my own body—because the person I am aroused by is myself. I look at myself in the mirror, or I watch myself on tape. For me, watching a tape of myself masturbating is the pornography I would use, to arouse myself while masturbating."

"Wow." Adam's face loosened, in a mixture of surprise, acceptance, and tipsiness. "I've never heard of that."

"The auto-sexual community surely has much to do, to gain the mainstream acceptance enjoyed by the gay, the lesbian, the bisexual, and the transgendered. We have no representation in movies, or television, or literature. Though many in our movement claim Walt Whitman."

"But," said Adam, "in your letter, you said, that after becoming a woman, you then would be a lesbian."

"In the eyes of the world," said Tent, "I allow myself to be assumed to be a heterosexual. I am not an activist for my people. But, perhaps you now better understand my passion for defending marginalized groups." Tent finished his gin with a swift tossing back of his head and tumbler, swallowing hard, and placing his glass upon the table by the bookshelf. He began again to be overtaken by a series of hacking coughs.

"Do you remember," Tent said, regaining his composure, and pressing the inner corners of his watering eyes, "the urban legend going around in the 90's, that Marilyn Manson had had two of his bottommost ribs removed, so that he could fellate himself?"

"Yes," said Adam.

Tent stepped toward the tall tinted windows, looked out upon the parking lot. "I cried when I heard that urban legend," he said, peering dreamily through the brown glass, at the vehicles beyond, "because it was so beautiful."

Adam had never felt so strangely moved.

"Come," said Tent, "let me show you," and exited the office, passing through the lobby, and toward the hallway in the opposing rear corner—his cane-assisted hobble maturing into a fluent stutter step, pressed on by the excitement of his task.

Adam, at this point having virtually forgotten any evil associations Hannah would have had him retain toward detective Tent, followed after him, curious what in the world he meant to show him, and afraid that it would cross that socially all-important line between the piquant and the nauseating.

The men arrived at the end of the hallway, which, as last time, terminated in a bookshelf filled with investigator tomes, to the right of which was the alcove containing the breakroom: its refrigerator, and countertop.

"What about that prostitute?" Adam asked him. "Baby?"

"Babby."

"Yes, Babby. What about her? I got the impression that something untoward had happened between you and her and detective Bethany."

"As you'll recall, Adam," Tent said, "that was for a case: a case we put ourselves on, but still. It was expedient to keep up the trappings of heterosexual appearances; also, I wanted Bethany to loosen up."

"I see," said Adam.

"But there has only ever been one person besides myself, that I have had sex without of a sincere desire to do so."

"That must have been a special person," said Adam, attempting sympathy. The two men stood facing the bookshelf. Adam knew that the rickety, old door to Tent's secret thinking closet was hidden behind it.

"It happened at a convention of fans of Roland's stories, put on by *Detective Stories Magazine.*

"I went to one of those," said Adam.

"This was the only one I ever attended," said Tent. "As you're no doubt aware, I am widely regarding as strictly a fictional character by the public at large."

"Yes."

"So, I attended under the guise of a Douglas Tent cosplayer."

Adam smiled, and tried not to laugh.

"I ended up coming in third in a Douglas Tent lookalike contest," Tent continued. "The man who came in first and I ended up back at his hotel room. Alcohol was consumed. We talked. He had an expansive knowledge of my cases. We had sex. But it wasn't the same, you know? He just wasn't me."

Adam's mouth, in a show of tense expressiveness, succeeded in portraying the sense of gravity that Tent seemed to be trying to convey, but Adam's eyes involuntarily failed not to look freaked out.

"Besides an abiding disappointment with the perfunctory affair, I also managed to come away from my sexual tryst with the man at the fan convention with an obscure and deadly virus; you've probably never heard of it."

"AIDS?" asked Adam.

"Maybe you *have* heard of it," said Tent. Setting his cane aside, he grabbed one end of the bookshelf and fecklessly began attempting to pull it into the breakroom. Adam joined in, and, as before, the bookshelf slid aside, revealing the rotten wooden door, a miasma of foreboding seeping from the blackness visible through the spaces in the broken portal.

As before, the leather book leaned against the dilapidated door. Tent picked it up, and handed it to Adam. "Here, hold this," he said.

Adam looked down at the book in his hands. He noticed for the first time the faint trace of grooves and ridges in the leather of its cover, suggesting a design that time had rubbed away, leaving behind patches of flakiness and discoloration. "This is the book," thought Adam, "the purported gateway to hell and murder."

Tent opened the closet door, and pulled the chain on the naked light bulb, which hung at a tall man's forehead height. The papering of photos, papers, newspaper clippings, and feverishly scrawled words had spread—like a rash—upward and downward on the closet walls. But this fact was exuberantly obscured by the absurdity of the object Adam saw filling the closet's center. It was a bare male mannequin, the body of it wearing its vague nudity with taciturn dignity. The head, however, was another story. Stuck to the mannequin's head was a slightly-larger-than-life-sized color printout of Douglas Tent's face, fetching a glamourous, masculine pose, the photo cut out of its original page, to achieve the roundness that a head deserves.

"You see, so it's all true," said Tent, in muted triumph. "I am an auto-sexual. I trust, as my friend, you will keep this a secret, along with the existence of my powerful meditation closet. I'm sure it's obvious what I do with this mannequin, so I won't condescend to explain it."

Tent took the magic book from Adam, replaced it against the now closed, darkened closet door, and, with Adam's help, returned the bookshelf to its original position, standing a silent stalwart, hiding the secret of the strange things in the seemingly innocent wall behind it. All the while, Adam fruitlessly pondered exactly what Tent thought was obvious about his relationship with the dummy version of himself.

Tent placed his cane under one of his arms, while retrieving a cigarette from the ever-present pack in his robe's pocket, placed it in his mouth, lit it, inhaled, and cleared his throat, stifling another coughing fit. With the back of one hand, he wiped the perspiration from his ghostly brow.

"I'm glad we had this talk, Adam," he said. "But if you'll excuse me, I'm due down at police headquarters. I'm to update detective Bethany on the Roland Bellwether case."

"What does he know?"

"I've given him a version of the truth, which he doesn't believe, in any case. He knows nothing of the concept of the existence of Malcom Esperanza, or even the name."

The men followed each other into the office's front room. Adam stood facing Tent, his back to the cloudy glass of the detective agency's front door, the backward letters of "Douglas Tent Investigations" caught by light, and shining through.

"As you already seem to know," Adam said to Tent, "the evidence I found against the preacher is that his cell phone called Roland and gave him the fatal trigger words, seconds before he killed himself. Pastor Lacuna's defense is that his phone was stolen, the day before the murder. The person he says that stole his phone is you, Detective Tent."

Tent showed no surprise at this. He looked at Adam like a forgiving teacher.

"Ask yourself," said Tent, "what would motivate him to say that? Either he's telling the truth, and I killed Roland Bellwether, or else, he happens to have chosen a very interesting target to frame. He has chosen exactly the person that Malcom

Esperanza would have wanted him to choose."

Tent's words hung in the air, then he wiggled the cane at his side. "I hope I didn't scare you with this thing," he said. "It isn't ever really loaded."

As proof of his statement, Tent raised the weapon toward Adam's head, and pulled the trigger. Instantly, a two-foot tuft of blue smoke shot out of the end of it, and dissipated: simultaneously, Adam heard the sound behind him of a pane of glass shattering and falling to the floor. Looking behind himself, he saw that a pane of glass had indeed broken and fallen from the detective agency's front door. A second pane, behind that one, had remained standing, but now had a smashed snowball of white cracks in its center, and a spider's web of cracks radiating out from that.

"I'm frightfully sorry, my boy," said Tent. "As I said, I am under the weather today. My virus is acting up. Still, it is a grace to see that my window's laminated glass has done its job."

"Did that really just happen?" asked Adam in shock.

"It's an interesting question," said detective Tent, "what really is happening, and what isn't. I suppose to be sure of things, one must be sure that he is in control of his own mind."

21

Sunday Morning Church

He'd been up all night, and into the morning, standing his usual vigil in the comfortably familiar square of solitude that is the guard shack guarding his particular break in the perimeter fence—and now it was 10 am, and he was with Hannah at church. They sat together, on an otherwise empty pew, second row back from the stage, at a 45-degree angle to it. The pew's green upholstery was cushiony under Adam, encouraging his sleep-deprived eyes to droop. He was revived by the radiant presence of Hannah beside him, resplendent in the flowing whiteness of her cotton dress, a light-brown belt high on her waist, a small jean jacket upon her upper body, and a flower-print scarf tied loosely around her neck. She absent-mindedly bounced the top knee of her crossed legs upon the knee below it. In true Texan fashion her shins disappeared into cowboy boots, the leather matching the hue of her belt. As always, her golden tresses cascaded around her face, and onto her shoulders, and her bright, light eyes shown with youth—as she concentrated on the events of the church service.

The elements of the service were as Adam vaguely remembered them from Presbyterian church of his youth—the congregation sang hymns, standing together in unison; there was praying, and church announcements, and a period between opening songs when the congregation was instructed to greet those situated around them: during this time, several pleasant persons walked over to Adam, from some distance away, to recognize him as a new face, and sincerely show interest in him —with a few questions and a handshake. Looking out on the rows of persons, filling the pews, in their shared orientation toward the stage—its pulpit, choir seats, baptismal pool, and giant wooden cross hanging above it all—Adam was struck with the varied ages in the auditorium. There were young children, corralled by their parents, threatening to break free, and run joyfully up and down the aisles, or else occupying themselves introvertedly with crayons and something to draw on, as the protocols of church went by around them. There were old men and women, in pairs, dutifully dressed in their Sunday best, worn by time, but faithful through life's storms. One old lady, Adam noticed on the complete other side of the auditorium, looked at her bible with a plastic magnifying glass, which was equipped with a small light, bright enough—in its pin-point way—to be almost blinding to Adam, from across the auditorium, if he looked toward it. The heavy, white-haired woman, in a flower-print Mumu, held her spyglass and her face, drawn tight with concentration, close to her open bible, intent on learning God's word.

The Baptist church service, Adam noticed—as the opening songs, announcements, and choir and solo-singer performances were drawing to a close—did not have the ancient pomp he remembered from the Presbyterian church services of his youth (borrowed as it was from Catholicism). Baptist church had no robes and candles and liturgy recited by the congregation in chanting simultaneity. The centerpiece of the Baptist observance, Adam would come to discover, was a pastor in a suit and tie, explaining to you a certain concept or passage out of the bible. It was not an attempt to reach God through ceremony and symbol—it was an acknowledgement of God's presence in the bible, and a spiritual rolling up of sleeves, to dig into what the bible says for an hour, bookended by the singing of hymns.

There was an awkwardness between Hannah and Adam on the pew. They had known each other, in the biblical sense, before marriage, and now here they were at church. She had kissed him, after he'd gotten saved from hell on that hilltop, but he found himself wondering now if he had the right to reach out and hold her hand, as they sat together there. An uneasiness and claustrophobia seemed to be closing in around him, in contrast to the lightness and joy of the atmosphere. The swelling feeling of the presence of God was not any longer the urgent, stinging call that it had been in his chest. That had been replaced, since Adam's salvation, with a calm assurance, that God is real, and that his word is true.

After the thirty minutes of musical preliminaries, it was time for pastor Moses Lacuna to stand behind the pulpit, smiling and famous on the stage, and open the King James bible. As he took his position, and became situated behind the lectern, as the auditorium chuckled at the pastor's opening witticisms, Adam took the transitional opportunity to softly grasp Hannah's hand with his, as their hand's lay upon the green upholstery between them. Hannah's palm and fingers returned a friendly grip.

"I've got an important message for you, this morning," began Pastor Lacuna, an earnestness in his face. "And I've got a confession." Adam's heart raced. Confession of what?

"I must confess," said the pastor, "that I've not been as clear with you, as I should have been, about a very important doctrine in the bible: in fact, the most important doctrine: the doctrine of salvation."

Pastor Lacuna removed his suit jacket, and placed it on a chair that was behind him on the stage. The sleeves of his dress shirt were already rolled up, as if in preparation for a theological fight. His neck tie was a deep red. He touched the right corner of his black, thick-rimmed glasses, with the fingers of his right hand, steadying himself to continue.

"I have done a disservice to this congregation by not taking sides in a factional debate that is occurring in Independent Fundamental Baptist churches today. Now, I know I will offend some people with what I am about to preach today. But it needs to be preached. A preacher isn't a preacher if he won't take a stand. And, if people leave the church over this, it's worth it to me, to preach the word of God."

A few men shouted, "Amen!" in support, but the rest of the audience sat under a shroud of uneasiness, at the pastor's confrontational tone. Adam gathered that this was something new in Lacuna's preaching career.

The pastor went on to argue that a plague of "easy believe-ism" was sweeping through Independent Fundamental Baptist churches today, falsely teaching people that repenting of one's sins is not a part of salvation from hell—that simply believing that Christ died for one's sins was enough to save a person. He singled out a particular preacher named James Sanderson, who apparently pastored a church in Tempe, Arizona, had a large following for his YouTube videos online, and was a prominent proponent of this "easy believe-ism" that pastor Lacuna wanted to implore his congregation to reject.

He quoted Jesus, from the gospel of John, when he said, "If any man will come after me, let him deny himself, and take up his cross, and follow me." Pastor Lacuna interpreted this to mean that a person, to really, truly be saved from hell—besides merely believing that Jesus died for their sins—must also be willing to take up the cross, to commit to living for Christ, and making Christ the Lord of one's life.

"In the original Greek," the pastor explained, "this word 'deny' has the sense of 'refusing to be associated with'. Literally, Jesus is saying, you must refuse to be associated with your former self. That's what true conversion, true salvation requires: that is repentance from sin: turning from sin to the Savior."

Next the pastor quoted a verse from the book of Romans —actually one of the same verses that Hannah had used, to give the gospel to Adam in the book nook, on that fateful first day of their meeting. "The Bible says," said Pastor Lacuna, "that 'if you confess with your mouth that Jesus is Lord and believe in your heart that God raised him from the dead, you will be saved'. Right there, the bible is clearly teaching that making Christ the Lord of your life is part of salvation, part of believing. But these easy-believe-ism, cheap grace teachers like Pastor Sanderson in

Arizona will lie to you, and tell you that it isn't so."

The next salvo in the pastor's attack was to go over the story, featured in the first three books of the New Testament —the synoptic gospels as they're sometimes called (Matthew, Mark, and Luke)—the story of Jesus and the Rich Young Man.

In the story, a rich young man approaches Jesus, and asks, "Good Master, what good thing shall I do, that I may have eternal life?" Jesus's first response is to say, "Why callest thou me good? there is none good but one, that is, God"; but then Jesus tells the man that, if he keeps the commandments, he will earn eternal life, and Jesus lists the bottom six commands of the famous Ten: "Thou shalt do no murder, Thou shalt not commit adultery, Thou shalt not steal, Thou shalt not bear false witness, Honour thy father and thy mother: and, Thou shalt love thy neighbour as thyself." The man assures Jesus that he does all of that already, and wants to know if anything else is required. Jesus tells him, "If thou wilt be perfect, go and sell that thou hast, and give to the poor, and thou shalt have treasure in heaven: and come and follow me." At this the young man becomes dejected, and walks away, because of his great possessions. After his departure, Jesus delivers to his disciples the famous line: "It is easier for a camel to go through the eye of a needle, than for a rich man to enter into the kingdom of God."

Pastor Lacuna told this story to argue that the rich, young man represents a prospective Christian that wants to be saved from hell, but is unwilling to repent of his sins, and submit to the Lordship of Jesus Christ. Like the rich, young man, a Christian, according to Pastor Lacuna, who is unwilling to turn from his sins—take up his cross, as it were, and follow Jesus—isn't doing what is required for true Biblical salvation from damnation, and therefore isn't saved.

The pastor then buttressed his point by quoting a famous verse from the 2nd chapter of the Letter of James: "faith without works is dead".

The pastor was animated and confident in his delivery, pacing around the stage, taking up the space, occasionally soliciting a chorus of amens from the crowd, their unease with his sermon thawing, and then warming to a boil as he progressed. At one particularly impassioned point, he stabbed the fingers of one hand emphatically into the air, as if poking the devil himself in the chest, with the power of the truth of his proclamation. At another point of enthusiasm, the pastor took his wristwatch off, and placed it on the pulpit. "You all know what it means when a Baptist preacher takes off his watch," Lacuna said. It seemed to be understood that it meant that he means business.

As the sermon advanced, Adam had observed, with growing alarm, higher and higher levels of rage building within Hannah at his side. First she let go of his hand, and crossed her arms, looking intently forward. Then redness gathered in her face and neck. Eventually, and finally, her frown matured into a grimace, and then into a deathly glower. When pastor Lacuna quoted James 2, she let out a barely subdued breath of exasperation, stood, and swept down the aisle toward the exit. The largeness of the auditorium, and the distance of the pews from the stage, allowed this to occur without the pastor or the assembled congregates being disturbed by it.

After a few seconds of hesitation, Adam followed her out. As he exited through one of the wooden double doors at the back of the sanctuary, he was just in time to see Hannah disappearing around the corner, into the hallway which led from the lobby to deeper rooms in the church-building complex. By the time he caught up with her, she had passed the bathrooms immediately around the corner and was approaching an off-shoot of the hallway, which led to some offices and a classroom.

"Hannah!" Adam called after her, with as much hushed authority as he could muster.

She spun around, and their eyes met, locked for an instant exchanging worry and exasperation. Adam looked behind himself and down the hallway before him, to see if anyone was being scandalized by their behavior. Finally, he stepped out of the main hallway, and Hannah joined him, in the small, perpendicular offshoot of hall, directly next to them.

The offices on either side of the smaller hall were unoccupied, but, in the classroom at the hall's termination, a mere fifteen feet away, a children's Sunday school class could be seen to be in session, through the narrow vertical window in the closed wooden door. A young woman with long hair and a jean skirt was kneeling in front of a gaggle of seated preschoolers, and reading and showing them a picture book. Presumably the picture book was about Noah and the ark, because a plastic toy ark was on the carpeted floor between the teacher and her students, large enough to fit its stuffed-animal passengers. Other stuffed animals, yet to be boarded onto the ark, were being held by various of the children. One big-eyed little black girl grasped onto a stuffed giraffe with desperate affection, in rapt attention to the story being shared. Others of the children displayed various degrees of attention to the proceedings, but behavior generally was good.

Outside, in the diminutive hallway, Hannah tightened her mouth, and squeezed her fists with outraged pressure, and said to Adam, "He's never been so bold before. He's hinted at his heresy, been equivocal and vague about it. But now, he's really taken sides: he's gone completely and finally over to the devil."

"Is it that bad?" asked Adam. "Could he still just be confused?"

"It's worse than you think," said Hannah. "Remember, we talked about the idea of a person being a reprobate? That there are some, who have rejected God, so finally and completely, that God has rejected them, and taken away their ability to believe, and hence get saved?"

"Yes."

"Well, besides homosexuality, and other unnatural desires, being a symptom of being a reprobate, there is another that the bible mentions, and that is: when a person is a false prophet: a false teacher."

"I see," said Adam.

"A person can be confused, can misspeak, can merely be

under the influence of reprobate false teachers," continued Hannah. "But when my father takes a stand, like he took today, for Lordship Salvation, for works-based salvation, as a pastor, as someone in that position... We might as well have found him in bed with another man, from the point of view of diagnosing the state of his soul."

"Wow."

"I can't believe it," said Hannah. "I can't believe what I just heard. You know it isn't true, right, Adam? He quoted Jesus, when Jesus said, 'If any man will come after me, let him deny himself, and take up his cross, and follow me.' The context of that quote is that Jesus is talking to his disciples, and telling them how to be good servants of God. In Luke, the same statement is quoted as 'If any man will come after me, let him deny himself, and take up his cross *daily*, and follow me.' Does my father think that salvation from hell is something that happens over and over again to the same person every day? Of course not! Because Jesus wasn't talking about salvation from hell! He was telling saved people how to be good Christians. And my father stands up there, pretending to know Greek. What a fucking asshole."

"Hannah!" said Adam in a loud whisper, gesturing toward the classroom. "Kids are trying to learn about Noah's flood in there." The class went on, undisturbed.

"And then he quotes Romans 10?" said Hannah. "He didn't even quote it from the King James, did you notice that?"

"It did sound a little strange."

"He quoted it as, 'if you confess with your mouth *that Jesus is Lord* and believe in your heart that God raised him from the dead, you will be saved.' The real bible, which is to say, the King James, actually says, 'That if thou shalt confess with thy mouth *the Lord Jesus*, and shalt believe in thine heart that God hath raised him from the dead, thou shalt be saved.' It's subtle, but the devil only needs a little rope to hang you with."

"When you read me that verse originally," said Adam, "I took it to mean that a person must confess that Jesus is God to be saved, and believe that he died for my sins—not that I had to agree to obey him, and follow rules to be saved."

"Of course that's what it means! It means, believe that Christ is God, and that he died for your sins—not that you have to 'make him the Lord of your life'. That's just another way of saying: do good works to be saved. But tell that to my reprobate father."

"He also mentioned the story about Jesus talking to the rich man," said Adam.

"That was the most ridiculous part of the sermon, I think," said Hannah. "The whole point of that story, if you read it, is that the young man is asking Jesus what he can do to earn eternal life—to earn salvation from hell through good works. And Jesus tells him: if you keep all of the commandments, you will earn salvation from hell. But he also leads the man to understand that he has fallen short of that requirement. Because, of course, we all fall short of it! Which is why we need salvation by grace, through faith! Instead of trying to earn it."

"He basically takes the exact opposite point," said Adam, "from what the story is meant to teach, when he interprets it to mean that the rich young man just wasn't trying hard enough to turn from his sins."

"Yes, a thousand times yes," said Hannah. "The blindness of heresy is astounding. And then, of course, he quoted the works salvationist's favorite verse of all time: James 2."

"What does James 2 really mean, in context?" asked Adam.

"To understand James 2," said Hannah, "as with any part of the bible, you have to understand it within the context of the whole rest of the bible."

"Sure," said Adam.

"A lot of people," continued Hannah, "don't understand that the word 'salvation', when used in the bible, isn't always referring to salvation from hell." Hannah straightened her purse on her shoulder, and gestured at Adam with her bible. "For example, in Philippians 2, Paul says a famous thing: 'work out your own salvation with fear and trembling'. In that chapter he is talking to believers, to people who are already saved from hell by faith in the gospel. What he is telling them to be saved from is a wasted life—by obeying Christ, and by being good Christians—that's what believers have to be worried about being saved from."

"I see," said Adam.

"I told you, when I gave you the gospel originally," said Hannah, "that there are punishments, in this life, for believers who act as bad children."

"I remember."

"But, it's also true that there are extra rewards in heaven," said Hannah, "for believers who work for God on earth. That's why Jesus said, 'lay up for yourselves treasures in heaven'. All it takes to get to heaven is believing that Jesus Christ was God in flesh, and died for one's sins, was buried, and rose again. But, the bible teaches that there will be saved Christians, who do nothing good on earth, and go to heaven, but miss out on these extra rewards. The bible says of such a person, that his 'work shall be burned', and 'he shall suffer loss, but he himself shall be saved'.

"That makes sense," said Adam.

"Being saved from that," said Hannah, "being saved from a wasted Christian life, is obviously what Paul is taking about in Philippians 2, when he says, 'work out your own salvation with fear and trembling'. Because he then goes on to say, in that same chapter—" Hannah flipped open her bible, and turned to Philippians 2. "He goes on to say, that the reason to do it, to work out your salvation with fear and trembling, is so that you can be, 'blameless and harmless' in this world, and so that Paul will not be disappointed with them, at Christ's return. It's not about going to heaven or hell."

"And James 2 is talking about that same salvation? Salvation from a wasted life?"

"Yes. And this is clear, if you read James 2 after reading James 1," said Hannah. She turned to James 1, and cradled her bible in her hands. "James says in James 1, 'receive with meekness the engrafted word, which is able to save your souls.' Save their souls from what? Again, he's addressing believers, who are already saved from hell. Eternal life is nowhere mentioned in these chapters. He is telling them to be saved from an unfruitful life on earth.

"A fruitful Christian life requires faith," she continued, "but not faith in the gospel—you believe the gospel once, and you have eternal life, the bible teaches. The faith that leads a Christian to good works is an additional kind of faith: faith that God will reward his children for their deeds: faith in the extra rewards available in heaven. Hebrews 11 is talking about this kind of faith—faith unto good works—when it says—" Hannah flipped to Hebrews 11. "It says, 'he that cometh to God must believe that he is, and that he is a rewarder of them that diligently seek him.' We come to God, we maintain a pleasing relationship with God, by having enough faith in the faithfulness of his heavenly rewards, to do good works for him on earth."

"And that's what James 2 is about?"

"Yes," said Hannah. "'Faith without works is dead,' means that a person who truly believes in the extra rewards, available in heaven through good works, will do the works. Otherwise, you don't really believe in the rewards. It's not talking about faith in the gospel, and it's not talking about going to hell."

"I'll have to read James 2 when I get the chance, with that in mind," said Adam.

"And this," said Hannah, "is how that a person is justified by their works: a person is justified before God, by believing the gospel and getting saved from hell; but, James wants us to know, a person is justified before his fellow man by good works, and thereby saved from a wasted Christian life. That's what James is talking about."

"Very interesting," said Adam.

They stood alone and close, in the small hall—Hannah's bible open, Adam's mind alive, tangled in thought.

"He took that dig at James Sanderson in the sermon, knowing full well that I'm a fan of his online preaching. I'd recommend his YouTube sermons, Adam. Him, and also Pastor Michaels from Good Ways Baptist Church in San Antonio. They'll blow your hair back."

"I'll have to check them out sometime."

"My father is so horribly lost," said Hannah, "with his wrong bible, and his false gospel. Pastor Sanderson said a thing once, Adam, and it's very true, and I hope you'll remember I told it to you. He said, quoting him roughly from memory: 'the ESV is a butter knife; the KJV is the sword of God.'"

22

Dilemma

A moment passed, as Adam and Hannah looked into each other's eyes, in that small offshoot of hall, she in her Texan best, and he also in his church clothes—or, at least, the only suit he owned, converted now into church clothes, because he was at church. The Sunday School class continued on close by, beyond the door at the hallway's end.

Hannah terminated the pregnant instant by replacing her bible into her purse.

"It's good that you're the one," said Hannah, "that will be going to destroy the murderous book, and not my father. As we've clearly seen today, he's not even saved—far from it. Far *and* close. To be close to salvation, and not to choose it, is to be far from it indeed. Such is the making of a reprobate."

"What?"

"My point, Adam," said Hannah, adjusting her purse again, upon the short slope of her jean-jacketed shoulder, "is that you're the man for the job. You are saved. I believe this gives you an immunity to Tent's powers."

"What do you mean?" Adam asked.

"As I said before," said Hannah, "this book wouldn't have the power to cause people to commit suicide if it was only operating through regular hypnosis. Regular hypnosis requires an impressionable and cooperating subject. This book's power is supernatural."

"Yes, you said, before," said Adam, "it is an object of black magic and demonic power. The rhythm of its words invites a demon to take possession of the hearer's soul, and that is how the suggestion of suicide, and the trigger words, are able to bring about the target's destruction."

"Exactly," said Hannah, "but a Christian—a saved believer—cannot be demonically possessed."

"Really?"

"Yes," said Hannah, "I believe so. Because, as you'll hopefully recall, upon salvation, upon being born again by believing the gospel, the Holy Spirit comes to indwell the believer, whereby, the bible says, 'ye are sealed unto the day of redemption'. That's why salvation is permanent: because of this permanent presence of the Holy Ghost within us."

"And someone," said Adam, "who is saved, with the Holy Ghost inside of them, cannot be possessed by a demon?"

"I don't think so," said Hannah. Because, the bible says, that 'greater is he that is in you, than he that is in the world.'"

"Is that verse talking about the impossibility of a saved person being possessed?"

"No," said Hannah, "but it's about the Holy Spirit being more powerful than the lying spirits who speak through false prophets." She thought for a second.

"There's another part in the bible, where Jesus tells a story, about a demon getting exorcised from a man. And the demon wanders around for a while, and then he returns to find his former home—within the man—'empty', so that he is able to move back in, with seven of his demon friends."

"Okay," said Adam, a questioning quiver in his voice.

"My point," said Hannah, "is that the demon was able to return, because the house of the man's soul was 'empty', i.e., not indwelled by the Holy Spirit. Ergo, a soul indwelled by the Holy Spirit cannot be demonically possessed."

"Okay," said Adam. "Very implicit, but okay."

Just then a lanky assistant pastor walked past, through the intersection of their small hall and the larger one, carrying in one hand his ESV, and in his other a copy of *A Defense of Calvinism* by Charles Haddon Spurgeon. He gave a perfunctory smile, and wave-like gesture as he passed. Adam got the impression, behind his show of pleasantness, that he knew Hannah and that he didn't like her.

When he was gone, Hannah continued: "My point is," she said, "your ace-in-the-hole is that you're saved. He's going to think that he can hypnotize you. In fact, with all of the time you've spent together, since Roland's death, he's probably already implanted the suicidal trigger words inside you, thinking he'll be able to use them when he needs to."

A rush of epiphany swam through Adam's mind.

"Hannah," he said, interrupting her as she was about to speak again. She looked in his eyes, recognizing that something startling was occurring to him.

"The first time I went to Tent's office," Adam continued, "he read to me from the atheism book. It was just two sentences, but I felt that I'd dozed off listening to them. At the time, I thought that I was only unconscious for, like, less than a second."

Hannah's eye's widened with alarm and determination. "That's it!" she said. "That's when he did it. It was all a part of his plan, you see? He hypnotized you then, implanting the suicidal suggestion, and the dormant evil spirit. Now he thinks that he can cause you to kill yourself, whenever he decides to expose you to the trigger words!"

Adam didn't like the sound of this at all. His eyebrows gathered together with worry.

"You mean, I was demonically possessed?"

"Dormantly," said Hannah. "But you're not anymore: the demon would have been banished, as soon as you believed the gospel and got saved, with me on Comanche Lookout Hill."

"Are you sure?"

"Yes," said Hannah emphatically. "You're better now. But Tent doesn't know that, you see? He doesn't understand the bible. He won't realize you are free from his hypnotic grasp. This gives us the advantage."

Adam was apprehensive. "Hannah, I..." he said with a slight tremble in his voice.

"What is it, Adam?"

"It's just... I'm not sure that I'm ready to be a Baptist." The words came out like a knot untying, like the first steps of involuntary fleeing. "I like you a lot," he continued. "and I believe the gospel, and that the bible is the word of God, and I'm grateful for it." Adam paused, and then resumed. "But it's possible that my destiny lies elsewhere than church, and marriage, and having kids."

Hannah was softly stolid.

"Detective Tent would say," said Adam, "that a detective must live a solitary life, as a lonely hunter for truth."

Hannah wanted to badmouth Tent again, but forbore.

"I'm not saying that I don't want to be an Independent Fundamental Baptist. But I don't know. I've got to at least finish this case first. Douglas Tent is working on his grand plan to finally catch Malcom Esperanza. The job he gave me is to find out who called Roland that night, and said the words that ended his life. I need to solve that once and for all, like a real detective would. Then I'll know. I'll know what's next in my life."

Hannah gave Adam a belabored but sympathetic look.

"Suppose your father didn't do it, and Douglas Tent didn't do it either," said Adam. "Then who does that leave? If it wasn't them, then there is someone that I've been overlooking. Tent said that it was someone close to Roland. Perhaps he said so, because he knows how Esperanza works. Perhaps it's his M.O. to plant someone into a victim's life, to get close to them, gather information, and ultimately betray them."

"What about the theft of my father's phone?" said Hannah. "He says he saw that the thief was Douglas Tent."

"Let's say Esperanza used someone who looked like Tent, disguised as Bethany—to frame Tent. He is a criminal mastermind remember. Then he delivered the phone to the real killer, the one positioned close to Roland, keeping tabs on him—the one I'm overlooking."

"Who are you overlooking?" asked Hannah.

Hannah and Adam both considered it for a moment.

Finally, Adam said, "My point is, I still believe in Douglas

Tent. I know he's an atheist. But he's also a crime-fighting genius. He's trying to help the world. He cares about combating global warming."

"Global warming isn't happening," said Hannah.

"And he's trying to end homophobia."

Hannah looked at Adam like he'd failed an open-book test. "Homophobia is good!"

"Be that as it may," said Adam. "This is what I have to do."

"So, you're breaking up with me?" asked Hannah.

Adam felt suddenly flattered, that Hannah already considered him her boyfriend. He took in anew the beauty of her.

"Yes, I am," he found himself saying. "I'm sorry."

Adam and his church clothes turned and sallied down the hallway and out the exit door at its far end.

"Son of a bitch," said Hannah—she thought—under her breath. But in the window of the classroom, the kneeling teacher in her blue-jean skirt turned and looked at Hannah with surprise and disapproval. So did all the children. Just then a small blond boy clutching a stuffed elephant on the carpet intuited that it would be the perfect instant for him to meet the situation by breaking into sobs.

Over the course of the next few days, Adam was struck with another killer case of detective's block, like the one that had struck him, before receiving the first letter from detective Tent. But, this time, no such letter came. And he was alone with his desire to solve the crime, not knowing how to proceed, and cursed with the paralyzing intuition that he was incapable of knowing.

Then, one day, three days in, something wonderful happened. In the storm and sorrow of his frustration, a still small voice came to him, and wordlessly showed him the way. He suddenly had a crystal-clear idea, surrounded by peace, that the way forward was simply to open the King James bible that Hannah had given him, and begin to read it.

More days passed as Adam, in paramilitary uniform, sat

up all night at work, in his little guard house, in the night, the moon looking down from above through wisps of clouds, a nude monarch, waiting to dive into the sea of the horizon, from up on its starry bluff, when the hours of the night watch ended. And Adam meanwhile was below, burning electric lamplight under the blanket of darkness, solitarily poring through the pages of God's word. A permanent replacement for the overnight supervisor position vacated by Roland had been found, and now Adam was free again to idly man his guardhouse—which freedom he used to read. He read the gospels of Matthew through John, and then moved on to the book of Acts, and then Paul's letter to the Romans (and his letter to the Galatians), in which were the verses that Hannah had used to save his very soul. In the gospels the person of Jesus taught, and loved, and warned, and died, and rose again. He spoke of hell for those that rejected salvation, of outer darkness, and wailing, and gnashing of teeth, and fire that would not be quenched. And he spoke of the gift of eternal life, and he promised the Holy Spirit would come, to comfort believers and show them the truth, and make possible many wonderful works. And then the early churches, and persecution, and preaching the gospel despite the forces massed against them. Adam could feel the sand of two-thousand-years-ago, from the holy land, between the toes in the sandals of those first New Testament Christians, as they were pressed on by the same divine breeze that was sweeping Adam toward falling in love with the words that he was reading. The sword of the Lord, as Hannah had told him.

Adam read the creation account in Genesis, and meditated on the overpowering reality of God's creation, his love for man, his perfect truth and goodness, and the evil of the devil's work in the world since that first epochal, sinful fall. In all this, Adam knew that he was tapping into a source of wisdom and authority that neither Douglas Tent nor Malcom Esperanza had any access to. Solving the death of Roland Bellwether was meaningless, Adam began to understand—as was everything—except to the extent that God would be glorified thereby. He needed this time to explore the majesty of the Lord's mind, in order to be spiritually prepared to face whatever evil conspiracy had killed the particular person that Adam's personal history had moved him to be curious about. He needed to do the big thing, to be able to rightly do the singular, smaller task.

And just like that, ten days passed. And it was late on Wednesday night. And Adam was in his apartment, with the night off of work. He sat on one of the wicker and iron barstools, pulled up to the peninsula of countertop that separated his apartment's front room from its kitchenet. Outside was rain and thunder, and sheets of water beat against the glass of the sliding door that led from the second-story apartment's front room to the small balcony just beyond.

On the countertop next to Adam was a shot glass and a bottle of whiskey that he was deciding not to consume. His bible was open before him, and he was contemplating a chapter in Romans. The apartment was dimly, but warmly lit. Visions of Hannah's face came to Adam's mind in dreamy, incandescent flashes. It had been two-weeks-ago, to the day, Adam realized, that she had called on him at night, and that they had resultantly performed the ceremony of their entanglement.

And then, impossibly, as if he'd willed it, there was a knock at Adam's door. What time was it? Adam asked himself, unsure in his nocturnality. He looked through his peephole, though he didn't have to. He opened his front door, and there was Hannah, young and beautiful, but rained-on and unhappy. A dark dress clung to her in its wetness, and her white trench coat was bedraggled upon her body. Her makeup had been made to melt and run down her face, creating a kind of mask of sad surprise. The face beneath was worried.

"Hannah," said Adam pleasantly. "Come in."

"I can't," said Hannah.

"That's right," said Adam. "We're not supposed to be alone together."

"Yes, I just wanted to come over—I had to… I have to tell you that I'm pregnant."

A trumpeting of thunder cried. Adam's heart ran toward his shoes.

"I was supposed to get my period today," said Hannah. "And I didn't. And I'd been feeling strangely anyway. So I took a pregnancy test, and it was positive. You can see it, if you want to see it."

"No, I believe you. But, please, now you've really got to come in."

"I can't," said Hannah. "I just wanted you to know: I'm not keeping it. I can't keep it."

"Keep it? Hannah, you mean, get an abortion?"

"Yes."

"Hannah…"

"I know it's wrong, Adam, I do. I know that the bible says that it's wrong."

"What does the bible say?" asked Adam.

"There are several verses," said Hannah, "that people point to, to take a biblical stand against abortion. For example, in Isaiah, in the prophecy about the birth of Jesus, it says that 'a virgin shall conceive', but the same verse is quoted in Matthew as, 'a virgin shall be with child'. So, to conceive is to be with child."

"Then don't do it," said Adam.

"And there is a law in Exodus," said Hannah, "that says that if two men are fighting, and a nearby pregnant woman gets struck, with the result that 'her fruit depart from her, and yet no mischief follow,' then the man gets whatever punishment the judge and the woman's husband find to be fair. But, it says, 'if any mischief follow,' then the punishment is 'life for life, eye for eye, tooth for tooth.'"

"What does that mean?" asked Adam.

"I think it means," said Hannah, "that if the woman or the child are killed, then the man who killed them gets the death penalty. Because killing a fetus is murder."

"Then don't get an abortion, Hannah," Adam pleaded.

"I can't stop myself. I know it's wrong, Adam. Believe me,

I do. But I can't go through with a pregnancy right now. I can't. My father would be shattered. I will suffer either way. I have to trust that the Lord will forgive me for this. I'm too young and unprepared to do the right thing. And I think that our child will forgive me too, Adam. Afterall, what would it be like, to wake up in heaven, never having known life on earth? In that case, what have you lost?"

Adam looked at Hannah with shocked and incredulous fear. "Two weeks ago, I was in favor of abortion, Hannah. But I'm a believer, now, and I've been reading my bible lately—the bible that you gave me. I haven't thought about the issue at all in that time, but confronted with it now, it's obvious to me that ending a pregnancy isn't anything that God would want somebody to do."

"I have no father," said Hannah, "and I have no pastor. And you are not my boyfriend, or my husband, Adam. So please don't try to stop me."

Adam looked at her, then down at the floor, and wondered if that meant that he was supposed to try and stop her.

"I told you when we met, that I wasn't a very good Christian, Adam. I hope you remember what I've taught you, and that you too can forgive me for this. Sometime in the next few days, I'm going to go to Planned Parenthood, and see about killing it. Goodbye, Adam."

With that she turned and left, and was gone.

A flicker of lightning wallpapered the heavens. A grumble of thunder pervaded the blankness where Hannah had just stood. He wanted to run after her, to grab her by her shoulders, to tell her she was wrong, and that she knew it. Feeling as hollow as a burned out church, Adam only closed his door.

23

The Killer

When Adam awoke the next day, it was Thursday afternoon, and he drove once again to Last Baptist Church on Backwoods Road in San Antonio, to attempt to find once more the church's pastor, seated in his office. Adam seemed to find that Pastor Lacuna figurately lived in his office, whereas Douglas Tent, Adam had concluded, literally lived in his.

Adam's purpose in visiting the pastor again was two-fold: a plan of attack, for finally solving the mystery of who killed Roland Bellwether had finally occurred to him: the key, he at last felt, was the man who'd stolen Lacuna's cell phone. If it wasn't Tent—but a detective-Tent look-alike perhaps—who was this look-alike? Where was he, and could Adam track him down? He had resolved that he would interview Pastor Lacuna in detail about his interaction with the phone thief, looking for any small clue, any seemingly-inconsequential detail, that Adam's investigative mind might be able to seize upon, and thereby unravel the whole shadowy affair. And, if the reality of the moment offered it as a wise thing to do, he would also tell the pastor that his daughter was trying to get an abortion. Adam had decided to play this last part of his plan by ear.

As luck would have it, Adam found the church empty, except for the pastor, seated in his small inner office, within the quaintly diminutive outer receptionist area (in which Adam had had his fateful first meeting with Hannah, and his subsequent adventure with that area's file cabinets). Pastor Lacuna was seated at his desk, when Adam made his way into the man's office. "Oh, Hello, Adam," said the pastor pleasantly. He was seated in his chair, behind his desk. His laptop was not present before him; rather, in an empty space among the ever shifting, ever-changing labyrinth of books and papers upon the desk, was the pastor's ESV bible, open to the last book. The pastor had looked up from his reading to greet Adam, his right hand still clutching a fork, that waded idly in a small white bowl of buttered spaghetti noodles. An old-fashioned portable desk radio was to the other side of his bible from the noodles. It had a wooden (or faux wood) casing, the top half of its front containing two speaker holes, and the façade's bottom half being a volume knob, and a tuning dial, between which knobs was the red plastic analog indicator line, positioned at the desired point along the possible radio station settings. Thusly the radio was gently projecting the crackle and wail of old-timey gospel music from the pastor's desk.

"You've caught me having a late lunch," said pastor Lacuna, "as I read the book of Revelation. Quite the fascinating and challenging section of the bible. Have you read it, Adam? Please take a seat."

"Not yet," said Adam, taking a seat.

"Buttered noodles are sadly about all that my heartburn will allow me to eat anymore." Next to the bowl of noodles was a plate, that the remaining crumbs seemed to suggest had recently been occupied by toast. On the plate was a used butter knife.

Suddenly the gospel music was interrupted, and the clean-shaven voice of a radio announcer came through the little unit's speakers.

"Attention: this is a KCHL news alert! San Antonio police are advising that a local mental patient, one Dio Macina, who had weeks-ago broken out of San Antonio's hospital for the criminally insane, only to be recaptured, has once again broken free of the high-security medical facility in which he had been receiving treatment for enflamed criminal tendencies and severe mental derangement. We repeat: violent mental patient Dio Macina is once again on the loose. Mr. Macina should be considered potentially armed, and extremely dangerous. This has been a KCHL news alert: your home for old-time gospel hits."

And just like that, the gospel music resumed mid-song. Pastor Lacuna seemed not to have noticed the dramatic radio announcement, distracted by something he was reading in the book of Revelation, while simultaneously bringing a forkful of noodles to his mouth. The noodles squirmed and flailed between the pastor's lips, then disappeared into his mouth, his eyes still trained upon the bible's open page.

Adam internally shook off the alarming news about Dio Macina, and resolved to press on, in his intended mission of questioning Pastor Lacuna about the theft of his phone.

"I'm actually glad that you've come," said the pastor, looking up from his ESV. "There is something important I need to discuss with you. We missed you last Sunday, but the Sunday previous to that, you were present for my sermon on Lordship Salvation—in which I preached against Easy Believism?"

Adam nodded, an ambiguously earnest look on his face, not wanting to appear to either agree or disagree with the sermon in question.

"My fear," continued the pastor, "is that my daughter has misled you on some very important theological issues. She seems to think that this detective Douglas Tent hypnotized Roland Bellwether to kill himself, and that, not only that, but also that Roland was possessed by demons to do so."

"Yes," said Adam Hume.

"Well," said Pastor Lacuna, "if that's true—if there's a killer who is calling in demons to kill people—"

"Through the use of a book," said Adam.

"What's that?"

"Hannah thinks," said Adam, "that he's using a treatise on atheism, the words of which have a hypnotic effect, that cause the person hypnotized thereby to become dormantly possessed. She thinks Tent implants trigger words at that time, which, when heard by the victim later, release a demonic, suicidal rage, causing the person to take his or her own life."

"Yes," said the pastor, "I remember." The pastor's aged, light-colored eyes looked at Adam over the top of his black, thick-rimmed glasses. "Do you believe that, Adam?"

"I think someone hypnotized Roland, but I don't believe it was Douglas Tent."

"I see," said the pastor. "It does sound far-fetched. But my point is, Adam; in case it is true, the best defense is to believe the right gospel. A saved person cannot be possessed by a demon. Did you know that?"

"Yes."

"Good," said Pastor Lacuna. "But notice, I said, the correct gospel. The bible clearly warns that there are false gospels out there: powerless to save one's soul. Everyone is counting on something to save them from death. Even the atheist has faith that the meaning found in this life, somehow, saves their existence from being made meaningless by the fact of their eventual annihilation. They either consciously or unconsciously believe that. That's the faith of the atheist."

"Yes," said Adam. "I thought like that when I was an atheist."

"And we know that the atheist won't be saved by that. But even among the versions of the Christian gospel, there are false gospels alongside the true one."

"I would definitely agree with that," said Adam.

"My fear," said the pastor, "is that my daughter has initiated you into a false gospel that cannot save you. If this is true, then you are not saved, and you will be vulnerable to hypnotic attack based on demonic possession—if in fact that's what killed Roland. I've personally never heard of it before."

"Oh," said Adam, uncomfortable at how far from his intended purpose their meeting had strayed, but interested nonetheless in the theologically pressing topic. "I... I suppose... well, I understand the gospel that Hannah explained to me, and I believe it. And I believe that I am saved thereby."

Pastor Lacuna squeezed his wrinkled chin between the thumb and forefinger of his right hand, and wore an expression of deep concern beneath his cotton-white hairdo. "But you heard my sermon? So you understand the issues involved?"

"Yes," said Adam. "But I disagree."

"The point of the sermon, if I were to boil it down, Adam," continued the pastor undaunted, "is that mere intellectual assent to the proposition that Jesus died for your sins isn't enough to save you."

"It isn't?"

"No," said the pastor. "You have to actually put your trust and faith in Jesus."

"On top of Camanche Lookout hill, I intellectually assented to the proposition that Jesus Christ died for my sins," said Adam. "If that isn't belief, I don't know what is. I believe that the line from unbelief to belief is crossed when a person sincerely confesses to himself, or to someone else, or to God, internally or externally, that he believes that Jesus was the Son of God, who died, was buried, and rose again, to purchase for the person the gift of eternal life—or words to that effect. That is why the bible says: 'by thy words thou shalt be justified, and by thy words thou shalt be condemned'."

"Look," said Pastor Lacuna, "what I'm saying is: someone has truly put their faith and trust in Christ, when they turn from their sins, and have a changed, fruitful life. That's true salvation."

"I'm sorry," said Adam, "but I don't believe that. What you are describing is works salvation. That is a false gospel. That gospel cannot save. '...by the works of the law shall no flesh be justified'."

"Have you been reading the bible I gave you, Adam?"

"No," said Adam, "I've been reading a bible Hannah gave me. It's a KJV."

"Very well," said Lacuna, stiffened by stifled annoyance. "The KJV then, along with the other valid translations, teaches that a believer, who is truly saved, will do good works. Perhaps you are familiar with Philippians 1:6: 'he which hath begun a good work in you will perform it until the day of Jesus Christ'.

So, you see, it is God that uses the believer to do the good works. That is why saving faith always has good work attendant with it."

"I haven't read Philippians yet," said Adam.

"Well," said Lacuna, leaning back and tenting his fingers, in satisfaction with himself, "you should. You should base your beliefs on a reading of the entire scriptures."

"But I'm sure," said Adam, "that it doesn't contradict the gospel preached in Matthew, Mark, Luke, John, Romans, Galatians, and Acts. Do you have a KJV here that I could look at?"

The pastor sat forward, taken aback by the question. "Yes," he said standing. He turned and inspected the bookshelf on the wall behind him, scanning its volumes replete with erudition. Then, remembering, he turned back to his desk, and moved a pile of papers—hidden underneath was a King James bible. He handed it to Adam.

"Thank you," said Adam, who opened the book, turned to Paul's letter to the Philippians, and began to read. A minute passed. "Okay," said Adam. "He's just greeting the Philippians, and he's saying that he thanks God for their fellowship. And he says that he's 'confident of this very thing'"—Adam glanced up at Lacuna and then back down at the text—"'that he which hath begun a good work in you will perform it until the day of Jesus Christ'. But then he says why he is confident: because they have been partakers with him in his persecution and his preaching of the gospel. He's just saying that their behavior makes him confident that they'll keep doing good works."

"But," said the pastor, "it says that God is doing the work."

"Obviously," said Adam, "it's the indwelling of the Holy Spirit, that empowers a person to do good works. But believers still have to choose to do them—to choose to walk in the Spirit, and not in the flesh. Paul is saying that he is confident that the Philippians will do that—because of their good track record—not because it's theologically necessary that they will."

"Have you read the letter to the Hebrews, Adam?" asked the pastor.

"Not yet," said Adam.

"Well, you might be interested to know that a verse in Hebrews says, 'Follow peace with all men, and holiness, without which no man shall see the Lord'."

"So, you're saying that means, 'if we don't act holy, we aren't really saved?"

"Yes—that there must be some change in behavior, for true conversion."

"I need to read that letter," said Adam. "But that verse seems perfectly in line with what I have read: that we should be holy, and follow the law—not to be really, truly saved—but because it is the destiny of believers to be sinless in the next life. So we should act in accordance with that destiny now. Like in Galatians—I skipped ahead and read Galatians, because it has this line that Hannah used."

Adam flipped to Galatians, Chapter 5.

"In chapter five," continued Adam, "where it tells us to walk in the Spirit, and not in the flesh, it says that the Spirit (of God within the believer) is against the flesh (of the believer) and the flesh is against the Spirit. And it lists drunkenness, and murder, and other sins, and says that they which do such things shall not inherit the kingdom of God. And they won't, of course, because the flesh of the believer won't inherit it! His spirit will, with a renewed, changed flesh. So, when we are walking in the Spirit, we are walking in eternal life, as opposed to walking in our sinful flesh, which won't inherit eternal life in its sinful current form. I assume that's what the verse from Hebrews that you quote is referring to: walk in holiness, to be the eternal you—the you that will see the Lord. It's not saying that a believer who walks in the flesh isn't saved."

"If I could just boil down what I'm saying," said pastor Lacuna, "what the bible is actually teaching: we are saved by faith alone, yes, but not by a faith that is alone." The pastor leaned back again in his chair, and put the palms of his hands on the edge of his desktop in casual triumph.

"What does that mean?" asked Adam.

"It means," said the pastor, "that faith in the gospel is what saves us. But if we are really saved, we will have good works. We are saved by faith alone, but not by a faith that is alone: not by a faith that is without works."

"I don't think that makes sense," said Adam, his face contorted by pondering.

"What doesn't make sense about it?"

"Well," said Adam. "Okay, for example, what if I said, 'Citizenship in American is free to anyone who lives here'? No money required. All you have to do is want citizenship. But then, what if I went on to say, 'However, anyone who truly wants citizenship will pay $100; and anyone who doesn't pay the $100, didn't really want it, and therefore isn't really a citizen'? Is citizenship free, in that scenario, or does it cost money? Obviously it costs money. Saying, in that case, I'm a citizen by desire alone, but not by a desire that is alone, would obviously be a circuitous way of saying that citizenship costs a hundred dollars."

The pastor let out a resigned, but paternal sigh. "I've stated the biblical case the best I know how. Repentance from sin is part of salvation. No less than the Westminster Confession says so."

"Well, then the Westminster Confession is wrong," said Adam.

The pastor chortled.

"The bottom line I would give is Romans 4," said Adam, "which says, 'But to him that worketh not, but believeth on him that justifieth the ungodly, his faith is counted for righteousness.' In other words, a man who does no good works whatsoever—a man who follows no commandments—will still go to heaven, if he believes the gospel."

"Romans 4—" began the pastor, but was interrupted by a cell phone ringing in the pocket of his pants. "Excuse me," said the pastor, reaching for the phone, and bringing it to his ear. "Hello?" he said, in a familiar tone.

Adam barely heard the murmur of a voice coming

through the earpiece, but could not discern its characteristics. Suddenly a crashing, breaking explosion of terror swept across the pastor's face. His vision locked onto Adam, with the eyes of a trapped animal—the eyes of a soul whose light had suddenly been eclipsed by the shadow of imminent death. Looking through Adam, Pastor Lacuna began to scream, "I'm blind! I'm blind! I'm blind!" in a berserker incantation. His right hand grabbed the butter knife from his crumby toast plate, and with a crushing grip, thrust the knife into the Adam's apple of his own throat, pulling it out, and then stabbing it back in again, and again, with a horrible mechanicality. With each meaty smack of cutting impact was a sound of juice and crumpling cartilage, and a tomato-red spray of blood as the weapon withdrew. In the midst of his gridlocked brain, Adam's mind recalled Italian westerns, confronted with the blaring redness of the hot splatter.

Finally, the stabbing ceased. The pastor's murderous arm fell exhausted at his side. The cell phone, in the confusion, had already been dropped, by his other hand, face-up upon the desktop. The pastor's eyes were dead like a lizard's and bloodshot, and he delivered a continuous moribund gurgle. Blood flowed from his butchered throat, and soaked into his dress shirt's collar, and impinged on the knot of his tie. Finally, his tortured attempts at breathing turned into an animalistic gasp, and the preacher drowned in his own blood. With an involuntary spasm, the body lurched forward, bringing Pastor Lacuna's face crashing into his English Standard Version of the bible, and a crimson pool began forming on and under the book. With a nauseating realization, Adam observed miniature circles of blood floating in the butter of the erstwhile clergyman's noodles.

Adam saw that the cell phone call the pastor had received was still engaged. The name of the person calling, as according to the cell phone's contact list, was displayed on the screen, along with the person's picture. The name and picture belonged to Hannah Lacuna.

Adam remembered that the pastor had said that, since

the theft of his phone, he'd been using his wife's—his wife who'd recently passed away. Adam imagined that the picture of Hannah, the one now being displayed on the cell phone in the middle of this carnage, was the one her mother had selected before leaving this world of heresy and violence.

Adam, despite his detectively compunctions about disturbing a fresh crime scene, picked up the phone from off of the desk, and put it to his ear.

"Hello?" he said with frantic assertion.

Silence. But the unmistakable aura of a person on the line.

"I know it's you," said Adam. "You were the killer of Roland all along. And you hypnotized Pastor Lacuna when you were stealing his phone—and you made him forget he'd been hypnotized. Just like you hypnotized me, and made me forget it."

With a chill running through his body, Adam wondered if the codewords would be forthcoming again, to turn the room into a double suicide. He took the phone a few inches from his ear, and noticed that the hand he was holding it with was smeared and speckled with blood. He felt the warmth of blood specks on his cheek and chin. He replaced the phone against his ear. The person on the other end spoke:

"I'm afraid that the evidence may show that *you* killed Pastor Lacuna. There was a witness at the Day's Inn motel who observed the pastor threaten you behind the porn store, shouting about your relationship with his daughter."

Adam was embraced by a claustrophobia of circumstances.

"Await my next letter," the voice concluded, then ended the call.

It was the orderly English voice of Douglas Tent.

24

Good Works

In San Antonio, there is a Planned Parenthood, on Perrin Beitel Road, across from a McDonalds, among the many stores, strip malls, and fast-food restaurants. The L-shaped strip mall that houses the Planned Parenthood also contains —among other things—a Firestone Auto Care center, the hydraulic lifts of its six garage entrances raising and lowering for the diagnosing of the problems of its customers beloved vehicles. In the opposing wing of the small strip mall, the Planned Parenthood is nestled between a nails place and a place called Zen Massage. The strip mall is painted a drab clay-yellow, and beneath the store's individuated signs, above the store-front windows, is an awning running across all facades, covered in hot-blue cloth. The sign for the nails place is red cursive letters; in the windowed façade below is a neon Open sign. One side of the windows is obscured by closeup pictures of women's nails, to entice with the workmanship of their designs. Likewise, the massage place, on the other side of the Planned Parenthood has a poster in one of its windows, of a woman lying comfortably, her bare back being massaged, a look of eyes-closed serenity on her face. The store-front windows of the massage place are blocked by red curtains draped across the entirety of them— cloaking in secrecy the art of massage within.

In between the two, the Planned Parenthood's façade strikes a more jubilant tone than either of the others. Beneath it's blue awning, one side of its windowed façade is merely reflectively tinted windows, and a sign declaring the disallowing of firearms on the premise. The other half of the windows —on the other side of the glass entrance door—is completely covered with two large photos, in rose-colored hues. In one, a multi-racial collection of three women are embracing each other, while facing forward and laughing triumphantly, as if they have just finished a marathon together, and then heard a hilarious joke. The oversized photo next to it is of a young, fit woman with big round glasses and big hair, literally embracing herself, while smiling self-confidently forward. Beneath one photo is written "Planned Parenthood is Health Care." And beneath the other is written, "#ThisIsHealthCare".

When Adam had imagined Hannah going to a Planned Parenthood to kill their baby, he pictured the facility as a clinical, clerical shrine to the banality of evil—the profundity of death turned into a sterile medical procedure. But what he found, when looking upon the entrance to the Planned Parenthood on Perrin Beitel Road, was a display that went beyond the perfunctory acceptance of the snuffing out of human life, to its enthusiastic celebration, as if abortion were some kind of fun new soft drink, loaded with caffeine and opportunities for empowerment and adventure.

It was 2 pm, on the Saturday following pastor Lacuna's brutal suicide, when Hannah Lacuna's white dilapidated Honda Civic lumbered into the strip mall's central parking spaces, near the front door of Planned Parenthood. As she walked determinedly toward the clinic, straightening the strap of her purse on her shoulder authoritatively as she went, she heard Adam's voice somewhere behind her call out, "Hannah!"

She spun around, and their eyes met, his: wounded and worried; hers: defiant and sad.

"I was questioned by the police for hours," Adam said. "They think I killed your father. I didn't, Hannah, I swear I didn't. I'm sorry for following you. I need to talk. Hannah, I think I'm going to be arrested tomorrow."

"I know what happened," said Hannah. "I told you about him: what he was, what he was capable of. You didn't believe me."

"I'm sorry, Hannah."

"They questioned me too, Adam. I think they think we did it together. That you killed my father, and then I called you afterwards, to see if it was done. It's working perfectly for Tent. He'll be able to say that my father killed Roland for sleeping with me—or that Roland killed himself because of me—and that you killed my father for disapproving of us. He'll get away with it. I told them the truth. I told them it was Tent. They didn't believe a word."

She noticed a torn-open envelope held in Adam's hand. "He sent me a letter," Adam said. "It was lying on one of my pillows next to my head, when I woke up this morning, horrifyingly enough. He wants me to come see him at his office tonight."

"Did you tell the police what really happened?"

"They wouldn't have believed me, Hannah. He's one of them. He has evidence against me, that the police don't even know about yet. They already think we did it. He'll make the case against us worse, if I don't cooperate. I told them everything, except that Tent was on the other end of the phone. I said that it was silence: that someone was there, but wasn't speaking."

"My family are all at my house now," said Hannah. "my brothers and my sisters, and their children. I've barely had time to cry about my father, Adam. But I've found time, when I can. It's a reservoir of tears, that is released in episodes. We've been eating, and remembering him. There's a funeral service for him on Monday evening at the church."

"I'm so sorry, Hannah," said Adam.

"I cry about *us* too," said Hannah.

They stood together, facing each other on the asphalt. The air was sultry and still. A broken-hearted play of strategies struggled languidly between them. The sun was vibrant but obscured by clouds, blanketing the world below in a patchwork of light and shadow.

"He used my phone to do it," said Hannah. "I didn't realize it till afterward. I was by myself in the house, when my father was at church. I was taking a shower. When I got done, I sensed things were amiss. There was a scent of cigarette smoke in my room."

"He used your phone to make the fatal call," said Adam absorbing the reality of it as he spoke. "We've got to stop him."

"Why do we have to do that?" asked Hannah. "There is no *we*, Adam. If you'll excuse me, I've got an appointment."

She turned to go, again adjusting the strap of her purse on her shoulder; the muscles of her back—as she turned her back to him—were tense with alienation.

"An appointment" said Adam. "To kill our baby?"

She spun around. In her eyes was the beginning of rage.

"We're going to discuss my options," said Hannah.

"The options for killing our baby?" said Adam, stony-faced.

Rage and sadness clashed and mixed within Hannah, softening and hardening her, as she stood ready to crumble or explode.

"I was wrong," said Adam. "I should have believed you that Tent is evil and reprobate. The clues were staring me in the face. You were right about him hating God, and even about his being a sexual pervert."

"He's a homosexual?"

"Sort of," said Adam. "It's very weird. My point is: you were right. I couldn't see it, because I was so in love with being the kind of truth-seeker that I thought I was supposed to be, that I wasn't loving the truth anymore. That was my bias."

"Which is how the devil rules the world," said Hannah.

"How's that?" asked Adam.

"Through creating and exploiting the biases of men," said Hannah. "You don't even need a conspiracy of men—they'll conspire for you, and not even know it, in order to protect the biases you've given them."

"Hannah," said Adam, "you know that what you are trying to do to our baby is wrong."

Hannah crossed her arms, rebellious but curious what he

would go on to say.

"You asked me, that night," continued Adam, "in the doorway to my apartment: you said, 'What has a baby really lost, if it wakes up in heaven, having never known life on earth? What difference does it make?' I've thought about that question, Hannah, and I've prayed about it. And I want to tell you what an aborted baby loses."

Hannah somewhat loosened her crossed-arm grip on herself. The jubilant Planned Parenthood customer in the giant photograph in the window continued her self-embrace as tightly as ever.

"What the aborted baby loses is his future," said Adam. "Before he is conceived, before the sperm and egg unite, Hannah, there is no specific person in existence, no individual DNA code, and therefore no unique person with a future to lose. But once that DNA is put together, Hannah, there is a human person growing inside of you, with a specific, individual future on earth to lose."

Hannah untied her arms all together, dropping them to her sides. Then one hand went absentmindedly to the strap of her purse on her shoulder. Her eyeline dropped, and one ear turned a little more toward Adam than the other.

"You say that aborted babies go to heaven," said Adam. "I'm glad to hear that, though I don't know where that's in the bible—"

"In Job, chapter 3," said Hannah, "Job says that if he'd never been born, he would have gone to a place of rest, free from weariness and oppression. Also, in 2nd Samuel 12, when the child that David had with Bathsheba dies, David says, 'I shall go to him, but he shall not return to me'—meaning that the child has gone where David is going: heaven."

"And that's a comforting thing to know," said Adam. "But any saved person that you could murder, at whatever age, would also go to heaven. My point is: killing a person isn't wrong, ultimately, because of the physical pain it causes, or because of the grief. Someone could be murdered painlessly, who had no friends or relatives. It isn't wrong because it's disappointing to the victim. It's wrong because a murderer steals from the victim the future life on earth that the victim would have had, if the murder hadn't happened. That's what Douglas Tent stole from Roland, and from your father. God has the right to strike dead whomever he wants, and we don't know how much future on earth he has ordained for any of us to have. But we have no right to take a human future on earth away. That's what the baby loses. That's what you'd be taking away. Then we'd be no better than Douglas Tent."

Hannah's eyes trembled and became bright with water.

"My father..." she said, distantly to no one. Her hand rose quickly, holding her lips. And her eyebrows tilted upward, creating furrows in her clear and lineless face.

"I know that you know all of these things, Hannah. You just needed me to be a man and tell you. Whether this baby is born or not, Hannah, I want to be your man."

Hannah walked quickly to Adam and fell against him in an embrace. She buried her face in his chest, and he felt the warmth and dampness of her tears, and the trembling of her sobs against his shirt. Adam became aware of the cars parked around them, of persons coming and going in the strip mall's shops. Then he put that out of his mind, and looked down at Hannah's golden hair, soft and fragrant against his chin.

"He was bad, my father," said Hannah's muffled voice, "but he didn't used to be. And he was my father."

"He convinced me to believe in the existence of God," said Adam remembering, holding her tight. "If he hadn't done that, I wouldn't have been prepared to hear the gospel from you, and get saved."

"God uses us all in different ways," said Hannah, her breath hot against Adam's torso.

"Even Douglas Tent," said Adam, "has presumably done many positive things. He caught all of those criminals. He just lost his way, and got too far gone. God gave him great talent. But that's led him to great pride."

"It's easy to end up in hell, I suppose," said Hannah. "You just have to believe in yourself."

Adam almost chuckled. A weary smile encroached on the corners of his mouth. Hannah looked up and gave a cubistic grin, through rosy eyes and crumpled youth.

"What time are you supposed to go see Tent at his office tonight?" asked Hannah, putting both hands on Adam's chest and pressing off slightly, to steady herself into an upright stance.

"At midnight," said Adam.

"Don't you work tonight?"

"No," said Adam. "I'm actually working day shift in the morning, instead. I'm covering for someone who needed it off."

"You've got to destroy his book, Adam—it's the source of his murderous power. Take a box of matches, and a bottle of high proof rum. When you get the chance, douse the book, and light it ablaze. Then get out of there fast."

"Is that still the best plan we can come up with?"

"It's simple," said Hannah. "That's its strength." Something occurred to her. "Oh! But you've got to get him to confess also. Does your phone record memos?"

"My phone's not very smart," said Adam. "I've still got a Windows phone. I assume there's an app I could download."

"Yeah, download the app," said Hannah, casual and energized. "Furtively record him confessing to the killing of Roland and my father, then burn up his book, and run away. Then our names will be cleared, and we won't have to go to prison for murder. I'll come with you to his office tonight."

"He said in his letter that I was to come alone," cautioned Adam.

"Okay, then I'll wait in the car."

"When last I spoke to him," said Adam, "he told me that his apprehension of Malcom Esperanza was at hand. I think he's going to show me who Malcom Esperanza is. That should be fascinating."

"Malcom Esperanza," said Hannah, and trailed off with bemused skepticism. She looked at the secretive glare on the windows of the Planned Parenthood clinic, and at its gaudy advertising. "Let's leave this wicked place," she said.

"Thank you!" shouted a female voice from somewhere beside them.

They turned and saw a woman sitting in the driver's seat of an otherwise unoccupied car, whom they hadn't noticed before, parked a few spaces from where they stood. The car was a weathered, tan-colored sedan. The woman looked like she was 20-years-old, or 35, depending on how the light struck her. Her hair was an abundance of tight blond curls. She wore bright red lipstick, and dangling silver earrings, but her clothing was yoga pants, and a baggy t-shirt. She held a burning cigarette.

"You two have helped me make my mind up about something. So thank you," the woman said leaning out of her driver's-side window. She tossed the half-smoked cigarette away, not looking where it landed. Adam noticed that part of the upholstery on her ceiling was falling down. He noticed in her backseat: an empty child's car seat, made of purple plastic with sturdy black straps.

The woman backed out of the space, and puttered away to face the music. Above, the cloud bank drifted in its place before the sun. And what was shadowed shifted, and what was illuminated changed.

25

Prelude

Adam sat in his car, in the parking lot of the Buy-N-Leave convenience store, across the street from Douglas Tent's office, at five minutes till midnight. Through his windshield he had a direct view of the building's front door, recreating the orientation at which Tent and Adam had been parked, when they had been surveilling Tent's office themselves. Adam's car's front-seat windows were cracked a few inches, and the silence of the hour fell in. A translucent layer of fibrous clouds streamed continuously past most of a moon, like blue and sienna smoke. Insects made a static of sound in midnight's unreachable penumbra. Adam felt physically vulnerable —like he'd felt in his guard shack, on that first night of his journey: the night of Roland's murder.

Adam stepped out of his car, closed the door gently, and opened a door to the backseat. He had installed a curtain rod sidewise along the middle of his car's interior, near the roof, and had fashioned two curtains from black cloth—which now hung from the rod. These curtains along with the tint that had been professionally applied to his back and rear windows transformed the car's backseat into a visually impenetrable surveillance nest, from which a stationary operative could spy on the surrounding environment undetected. These tricks had been suggested to Adam by Douglas Tent himself, when they'd had their surveillance lesson together on this very spot.

Adam entered the furtive enclosure, shut himself in, and sat next to Hannah Lacuna, who wore her white trench coat, overtop of her jeans and a faded gray t-shirt which read "Last Baptist Church of San Antonio". Her hair was pulled back into a ponytail, a few strands from the sides and top of her hairline hanging free, framing her face. On the seat between them was a digital video camera, binoculars, an open notebook and pens, and a few bottles of water—the tools of the art of espionage.

"Okay," said Adam, "this is it."

Hannah looked at him, worried and strong. She retrieved two things from the floor.

"Here is your bottle of high-proof rum," she said, and handed him the glass bottle, filled with its amber fluid, the weight of which he cradled like an unsure weapon.

"And your box of wooden matches," she said, handing him the slide-open box, filled with wooden matches, strikable on the box's side. He took it with the other hand, then put both objects on the seat between them, among the surveillance supplies.

"Is the audio recording app ready?"

"Yes," said Adam, checking his phone, and then returning it to the inside pocket of his blazer. Adam wore jeans, like Hannah, and a black golf shirt beneath a gray blazer. He had chosen the jacket, because he reasoned that its inside pocket would provide a place from which his phone would be able to record sound inconspicuously. He and Hannah, earlier that night, had tested the new app's recording prowess from inside the blazer, and had practiced setting a book on fire, with rum and matches —using a second, spare bottle of booze. Adam wondered if his semi-formal appearance would be strange to Tent, as he'd not presented himself that way before. But Adam finally decided that it was an occasion that called for some formality: he was saying goodbye to his friend and hero.

"Okay," said Hannah, "so, according to our tests, your phone will record for sixty minutes on one file, before stopping. So, that's how long you've got in which to get him to mention his murder of Roland and my father."

"Yes," said Adam, taking a deep breath, and then exhaling it loud and slow.

"Once he's confessed, grab the book, set it on fire, and

then get out of there. I think you should also take this." Hannah reached into her purse, which sat on the far side of her, and brought out a stainless steel revolver, offering it to Adam, with a metallic rattle.

"It's loaded," said Hannah.

The muscles in Adam's face tried to create a scandalized expression, but were mostly too paralyzed with nervousness to do so.

"Is that your father's gun?"

"Yes," said Hannah.

"No," said Adam. "Thank you, but no. Tent has a way of knowing things. If I go in there with a gun, I'm afraid he'll know, and it won't go well. I don't believe his intentions toward me are violent. I think all that he's done, the murder, has been in the service of catching Malcom Esperanza. And I think he wants my loyalty. He's threatening to frame me for murder, to ensure that I'll go along with whatever he has planned."

"Okay," said Hannah acquiescing, and returned the gun to her purse.

"Here are my keys. If I'm not back out by 1 am, leave, and contact the police. You have the binoculars. If you see things going bad before 1 am, then leave and call the police. Okay?"

"Okay, Adam," said Hannah.

Adam grasped her left wrist, and checked her small wristwatch, with its pink leather band. He remembered noticing it, when they'd first met. Her watch and the black one he wore on his wrist were in synch.

"Okay," he said, and a preparatory calm came over him. He took his phone out of his inside jacket pocket, pressed record on the sound-recording app, blackened the phone's screen, and replaced it inside his blazer. He opened the car door, and began to exit.

"No, wait—" said Hannah reaching out to stop him.

Adam slid back into place beside her, and reclosed the door.

"Aren't you forgetting something?" Hannah asked.

Adam's spinning brain groped around within itself, for what he might be missing.

"A prayer," said Hannah.

"Oh yes, of course." Adam lowered his head, Hannah lowered hers, and turning toward each other, his hands enclosed hers upon the detection paraphernalia.

"Heavenly Father," Adam began, clearing the tremble in his voice with a modest grumble. "We thank you for this chance, to stand for the truth, against the forces of lying and murder. We know that, without you, we don't stand a chance. Please fight this battle for us, Lord. Forgive us our trespasses, Lord. And glorify thyself, by using us, your servants, to bring to light the evil that's been done, and to bring the true criminal to justice. Put your Spirit upon us, Lord. We are your children. We love you, Father. Somehow, if it be your will, cause us to win. In Jesus' name we pray. Amen."

"Amen," said Hannah Lacuna.

They opened their eyes, and Adam continued to hold her hands.

"Hannah," he said, "and looked down at the space between them. "If I don't make it back: if something happens to me—"

"Don't say that, Adam."

"I just want you to know," said Adam, and sputtered and struggled to say the words.

"I love you, too," said Hannah, and kissed him.

Adam's face was raised now, buoyed up by joy, and bright with happy disbelief.

"Now, get in there," said Hannah, "and catch the bad guy."

Adam smiled, kissed her, and energetically but carefully, taking the rum and matches, exited the car, closed the door, and began the very short walk across the road that separated the convenience store (and the doggie barber shop next to it) from the small parking lot attached to Tent's building.

Looking briefly behind himself, he was reassured that Hannah was invisible, cloaked in the darkness of the seemingly empty car's backseat. He made his way deliberately but apprehensively toward the front door of the dentist's office/detective agency that stood before him, looming in the darkness. He noticed that Tent's golden station wagon was the sole vehicle parked in the lot. The tall windows of the detective's office reflected unforgivingly the images of the night—giving up no clues as to what was in store.

Adam heard the almost-imperceptible scraping of his shoes on the pavement, as he advanced, and remembered the similarly frightening walk, that had resulted in his discovery of Roland's body—a month ago. He felt absurd, holding the booze and matches, like some midnight party goer. He realized he shouldn't be holding the matches, and placed them in the right-side pocket of his blazer. He walked—his mind blank with fear. The night air fondled Adam's perimeter. The moon sang an otherworldly song. And then he was at the deserted front door, and opening it, he entered the building's foyer.

The foyer was shadows and silhouettes—muted moonlight haphazardly beaming in. The entryway's fountain was silent—its flow arrested. Tent must have keys to the building's front door, and the code to whatever security system, Adam reasoned—must have left the building open for Adam's arrival. The only light glowed forth from the snowy skein of fissures that was the shattered widow, in the detective agency's front door—its lettering rendered illegible. It called like a broken beacon.

This plan is ridiculous, Adam though. How could he possibly expect to defeat a crime-fighting genius (and a devious murderer) with such a simplistic plan? Had he and Hannah been insane? Had Tent been watching him approach? Had he seen him put the matches in his pocket? But he couldn't back out now. He had to comply with Tent's demand to meet tonight, or else be further framed for murder. And if Tent wasn't stopped as soon as possible, how many more innocent people would die?

Adam and Hannah could not defeat Tent, Adam realized. That was obvious. Only God could do that. And if, by God's grace, a lowly security guard, with delusions of being an amateur detective, could defeat the world-famous Douglas Tent, then God's hand in that would be clear. God would receive the glory. Adam accepted his complete inadequacy. But he trusted in God's supreme power and goodness. He remembered something he'd just read in Paul's second letter to the church at Corinth: "...when I am weak, then am I strong."

Adam looked at his watch. It was 11:59 pm. He had an hour. Reaching out, and taking hold of the doorknob, Adam stepped through the detective agency's door, his entrance announced with the familiar and unsettling electronic chime.

26

The Showdown

Detective Douglas Tent was standing in the front room of his offices, with his back to the door, when Adam arrived. The room was as Adam remembered it: the receptionist's desk, sans receptionist, piled with files, chemistry, and ashtrays—the rest of the room likewise disheveled and smoggy.

Detective Tent turned nonchalantly around, to greet Adam with a cocksure silence. He was dressed as Adam remembered him, from the night of their first meeting, at the hospital, after Roland's murder. Tent again wore a tightly-tailored suit, and tie, donning his wool fedora atop his porcelain forehead and spherically combed-back oil slick of hair. His bright green eyes burned like two all-knowing suns. His transformation from the hospice patient he resembled two weeks ago was amazing. His eyes were sunken, and underscored by purple shadows, but the strain on his face now seemed to be the product of assiduous thinking, rather than drugs and disease.

Adam did however note one flamboyantly new element in the room. Leaning with its back against the wall, behind the reception's desk, was the mannequin from Douglas Tent's secret thinking chamber, out in the open now, still adorned with detective Tent's face vivaciously taped to its head. The mannequin stood wearing Tent's blue, kimono-style bathrobe closed and tied around its torso, like a post-coital doppelganger paramour, who'd wandered in, and whose beaming countenance was eavesdropping on their conversation. The unsaved part of Adam couldn't help but feel a sense of pride for Tent, for bringing his travesty of a romance out of the closet.

"I'm glad you were able to come by, my boy," said detective Tent, his speaking full of gravity and English irony. He approached Adam, and—surprisingly—embraced him in a hug. Tent held Adam for a moment, and then withdrew to an arm's length, using his hands to pat up and down Adam's back and sides.

"What's this?" asked the detective, withdrawing the box of matches from Adam's pocket. Tent's eager eyes scanned the box, and he turned it over. He sniffed the striking surface on the side of the matches, opened the box, looked inside, then shut it up again.

"These matches appear to be new, and yet, half of them have been very recently used," said Tent, touching the matchbox to his chin meditatively and then placing them in the right-hand pocket of his own blazer. Next Tent removed Adam's cell phone from his inside jacket pocket, and cradled it in his hand, while retreating to the back of the room, to stand in front of the wooden sideboard, which ran along the back of it—Tent's framed newspaper headlines, as always, announcing his crime-fighting strokes of genius from the past, on the wall above.

"I've never before seen you wear a jacket," said Tent. "Though you have worn jeans. Why would a man, not accustomed to wearing a jacket, but accustomed to wearing jeans, keep his phone in the jacket, rather than leaving it in his jeans?"

He knows. The words rang echoingly in the feverish cave of Adam's skull. *Of course, he knows.* How could Adam have expected otherwise? Tent opened a drawer on the sideboard, placed Adam's phone within, then shut the phone impotently inside. He removed his wool fedora, and discarded it upon the surface of the sideboard. Adam noticed a knee-high metal trashcan, next to the sideboard, by where Tent's fedora rested. He pictured burning the book inside of it.

"Is this a gift for me?" said Tent, referring to Adam's bottle of rum. Tent took it from him, and examined the label. "Too kind of you. I thank you."

He placed the bottle on the sideboard next to his hat.

"Now," said Tent, "the reason I've called you here." He

took Adam's matches out, along with a pack of cigarettes, lit one in his mouth, returned the matches and cigarettes to the detective's right-side jacket pocket, and took a long, contemplative pull on the burning fag.

"It's time for you to meet Malcom Esperanza," Tent said, and walked away, down the hall which led to the secret closet behind the bookshelf.

Adam, for a moment, was frozen. He could run now. The plan was fucked. He could simply run, face the music in court. He was innocent; surely he and Hannah wouldn't be found guilty of a murder they didn't commit. Would they? Adam heard Tent struggling to move the bookcase. If he left now, he wouldn't know what was in the closet this time—who was in it. He wanted to meet Malcom Esperanza. And he could still destroy the book, or steal it and escape—the book: the source of Tent's hypnotic murders. Pushed on by weakness, or foolishness, or the leading of the Holy Spirit, he found himself walking forward, and suddenly he had rounded the corner, and was in the orbit of the destiny of that choice, moving toward the hallway's terminal end. He glanced at his watch: 12:05. He prayed that he could find a way out by 12:55. He prayed that Hannah would leave without him, if he couldn't. He prayed she would be safe.

Tent's tall but thin limbs were doing an admirable but slow job of dragging the bookcase into the break nook. As before, Adam lent his strength to the task, and the shelf was pulled clear of the old, rotting, wooden door it had been concealing. A flutter of panic caressed Adam's heart, when he saw that the book was not where it had been: it was not resting against the clandestine door. It was nowhere to be found.

"You may want to be sitting down for this," said detective Tent, and rolled an office chair in from the abandoned room off of the hall, opposite the break nook, and positioned the chair for Adam to sit in, facing the closet door. Adam sat, fear metastasizing in the pit of his stomach.

Tent parked his smoke beneath his aquiline nose, bogarting it while he gave Adam a sizing-up gaze, before turning and placing his hand on the knob of the alien door. Then the door was flung open, and the cord to the naked lightbulb dangling inside was pulled, causing light to bathe the closet's occupant in modest illumination.

And with that, whatever semblance of reality remained for Adam, whatever shred of it had survived the foregoing month of murder and hypnosis, of angels and demons, of a hero walking off the page, and of a hero fallen, whatever sense of reality had survived this month of romance, detective work, and God now fell and shattered in slow motion, like a piece of candy against a concrete floor. Time stood still, and Adam involuntarily held his breath—as it is when one is looking at an impossible thing. It was not an impersonator, it was not a prank. There in Tent's thinking closet, his hands tied behind his back and behind the chair he was sitting in, and with his ankles tied together, and a gag of cloth across his mouth, was current President of the United States Donald John Trump.

The president looked sideways at Tent, and grunted a disrespectful hello. Adam was bug-eyed with shock. Tent untied the president's gag, and it fell aside.

"Never mind how it was done," said Tent. "Let's just say that I'm a genius, and I did it."

"I should have listened to the Secret Service," said President Trump. "I should stop taking Ubers to McDonald's."

President Trump was in a black suit, his jacket unbuttoned, and his long red tie hanging down the front of him. A miniature American flag was pinned to his left lapel. He was a tall man, Adam noted—as tall as Douglas Tent. The president's silvery blond hair was combed back and over in its trademark way. Had the President of the United States been at a rally in Texas tonight? He must have been. This was the craziest thing that Adam had ever seen.

"Buddy, you look like a good character," said President Trump. "Go get help. This guy is a wacko. I'm talking seriously crazy."

Tent bent over, grabbed the sides of the president's chair, and with a grunting effort, slid the president and his chair out into the hall, in front of the open closet.

"I give you," said detective Tent, "Malcom Esperanza."

"He keeps calling me that," said Trump, his face pulling back against his skull in mocking disbelief.

Tent took a drag on his cigarette, and then began pacing next to the president's chair, gesturing with his cigarette held between two fingers—the smoke dissolving into the air—his other hand authoritatively in one pocket, propelling his upright form along its tight, circuitous trek.

"As you know, Adam, from reading Roland's accounts of our adventures together, I first became suspicious of the existence of Malcom Esperanza during *The Case of the Missing Bank Vault*. Now, in that case, the criminal turned out to be a mousy, though not unattractive teller, who'd contrived the whole affair using an ingenious device constructed in her garage out of disassembled appliances from her kitchen and bathroom. But the pure brilliance of her scheme, Adam—as you recall, that's when I first suspected the operation of a criminal mastermind, a consulting demon, who aided everyday criminals in the accomplishing of their crimes: a true artist, who profited to some extent from the pittance paid him by his ne'er-do-well clients, but whose true profit came from seeing his insidious web of corruptions play out in the news, whose true glee is from watching morality burn, and from watching me attempt to put out his fires.

"As I told you before," continued Tent, "I even believe the man now sitting unmasked before you has made my acquaintance before over the years, but always appearing in disguise, of course. In *The Case of the Murdered Bachelor Party*, he appeared to me in the semblance of an unassuming elderly woman; in *The Case of the Dinosaur Museum*, he went as far as to take the form of the statue of a bear. In each case, and there are others, I only was able to infer his dissembling physical presence in retrospect, just as his existence in general has been merely inferred through its virulent effects—though, nonetheless, a presence of unmistakable reality.

"But it was only recently," Tent went on, pausing to take a drag, "that I realized that it was not just these charming and dastardly crimes—these delicious puzzles of lawbreaking—that were more black, more sinister than they should be. Once I began my self-hypnosis—through use of the psychoactive text that I showed you—it was only then that I realized that all of human history likewise evinces the shadowy fingerprints of Malcom Esperanza: the Kennedy Assassination, 9/11, Global Warming, New Coke. How were these things allowed to happen? Homophobia, racism, hetero-normative, cisgendered, patriarchal society, in general: how were these things written on the unsullied canvas of the human heart? There can be only one answer: Malcom Esperanza."

President Trump shot a wide-eyed look at Adam, and waved his eyeballs toward Tent, silently saying, "This guy is crackers, big-league."

"What are you going to do?" asked Adam, sitting stiffly with his hands on his knees.

"My intentions are not violent," said Tent. "I believe that Esperanza wants to confess. He is a narcissist of the highest order. He wants to tell me of his network through which he's run the world for hundreds of years. He's dying to tell it. Not being able to broadcast his full list of accomplishments is mental torture for him—torture beyond any physical stress I could apply. I won't record his confession electronically—the sight of his current state, perhaps the distress in his voice, might cause his words to appear coerced. No, I will hear his confession with my own ears, and I will be believed when I tell it to the planet: I will get my own show on CNN."

"He probably will," said President Trump.

"Tell us," said Tent to Trump. "How did you acquire your infernal time machine?"

"Time machine?" the president asked.

"Don't you see?" said Tent. "He has to have a time machine, Adam. It's the only logical deduction based on the facts. Those letters I sent you represented an invented narrative of my own fashioning. But their implication was nonetheless true. Something like that must have happened. And what he was preparing to do to me in that story must be something like what he really wants to do. I referred in my letters to Malcom Esperanza as a rich New York billionaire. You saw the photo of Ronald Reagan on my list of suspects in my thinking closet. Surely, Adam, you deduced whom I believed Esperanza to be."

Adam sat silently. He had not deduced it.

"You've lost your mind," said Adam finally, a lightning of courage firing in his chest. "Why?" said Adam. "Why did you murder Roland and the pastor?" His voice was a trembling rage.

Tent's eyes narrowed with meditation. He held the smoke in his mouth, and then inhaled it.

"Roland was my best friend," said Doulas Tent. "He was my partner in crime-fighting, and my biographer, for which I loved the man." Tent's arms dropped to his sides, and he faced Adam plainly. "And that is why I had to kill him," he said with a melancholy resignation. "This world we live in—this world poisoned by the spell cast over it by Malcom Esperanza—what is, at bottom, its fatal flaw? I'll tell you: it is a lack of rationality—a paucity of dispassionate scientific outlook.

"We are taught by religion, by traditionalism, by the patriarchy, that our family, our neighborhood, our country, should weigh more heavily on our hearts than some other fellow's family, some other woman's neighborhood, more than the country of a Chinese person of non-conforming gender. This undying parochialism is at the center of humanity's inability to collectively stand up to Esperanza's propaganda."

Adam began to almost imperceptibly nod his head. He didn't understand. But he thought that perhaps he was beginning to.

"If I could kill my best friend," said Douglas Tent, "then I knew I could be detached enough, enlightened enough, scientific enough to lead the charge against the bigotry of Esperanza's xenophobia. Then we could collectively begin to do the hard things: to reduce our carbon emissions, to halt the excessive birth rate that is crippling the planet with overpopulation. We could do these things because we would have sloughed off the primitive, evolutionarily vestigial emotion that inspires one to care more for his or her own, rather than caring equally for those that one has never met. We could be motivated by a utilitarian calculus, rather than by our consciences. Did not even Christ say, 'love thy neighbor'?"

"Yes," said Adam, "but your neighbor is someone whom you've met—someone local."

"He's got you there," said President Trump.

"Which brings me to the pastor," said detective Tent. "This pastor that has poisoned your mind with Bronze Age fairy tales." Tent wagged his cigarette with scolding stabs as he said the words. "Roland and I had a bond that can only be forged in the furnace of shared danger—a shared striving toward greatness. He himself was not a Christian, but I grew to hate his tolerance of that virulent culture—that cesspool of pusillanimous philosophies. Imagine my horror upon witnessing the same pastor poison you with the same ideas. But you've actually fallen for it in a way that Roland never did, haven't you?"

"I have," said Adam. "I am a Christian."

Tent made the face of a man viewing a disgusting display. "It's clear to me now, that Esperanza wrote the Christian bible, or had someone do it, to prop up the capitalism and patriarchal, cisgendered heteronormativity that's made him rich. If you can fall for Christianity, Adam, then you really were never meant to be my partner in detection."

Adam felt a calm come over him—he felt a deep sense of knowing who he was.

"We are defined, my boy," continued Tent, "by whom we know the bad guys in this world to be. I could have made your heroic dreams come true. You could have been a genius. The only god in this room right now whom you should have concerned yourself with is me."

"I've made my choice," said Adam.

"I see that you have," said Tent.

"And you will spend the rest of your life in prison," Adam said.

"Prison, my boy?" said Tent. "Why ever should I go to prison? Because of my confession to the murders in the hearing of yourself and President Trump? Neither of you has any credibility. You, my boy, will be arrested for the murders of Roland and the preacher. Once I have secured Esperanza's confession, I will be pardoned for his kidnapping, and celebrated as the savior of the world—the catcher of Satan himself—the crowning achievement of my illustrious career."

Tent took the last drag of his cigarette, tossed it onto the floor, and crushed it under his shoe with contempt.

"Before you go," said Tent to Adam, "let me give you a gift."

Tent reached into the open doorway of the unused office room behind him, and retrieved a sheathed saber—the same ancient weapon with which he had threatened Adam upon Adam's first visit to Tent's office, an emotional lifetime ago.

Tent placed the sword, its ornate metalworking and its threatening heft, into Adam's hands as he sat in the chair, looking at Tent—the President of the United States sitting to one side between them. Adam glanced at his wristwatch, and saw that it was 12:15. He hoped that Hannah was safe and unafraid.

"I have just four words, to say to you," said Tent. "I say them in place of 'goodbye'."

Adam knew what was coming: the trigger words. Tent intended to activate the hypnotic programing that he had implanted on that first office visit. He intended Adam to experience hysterical blindness, and to subsequently become a machinery of suicide, a screaming outburst of self-immolation, as the others had done.

Their eyes locked—and Adam saw, in the glaring orbs of detective Douglas Tent, the soulless hatred of a calculating killer.

"Do as thou wilt," said Douglas Tent, and waited.

Nothing occurred. Adam remained his sighted self, and in that moment, as the Holy Spirit rallied within, to protect him from the demons on Tent's side, a secret was spoken into the ear of Adam's soul: and suddenly, as if delivered with an overwhelming sense of peace, he knew where Tent had hidden the book. It was with the only one it could be with. It was so clear. He'd left it with the only one he really, truly loved.

"Do as thou wilt!" repeated Tent, perturbed—losing his cool.

Adam looked at Tent, confident and unaffected. Tent lunged toward Adam in anger, and as he did, President Donald Trump raised his tied-together legs, at just the right moment to send Tent lurching forward and colliding with the ground with a resonating smack.

Adam tossed the sword aside, and bending down, shot his hand into Tent's jacket pocket, retrieved the book of matches, and ran sweepingly down the hall. When the hall opened into the receptionist's area, Adam ran toward the mannequin dressed in Tent's blue bathrobe and wearing his face. Unraveling the sash, and throwing the wings of the robe asunder, Adam saw —tucked into boxer shorts that Adam could only assume were a loving gift from Tent—the noxious, leather-bound book. Adam heaved it free, and ran toward the trash can by the sideboard. As he did, he considered simply holding the book, and running out the door with it. But he simultaneously had the idea that it would be better to set it ablaze right here. Then Tent would be distracted, from following him back to his car, and possibly doing violence to him or Hannah. Based on the intensity of Tent's impact with the floor, he desperately clung to the idea that he had at least a few seconds to complete his task.

He dropped the book into the trashcan with a thud, and frantically popped open the screw off top of the rum, doused the book, and replaced the open bottle on the sideboard. Giddy that he'd gotten this far, without Tent appearing and apprehending him, Adam hurriedly opened the matchbox, and prepared to strike one. Then a sudden and familiar feeling made his legs become rubbery, and Adam collapsed, paralyzed, to the floor.

Tent strolled into the room, banged up and bleeding from his fall. He held the ancient saber, which he placed against the sideboard.

"An excellent piece of deduction," he said. "You seem to know all about the uses of my book, and even where I hid it. You've become a capable pupil, under my tutelage. Unfortunately, for you, there is one thing you did not expect."

Tent took the matchbox from where it'd fallen from Adam's hand, and lit a cigarette—its tip glowing orange in the room's fluorescent light, as Tent inhaled triumphant.

"You didn't expect, my boy," said Tent, "that I had adapted my experimental paralysis drug—the very drug that you experienced upon your first visit to my office—into a powdered form, which works through transdermal absorption, and which paralyzes its victim from the neck down. You received a full 8-hour dose, when you touched the book, I'm afraid. Of course, there is the antidote."

Adam's flaccid limbs lay like weights upon him, as Tent walked to the collection of chemical bottles on the cluttered desk nearby. He brought from among the objects and papers a coffee mug, filled shallowly with an odorless fluid and placed it on the sideboard, by his fedora.

"The antidote, as you recall, is as fast-acting as the poison. I've consumed some of it today myself, as a prophylactic measure, before applying the powder to the book." Tent's damaged, sunken-in features hung like a drooping mask, as he tilted his neck to look down at Adam's helplessness. "I'm sorry, Adam. This time, I cannot save you," he said and placed his hat over the mug, to demonstrate its unavailability. Adam only retained sufficient control of his muscles to ripple his face in the agony of defeat, and turn his head slowly from side to side, in a futile attempt to spur his body back to life.

Tent drew the sword from its sheath, with a slow and deliberate savoring of its menace. He tossed the metal casing free, and took a reinforced stance, the saber gripped expertly in his right hand.

"It's a shame you didn't kill yourself, Adam," said Tent. "But it's just as well. Your death at my hand will be just as easy to explain. You came here to do me bodily harm, because of what I know—and I defended myself. I don't know how you escaped my hypnotic control, but what comes now will be beyond your power to stop. Goodbye, my friend."

With a thumb and index finger, Tent solemnly pulled the cigarette from his mouth and snuffed it out in an ashtray on the sideboard. He tightened his hold on his artful weapon, preparing to strike. Then a loud, violent thump was heard emanating from the row of tall, one-way windows in Tent's darkened inner office, by his personal desk. His office door being open, Adam, raising his head from the floor, and Tent, looking upward, put their attention on the source of the sound, at which instant another impact sounded. Then, in view of the men, one of the black windows split into pieces and fell, like a section of night sky breaking into jagged shapes and spilling to the ground. And moving through the hole made by the disappeared window, stepping out of the blackness and into the shadows, was the escaped maniac Dio Macina.

Moonlight played off of his features, distorted by insanity—his one perpetually raised eyebrow raised with a violent intensity. He held joyfully in his hands a red fire axe, its silver edge sharpened to a surgical point, the newness of its paint and wood contrasting with the rot and wear in the ill-intending mind of the man who held it.

Macina ran straight at Tent, with a white-hot sense of purpose. Tent did not flee, did not even lift his arm—for in some dried up, neglected part of Tent's heart, the realization flooded in like calming water, that a God he didn't believe in was at this moment visiting judgement upon him. Macina took a running, windmill swing, and the edge of his axe sank into Tent's sternum with a sickening wallop, severing the muscles of his heart, and rendering the man deceased, before his crashing, lifeless body had had time to fall earthward.

Pushing off with one leg, Macina extracted his weapon from Tent's body, like a firewood cutter pulling his axe out of a stump. Then turning to loom above Adam now, Macina raised the axe high above his head with both arms, his face alight with a childlike anticipation of the carnage to follow.

This was it, thought Adam. He wasn't going to make it. He thought of marrying Hannah, and having children with her. The life they would have had together flashed before his eyes. He bid it farewell and held in his heart the expectation of seeing Jesus face to face.

The door's electronic chime sounded. Three gunshots rang out sonorously, and the madman Dio Macina slumped limply into a corpse's position next to Tent—the axe dropping harmlessly upon the vacant clothing of their flesh.

Adam turned his head and saw her, holding her father's gun—a gun her father had never fired in an emergency. A draft of air came through the broken window, causing the back of Hannah's trench coat to flutter upward like a curling white cape.

Then Hannah's face was upside-down above Adam's, like a very worried surgeon. Her eyes were an ocean of rescue, to flee to from the burning mainland. The focus of Adam's gaze drifted to the acoustic squares of office ceiling above them—beyond which Adam knew was night that was newly making its way toward day; beyond which Adam knew was outer space; beyond which Adam knew lived the emerald aura of the throne room of God.

"Thank you," said Adam with a shiver, as two beads of tears broke and glided down his temples. "Thank you."

27

The End

Hannah and Adam arrived together, the next morning, at Adam's guardhouse, the site of the beginning of the story that had ended up bringing them together—so that Adam could begin the rare morning shift, that he'd agreed to cover for his coworker.

They'd both been up most of the night, talking to the Secret Service, and the FBI. Finally, they'd gone to Adam's apartment, and had a miniscule amount of sleep together. Then Hannah had come with Adam in his car to work. They couldn't say why. The intensity of the previous night's events had wedded their emotions together, made them feel that separating too precipitously would leave them vulnerable to unforeseen aftershocks. And they were in love.

The familiar nightly environs—the pavement, the lampposts, the agave plants, and prairie blues—surrounding Adam's guardhouse were a different world wearing their new suit of day: like a polished and rebuilt ruin, like a submerged continent returned to the surface. The beleaguering spell of night had been lifted—leaving behind a glow, a hue, like an undiscovered shade of blue added to eyesight. Adam could see in multichromatic detail what had been gray and gross; he could read the lettering on signs that he hadn't even noticed were there. On multiple occasions, recently, Adam had been offered the chance to transfer to the a.m., having always chosen instead to remain ensconced in the anonymity of the graveyard hours. Now, at this moment, the bad guy defeated, and Hannah by his side, he realized that he'd been guarding the nighttime long enough: it was time to join the dayshift.

"Should I even be here?" Hannah asked, standing close, and caressing Adam between his shoulder blades, while he sat in his stalwart chair, considering the shift's preliminary paperwork and checklists.

"No," said Adam, embracing her, and pulling her onto his lap. She put her arms around his neck, with a coquettish smile.

"We should be at church. It's Sunday morning," Adam said.

"That's right," said Hannah. "You'll be disappointed to know that, with my father's passing, the pastoring duties of Last Baptist Church of San Antonio will be taken over by the staunch Calvinist assistant pastor that never liked me. So, the false repent-of-your-sins-to-be-saved gospel is in no danger of being defeated at our poor church."

"Why don't we start going to Good Ways Baptist? You said you like the sermons Pastor Michaels puts on YouTube. That church is just thirty minutes south of here."

"I suppose we should now," said Hannah. "You're full of good ideas." She smiled again, framed his cheeks with her palms, and kissed him.

"We're on camera," said Adam, "They'll be calling on the phone any second, asking what in the hell I think I'm doing."

"Don't get fired, Adam," said Hannah. "You're not a highly sought-after private investigator yet. You've only just now solved your first case. Though the President of the United States was impressed with us. You didn't need to record your conversation with Tent, after all. Donald Trump heard his confession. And he's the head of the executive branch."

"I don't want to be a private investigator anymore," said Adam.

"Oh?"

"I want to be a Baptist preacher. That's the deeper detective work—finding deeper clues to higher mysteries."

"Everything is the truth, or else it's hypnotism," said Hannah.

"What—" said Adam, perplexed. "What is that from?"

"It's from the first Douglas Tent story that Roland ever wrote. *The Case of the Vanished Magician*. Under your influence, I've started reading them."

"Oh, yeah," said Adam remembering.

"You know," said Hannah, "the bible says that you have to be married to be a pastor."

"Does it?" asked Adam playfully.

"But one thing bothers me," said Hannah, perusing the guardhouse windows, and the spartan arrangement of necessities on the metal shelf that acted as the guardhouse desk.

"What's that?"

"We didn't destroy the book," said Hannah. "In the commotion of giving you the antidote, and calling the police, and the aftermath—we left Tent's book of evil hypnotic power soaking in rum in the trashcan. What will become of it? Where will it be taken by the police?"

"I don't think it matters," said Adam.

"It doesn't?"

"No," said Adam, "because, look at what happened to me. You were right that the saved cannot be demon possessed. And there will always be other books. The hypnosis of Tent's book only caused bodily death. But what about the meaning of the atheistic words inside? What about the books of false religions, that likewise send the souls of those who believe in them to hell? We can't burn all of those with high-proof rum."

"An excellent point," said Hannah.

"The solution then," said Adam, "is to get souls saved, by preaching them the biblical gospel. Then they'll be immune to Tent's book, as well as other enchanting lies."

Hannah looked into Adam's eyes, preparing to kiss him again, but was interrupted by a police cruiser pulling up to the guardhouse and scooting its nose up close, parking between the lanes. Police detective Richard Bethany got out of the passenger side. A patrolman remained waiting in the driver's seat.

"Hello, Adam; Hannah." said detective Bethany—entering the cramped quarters of the guardhouse—who'd met Hannah in the chaos of the previous night, when he'd arrived at the detective agency, to represent the local authorities, among the cacophony of emergency lights and cross-purposed law-enforcement acronyms.

"This officer," said the detective, gesturing to the police cruiser, "was just taking me somewhere, so I decided to have him stop me by here on the way."

"It's good to see you, detective," said Hannah.

"The SAPD appreciates what the both of you did last night. And the whole country will appreciate it," said Bethany. "Unfortunately, any minute now, CNN and Fox News and everybody else are going to learn what happened last night, and are going to learn where both of you live and work. And I'm afraid that both of your lives are going to become a circus into the foreseeable future."

Adam and Hannah exchanged a cautious look. They hadn't considered the media.

"We'll talk into the microphones," said Hannah, "and tell the world about Christ."

An inveterate lawman's grin formed below Bethany's bushy red mustache. "I hope that you will," he said.

"Oh, there's one other thing," said Bethany, producing a windowed, letter-sized envelope, from the side pocket of his trench coat, and holding it with both hands. "This is the last paycheck from the San Antonio police department, made out to Douglas Tent, for his latest help on various cases. Since I was the liaison between the department and Tent, I always brought him his paychecks. We'll be stopping payment on the check, now that he's deceased, while all of the legal niceties are squared away in probate court. So the check has no monetary value, but... It may be a strange idea, but I thought, Adam, that you might want it as a souvenir."

"I—" said Adam, and was at a loss. The genius and the evil of Douglas Tent stood like a burning monument in Adam's feelings and memory. "I do—I would like it. Thank you."

"I think I'm the only person," said detective Richard

Bethany, "besides our H.R. lady, that actually knows that 'Douglas Tent' was only his professional name. His legal name is different. Even Roland didn't know that, I believe. But I'm not an expert on what Roland knew. I never read his stories."

Adam took the letter, and looking through its cellophane window, saw the check itself. In the address line, it was addressed to Malcom Esperanza.

Made in the USA
Coppell, TX
01 December 2022

87501525R00146